A woman's shrill scream woke him.

The penetrating sound brought him bolt upright. A fierce pain lanced through his head, and his gut churned like a flood-swollen river. He moaned and squinted against the sunlight streaming through the window.

Was it morning, already? Had he ever been asleep?

A woman stood in the doorway, her sallow face set in a horrified mask. "Horace!" she screeched. "Come here!"

Chase shook his head, trying to dispel the ringing in his ears and the thick fog in his head. A moment later, a short, pudgy man pushed past the woman and entered the suite. Chase groaned. Why the hell were these people in his room?

A soft gasp sounded beside him. Turning, he spied a young woman clasping the coverlet under her chin. She stared at him with whiskey-brown eyes widened in alarm. A shudder passed through him that had nothing to do with the cool air swirling around his bared chest. God, he didn't remember...a girl? That had never happened before. He always remembered...although, he barely recalled returning to his room last night. Had the girl come with him?

She certainly was his type, a lovely, little, raven-haired vixen with luscious lips that begged to be kissed. Strange how he couldn't recall tasting such sweetness.

The Cavalry Wife

by

Donna Dalton

The Cavalry Wife

Cover Art by *Angela Anderson*

The Wild Rose Press
PO Box 708
Adams Basin, NY 14410-0706
Visit us at www.thewildrosepress.com

Publishing History
First Cactus Rose Edition, 2007
Print ISBN 1-60154-116-3

Published in the United States of America

Dedication

I dedicate this book to my mother, Peggy Alley, who has always stood behind me and encouraged me to reach for the stars and make my dreams come true.

Winner of the Historical category of the Northeast Indiana Romance Authors 2004 Opening Gambit Contest.

ONE

Washington, D.C.
March 1869

All goes onward and outward...and nothing collapses.
And to die is different from what anyone supposed, and
luckier.

"Callista Louise!"

Callie Grant jumped at the harsh tone. Whitman's words flew out of her head like a startled pigeon. Oh, what she wouldn't trade to be back in her hotel room, reading her book instead of suffocating in the crowded Treasury Building.

"Callista!"

Cringing inwardly, she faced the owner of the voice. "Y-Yes, Aunt Eunice?"

Dark and ominous in her usual mourning ensemble, Eunice Boggs pursed already thin lips and glared through narrowed eyes. "Julia stopped to speak with you. If you weren't so busy wool gathering—"

"Good evening, Callie," a sweet, familiar voice interrupted. Dressed in a beautiful, dark green, silk gown trimmed in pristine lace, Julia Dent Grant, wife of the newly-elected President of the United States, looked the perfect, poised First Lady.

Callie's heavy heart lightened. A smile lifted to her lips for the first time that day. "H-Hello, Julia," she murmured.

Her cousin's wife leaned forward and gave her an affectionate peck on the cheek. "It's been a while since I've seen you. You've grown into quite a lovely, young lady."

Heat suffused her face. "Th-thank you, Julia. It's good to see you, as well."

"Lyss and I are so pleased you could make it to the

1

Inaugural ceremony, though we heard you'll be remaining in Washington permanently with your guardians."

Callie nodded. "We're staying in a hotel until—"

"Horace has contracted a rental home in Georgetown," Eunice cut in. "He hopes Ulysses will consider him for some financial appointment. Horace *is* an expert in trade economics, you know."

"Yes, well, he will have to speak with Ulysses regarding that subject." Julia furnished Eunice with a gracious smile, then returned her attention to Callie. "I'm glad you'll be in town. It will give us a chance to visit more often."

"That would be nice." Her heart swelled. It *would* be nice to visit with Julia. Though infrequent at best, Lyss and Julia's visits always brought a ray of sunshine into her cold and dreary life.

Julia rested a hand on Callie's arm. "I'm sorry we missed your birthday. How did you find *Candide*, dear?"

"Most enlightening. Thank you for the gift. Voltaire is wonderful."

"I'm happy you enjoyed it. Lyss thought you might." She glanced at the gathering crowd. "It looks as if we're about to begin receiving. If you'll excuse me?"

Callie heaved a soft sigh as she watched Julia head for the other end of the chamber, cheerfully greeting everyone in her path. How she wished she could be like her cousin's wife—poised and confident, never stuttering or shying away from a crowd.

The approaching swarm moved down the receiving line. Heart thudding, Callie eased backward until she reached the comforting hardness of the wall behind her. She prayed the flood of guests would keep Eunice from noticing her absence. Crowds turned her insides to porridge and her tongue to stone. She liked people—she just preferred them one at a time.

Safely tucked beside a large, potted fern, she glanced around the room. Chandeliers bathed the Treasury Hall in soft, golden light. Gilt-framed paintings lined the walls, the rich oils glistening in the candlelight. The warmth filling the chamber was a welcome change from the cold drizzle she'd endured earlier that morning while Ulysses took his oath of office on the White House lawn.

Her gaze strayed over the crowd, a mixture of civilians, diplomats, and—of course—a large contingent from the military. One officer in particular towered above the others. He lifted a gloved hand and swept back a stray lock of blond hair. He was incredibly handsome, even with a scowl.

He doesn't want to be here any more than I do.

As though he heard her thoughts, he turned. Cold gray eyes met hers with a look that could melt stone. Callie snapped her head around and focused on Eunice's rigid back. She'd often dreamt of marrying a military man—a man like her father, cheery and compassionate, dedicated to his country. She risked another glance at the daunting, steely-eyed officer.

She'd never have the courage to wed a man such as that.

As the last guest exited the Hall, the receiving party moved into a spacious dining chamber. All thoughts of the intimidating officer disappeared as she admired the colorful banners and garlands strung amongst the flags and shields adorning the walls. They were steered toward one end of the room where a raised platform had been placed for the President and his entourage.

Seated with her guardians at one of the linen-draped tables, she watched, mesmerized, as the crowd swarmed about the vast chamber. Billowing gowns blended into a kaleidoscope of beautiful colors. How would it feel to wear such lovely garments? She fingered her drab, high-necked gown. Eunice never allowed her to wear anything brighter than gray, as though she wanted to keep her charge clothed in perpetual mourning.

A massive girth abruptly blocked her view. Callie looked up and cringed at the sight of Edward Carroll, her uncle's associate, standing before her. His bulbous nose appeared redder than usual. That meant more ugliness than normal would pour from his drink-loosened lips.

Uncle Horace motioned to the empty chair next to her. "Edward, here. I believe that's your name on the table placard."

"Thank you, Boggs." He settled onto the seat with a grunt.

Uncle's face split into a wide smile. "Callista, you

remember Edward Carroll?" His voice dripped with honeyed pleasantness. "He's supped with us on numerous occasions."

Panic tumbled inside her like waves in a gale. What was her guardian up to? And how had he finagled a seat for his associate at a family dinner table? She swallowed hard. "Yes, I remember. H-how do you do, Mr. Carroll?"

Beady, black eyes devoured her. "I'm doing well," he said. "*Very* well."

She peered down at her hands and twisted her napkin into a knot, struggling not to gag when Mr. Carroll's cloying cologne wafted around her. Why did this man have to intrude on their celebration? The festive room didn't seem quite so bright in his presence.

A waiter approached and began pouring wine. Others served from platters and filled the guests' plates with steaming food. Callie lifted her glass, took a sip, and winced. The wine tasted sweet and fruity—and potent—not at all like the watered-down spirits her aunt usually served. She shrugged. Perhaps it would help settle her churning stomach.

As the meal progressed, the clink of silverware joined the enthusiastic hum of conversation filling the chamber. Callie drank her second glass of wine while absently pushing the food around on her plate. Her appetite, along with her enthusiasm, had fled.

Halfway through his meal, Edward Carroll leaned toward her. "You're looking quite lovely this evening, Miss Grant." His heated gaze lingered on her breasts before rising to her face. He swallowed and then flicked his tongue over his bottom lip. "Are you enjoying the celebration?"

The sting of bile burned in her throat. She shuddered and averted her eyes.

"Speak up, Callista," Eunice admonished. "Edward asked you a question."

Heat rose in her face, but she remained silent. The way her stomach rolled, she feared if she spoke, more than words would spill from her mouth.

Eunice issued an exasperated harrumph. "Lordy, girl, you need to learn to overcome your shyness. No man will want a wife who can't string together more than two

4

words."

"A firm-handed husband will break her of such nonsense," Mr. Carroll replied, his tone pointed and harsh.

Callie stiffened. Break her? Like a horse? She could certainly see how Edward Carroll would treat a wife, like a brood mare to be used as he saw fit, regardless of the woman's feelings. Not the type of man she would ever want to wed. A thought flared, and ice filled her veins. Surely her guardians wouldn't—

Buck Grant approached, interrupting her unpleasant thought. He nodded toward the Presidential table. "Father is asking for you, Callie."

Thank you, Ulysses. She rose and followed her younger cousin across the platform. A mob surrounded the President—an exceptionally large mob of uniformed officers, well-dressed gentlemen, and bejeweled ladies. Familiar fingers of fear gripped her insides.

Buck stopped at the edge of the cluster, and Callie paused to swipe damp palms down the sides of her gown. She tossed a silent prayer heavenward that she wouldn't stutter in front of Lyss' well-wishers.

A low-pitched, musical voice lifted over the chatter. She smiled at the sound. *So much like Father's.* Beyond the press of bodies stood her cousin, stroking his bearded chin with his left hand in a familiar gesture. His shoulders sagged wearily, his back more stooped than usual.

Her heart lurched. *Poor Cousin Lyss.*

The new President turned, spotted her in the crowd, and pinned her with twinkling eyes. He stepped forward, extending a hand as he moved. "Little Callie, there you are. Thank you for coming."

All eyes rolled in her direction. Her throat constricted around a knot of fear. She could do little more than lift her hand to him. Lyss grasped her trembling fingers and gently pulled her into the center of the huge crowd. Heat flamed in her cheeks and scorched her ears. She should have remained at her table and endured Mr. Carroll's crassness. Now, she was the focus of a *hundred* people's scrutiny.

Lyss lifted his lips into a tender smile. "Julia was

5

correct," he said. "You have grown since we last visited. How have you been, Callie?"

"I-I've been doing well, th-thank you, Cousin," she stammered, despite her efforts.

"Are you enjoying yourself?"

"Y-yes, it's been a very exciting day."

"I'm glad. I just wanted to see you before my duties begin. I'm afraid I won't have much time for family for a while."

"That's understandable," she murmured.

"I'm sorry I didn't get to visit you more often in the past. I always enjoyed our debates." His eyes crinkled at the corners. "Especially the ones regarding General Washington's presidency. Most stimulating."

Her fear evaporated as she recalled their animated discussions. She smiled. "I enjoyed them as well."

He gave her hand a soothing pat. "I won't keep you any longer. Go, my dear. Enjoy the rest of the evening."

Callie nodded and eased out of his grasp. After threading her way through his well-wishers, she crossed the platform, only to find another large crowd blocking her path. Elbow to elbow, nary an inch of light glimmered between the noisy, chattering horde. She drew to a halt. She'd rather cut off her arm than try to prod through *that* press.

Pivoting on her heels, she circled around them and weaved her way through a maze of tables and empty chairs. Callie finally located her table by the glare bouncing off the back of Edward Carroll's balding head. A waiter carrying a dish-laden tray stepped in front of her. She paused to allow him to pass.

Her uncle's voice drifted across the short distance. "Callista will do as I say."

"Glad to hear it, Boggs," Mr. Carroll replied. "I expect a swift betrothal and wedding. I'm not getting any younger."

Eunice sniffed loudly. "You can't do any better than Callista Louise. She's very mature for an eighteen-year-old. I know she'll be a dutiful wife and mother."

Callie reeled on unsteady legs and grasped an unoccupied chair to steady herself. Dear God, they were talking about her, betrothing her to that lecherous, disgusting old man. She knew she owed Eunice and Horace for taking her in, for accepting the responsibility of raising her. But this...

She closed her eyes and pictured her aunt sitting on a picnic blanket with a small girl dancing beside her. Eunice caressed Deanna's golden locks and gave the child a loving smile. Seated next to his wife, Horace chuckled, a foreign sound that rarely passed his lips nowadays.

Callie's throat tightened as she recalled that day thirteen years ago. If only she had obeyed her father's orders. If she'd stayed clear of those fascinating cannons. If she'd not urged her younger cousin to follow...

Perhaps the Boggses would not have become such resentful, anguished individuals. Perhaps her parents and Deanna would still be alive.

Sickened by her thoughts, she forced her eyes open and crossed the remaining distance. Eunice gave her a cursory glance and then turned her attention to the newly arrived visitors to the table. Freed from her aunt's scrutiny, Callie sat, downed the remainder of her wine, and motioned for the waiter to pour more. She knew she shouldn't overindulge, but she just couldn't help herself. The potent spirits tamed her rebellious stomach and dulled the ache stabbing her heart.

When Horace finally announced that it was time to leave, relief flooded her. She could bear no more of the wine or Edward Carroll's leering glances.

During the ride to the hotel, she sat in numbed silence and stared out the window at the darkened city. Exhausted from the trip to Washington and the long Inaugural celebration, she wanted nothing more than to crawl into bed and fall into mindless slumber—a sleep where she wouldn't have to think about her guardians or Mr. Carroll.

On the opposite seat, Horace cleared his throat. "Your aunt and I have important news for you, Callista."

"N-News? Wh-What news?" she asked, even though she already knew what he was about to say.

"Edward Carroll has asked for your hand in marriage. And we have accepted his offer."

Her pulse skipped. "B-But, Uncle, I don't want to marry Mr. Carroll."

Horace snorted. "Edward is a prosperous merchant in Washington and a well-respected Senator. You should be glad to have such an important man interested in you."

"H-He's old enough to be my father."

"Bah. An older man is just what you need. Someone who has learned from life and can guide you through it."

Panic surged inside her. How might she convince him to change his mind? "Please, Uncle. I don't—"

"Silence!" he stormed, his face contorting with rage in the lantern-lit coach. "We are your legal guardians. You'll do as we say. Two months hence, you *will* wed Edward."

She closed her eyes, battling her rising nausea. Marry Edward Carroll. If she refused, she would stay with her guardians, remain with heartless individuals who could pass by a child's bedchamber and not stop to investigate the mournful weeping.

Yet if she agreed, would her life be filled with more of the same? Edward Carroll was a man much like her uncle, strict and hard-hearted. She recalled his remark about breaking her shyness with a firm hand, and she shuddered. Nothing short of a miracle would save her from a life of emptiness.

Horace thankfully grew silent for the remainder of the trip. Once inside the hotel, Callie slowly navigated the steep staircase. Her head whirled like a toy top, and she gripped the rail tightly to keep from stumbling. The last thing she needed was to have Eunice berate her for overindulging and add to the misery pounding in her skull.

Callie bid her guardians goodnight and waited for them to enter the suite next to hers. As their door clicked shut, she extracted her key from her purse and fumbled with the lock. The number on the door caught her eye. *Six*? She was in room nine.

She glanced down the hallway and counted the doors. This was the right room. She leaned closer, squinted, and then frowned. The brass numeral dangled unevenly on the wood panel. Callie reached out and flipped it upright. Six became a nine. A missing nail appeared to be the culprit. She released the numeral, and it spun down to become a six again.

Nothing seemed to be going right for her this day.

With a sigh, she returned her attention to the lock and finally succeeded in opening the door. She tottered into the darkened bedchamber and crossed to the bureau. Though her head spun wildly, she managed to undress in the icy darkness.

Hair braided and nightgown buttoned to her chin, Callie slid into the bed and pulled the coverlet over her. Outside the window, the wind howled mournfully and bashed against the panes in furtive gusts. She stiffened against the urge to curl into a ball and wail like the wind. It would be futile. Tears hadn't brought back her parents, or her cousin, and they certainly wouldn't alter the course of her life now.

****

Captain Chase Brooks weaved along the hotel corridor, trying to control the placement of booted feet that seemed to have a mind of their own. Halfway down the dimly-lit hallway, he paused and leaned against the wall for support.

Christ, he never should have allowed Captain Lewis to talk him into that last drink at the Inauguration dinner. The whiskey's ambush on his speech should've been warning enough. Chase ran a hand through his sweat-soaked hair and pushed upright. A door loomed before him. He squinted, straining to confirm the number dancing before his eyes like a wily Indian.

Six. Finally, he'd found his room. He shouldered against the doorframe, dug his key from his pocket, and attempted to shove the key into the keyhole. It was like trying to hit a moving target. His hand slipped. He pressed against the knob, and the door swung open. He lurched inside.

Damn. Hadn't he locked it that morning? He grimaced. Evidently not.

Chase pushed the door shut and darkness enveloped the room. Head spinning, he took a step toward the bureau and a lamp. The floor pitched under his feet. He ground his teeth. To hell with the lamp. He needed a bed.

Hands outstretched, he stumbled across the carpet until he found the bed. Fingers as ornery as his legs fumbled with buttons, buckles, and boots. Wavering unsteadily, he managed to strip off his uniform and slide naked under the coverlet.

He burrowed his head into the pillow. Thank God the festivities surrounding President Grant's Inauguration were over. He'd soon be heading back to his outpost where he belonged, not suffocating in this filthy, over-crowded city. Chase turned on his side, melted into the soft mattress, and welcomed the blissful oblivion of sleep.

A woman's shrill scream woke him.

The penetrating sound brought him bolt upright. A fierce pain lanced through his head, and his gut churned like a flood-swollen river. He moaned and squinted against the sunlight streaming through the window.

Was it morning, already? Had he ever been asleep?

A woman stood in the doorway, her sallow face set in a horrified mask. "Horace!" she screeched. "Come here!"

Chase shook his head, trying to dispel the ringing in his ears and the thick fog in his head. A moment later, a short, pudgy man pushed past the woman and entered the suite. Chase groaned. Why the hell were these people in his room?

A soft gasp sounded beside him. Turning, he spied a young woman clasping the coverlet under her chin. She stared at him with whiskey-brown eyes widened in alarm. A shudder passed through him that had nothing to do with the cool air swirling around his bared chest. God, he didn't remember...a girl? That had never happened before. He always remembered...although, he barely recalled returning to his room last night. Had the girl come with him?

She certainly was his type, a lovely, little, raven-haired vixen with luscious lips that begged to be kissed. Strange how he couldn't recall tasting such sweetness.

"You strumpet!" the red-faced man bellowed from the doorway. "Get out of that bed and go with your aunt to our suite."

His mind still clawing toward reality, Chase watched the remaining color drain from the young woman's pale face. With a trembling hand, she tossed aside the quilt and slid out of the bed. A long, black braid stood out starkly against her white nightdress as she rushed barefoot across the floor. The stout man lifted his hand as though to strike her.

Chase stiffened and prepared to leap out of bed. Men who mistreated women were the worst sort of slime, deserving threefold the same punishment they dished out. "Mister, you'd best not lay one finger on her," he warned.

The man glanced at Chase and then at the cowering girl. Apprehension replaced the anger furrowing his thickset face. He lowered his hand and allowed the girl to pass untouched. The two ladies disappeared into the hallway.

Chase relaxed and addressed the man, who still occupied the doorway. "What exactly is going on here?"

"What indeed?" the man snapped.

The stabbing sound reverberated in Chase's throbbing head and stampeded down his spine. He groaned and rubbed his temple.

"How did you come to be in my niece's room?"

Niece's room? "This is my room!"

"My *niece's* room," the man repeated.

Chase glanced around. A woman's hat sat on the bureau. Gowns hung in the wardrobe where his uniforms were not. Something was wrong, unbelievably wrong. A sinking sensation hit his already turbulent gut. What had he gotten himself into?

"What's going on here, Captain?"

Christ. Chase jerked his head toward the doorway at the sound of the familiar, authoritative voice. He winced from both the pain stabbing into his skull and the ill-timed appearance of his commander.

The fat man, presumably the uncle of the captivating lady in his bed, jabbed a finger in Chase's direction. "This soldier has despoiled my niece. I found them in bed together."

Colonel Grierson pushed past the man and entered the bedchamber. He glanced from Chase to the furious uncle and back to Chase. "That true, Captain?"

Chase moaned again, trying to make sense of the bizarre situation. He couldn't possibly have been that drunk. Besides, if he *had* tumbled the girl, she wouldn't still be clothed in that virginal nightgown. "Colonel, there's been some mistake. I didn't—"

"Mistake?" the uncle barked. "You can be certain there's been a mistake. And you, *Captain*, made it."

11

Chase suppressed the urge to leap out of bed and throttle the arrogant fool. Years of discipline kept him rooted in place, his face schooled into an expressionless mask.

A frown creased Grierson's forehead. "Captain, can you explain—"

"Are you aware," the uncle interrupted, "that his bed partner is President Grant's cousin?"

Instantly the fog lifted from Chase's drink-addled brain. Christ, he remembered the young woman from the Inauguration dinner. She'd slid shyly through the circle of family and friends gathered around Grant. The new Commander-in-Chief had called her "Little Callie."

His stomach sank like a chunk of granite. Whether he'd consorted with the lady or not, his career in the Army was over.

The colonel thinned already taut lips. "Captain Brooks, dress and meet me in my room in ten minutes. Mr..?"

"Boggs, Horace Boggs."

"Mr. Boggs, if you'll come with me, I'm sure we can resolve this matter without involving President Grant." Grierson motioned to the doorway, the brass buttons on his uniform glinting in the sunlight.

The two men exited the room and blessed silence returned. As his commander pulled the door closed, Chase spied the numeral six swaying crookedly on the wood panel. A fist clamped down on his innards.

Good God, he was in for it now.

****

Legs braced apart and arms tucked behind his back, Chase stood in the middle of Grierson's hotel room and watched as his commander shuffled papers into a neat stack on the small secretary near the window. The obnoxious Horace Boggs had departed earlier. Chase grunted. Thank God. Much more of the man's pompous whining and his throbbing skull would've exploded.

His task complete, Grierson looked up. Concern lines creased his brow, softening the stern commander-to-subordinate expression he'd adopted while in the presence of Boggs. "You made the right choice, Chase."

He clenched his teeth together. Had he? How did one

12

choose between a bullet and a knife to the heart? Both killed a man. Toes to the sun dead.

The colonel strode toward him and placed a hand on his shoulder. "I know your first marriage wasn't perfect—"

"Damn right it wasn't," he snapped and then stiffened with a jolt of realization. "Beg your pardon, Colonel."

Grierson gave his shoulder a reassuring squeeze and removed his hand. "No need for an apology, my boy. You had a difficult choice to make, though I'm selfish enough to admit I'm glad you didn't give up your commission. I need dedicated officers like you to lead my men."

His heart pitched. And he needed the Army. It was the only life he'd ever known. He couldn't give it up because some ranting, rattlesnake of a man wanted satisfaction for a bedding that never happened.

But marriage? *Godamighty*. He'd avoided that trap for nearly three years. Ever since...

Ice flowed through his veins at the thought of the hell his first wife had put him through. Lies and betrayal. Pain and death. He wouldn't go through that again. Ever.

Grierson read his thoughts. "Not all women are like Miranda. Perhaps if you give this girl a chance...?"

His anger rose to dangerous levels. He hadn't met a woman yet who didn't have at least one trait in common with Miranda. And now this one, this Miss Grant, who could set things to right with only a few words, was using a lie and her family name to ensnare him. No, from Eve right on down to Callie Grant, women couldn't be trusted. Except perhaps the colonel's wife. But then, Alice Grierson was one of the rare ones.

Chase dropped fisted hands to his sides. "I'll marry the girl," he said. "But she's not coming with me to Fort Arbuckle. She'll stay here with her guardians. They've done a *magnificent* job of looking after her so far." His sarcastic snort echoed off the walls.

"If that's how you want it..."

"That's the way it has to be."

"Well then, I'll just go down to the lobby and wait for the chaplain." Troubled eyes probed him for a second longer, then Grierson tugged on his hat. "Join us when you're ready."

Chase closed his eyes and listened to the colonel's footsteps fade until he was alone. He shook his head. Christ, he needed a drink, something to take the edge off this foul morning. But he knew he wouldn't find a drop of whiskey in Benjamin Grierson's suite. The man was a devout teetotaler.

And the best friend and commander a man could ask for.

The colonel was probably the only reason Chase was still alive. After Miranda's death, Grierson had wisely kept him busy with duty assignments and long, mind-numbing patrols, until he'd managed to stuff his pain deep into a dark pit. And he'd kept it there, had hardened his heart to all but his men and duty to his country, much to the dismay of the nosey busy-bodies at Arbuckle.

A thought reared up and took hold. Perhaps marriage wasn't such a bad idea after all. With a wife tucked safely away in Washington, the matchmakers would have no choice but to leave him alone. No more uncomfortable socials with officers' wives and their unmarried lady friends to endure. No more chatty females hanging on his arm and hoping to snare a husband.

For the first time that morning, his gut stopped rolling.

TWO

Callie sat in numbed silence and stared at the faded carpet. The silken swish of her aunt's skirts kept pace with the frantic thoughts grinding inside her head. How had that man ended up in her bed, and why hadn't she heard him? Felt him? She knew she was a heavy sleeper, but...

She rubbed at the throb in her temple. Too much wine, most likely. She glanced up and met Eunice's narrowed gaze and exasperated "hrrmph." Callie cringed and looked away.

Another disturbing thought blossomed. Had he...?

Heat burned in her face as she recalled the man's naked, sinewy back rising from the quilt. No, certainly he hadn't touched her. She shifted uneasily. Surely she would know if—

"You've ruined everything," her aunt ranted, startling Callie almost out of her seat. "Edward Carroll will not accept a defiled girl for a wife. A highly regarded senator cannot be tainted with such scandal."

"But Aunt, we didn't—"

"You've always been a stupid, insensitive—" Eunice broke off with another "hrrmph."

"We didn't, Aunt Eunice."

"I saw the man's indecent display of..." Her aunt clutched a hand to her chest. "I've told you about men, Callista Louise, but apparently you didn't listen. Men will take advantage and most certainly a man like...well, it's quite obvious what transpired."

A man like what? she wanted to ask. Instead, she bowed her head and remained mute. It was useless to argue. Eunice would believe what she wanted, regardless of Callie's claim.

With a heavy heart, she forced her aunt's fuming and

disgusted clucks out of her head, only to have them replaced by images of the stranger's tanned face and sleep-tousled hair. Recollection tweaked a memory, and she tensed. Dear God. He was the officer from the receiving room, the one with the steel-hard, emotionless stare.

The door exploded open, jolting her back to attention.

Her uncle strode in and pinned her with condemning eyes. "You're quite fortunate to have selected such a noble bed partner," he fumed. "Faced with losing his commission or marrying you, the gallant captain chose the latter."

Her pulse skipped. *Marry her?*

Eunice halted her pacing and sank onto the chest at the end of the bed. "Thank the Lord. I was so worried what her foolishness might have cost us."

Horace nodded. "Marriage to another will keep Edward's name out of any scandalous tattle, and thus salvage our relationship with him."

"When will this marriage take place?" Eunice asked.

"His commander is sending for a chaplain as we speak. The ceremony will be conducted in the hotel foyer."

"Good Lord, Horace, that doesn't give us much time."

"It cannot be helped. The captain is leaving tomorrow, headed back to his western outpost."

Eunice leapt to her feet, suddenly energized. "I'll spread word to the family members still at the hotel. We'll tell them..." She tapped a finger to her pale lips and then gave a satisfied smile. "We'll tell them Callista was swept off her feet by the handsome captain, and they wanted to wed before he departed. That should keep any tittle-tattle about them being found together from growing."

Callie stiffened. She had to do something. She couldn't just sit there like the mindless rag doll they believed her to be. "But Uncle," she managed to blurt out. "I don't want to get married." *To Edward, or to the intimidating captain.*

Horace turned hard, reproving eyes on her. Callie pushed back against the chair to brace herself. She'd felt the sting of his hand too many times not to be on guard.

"Do you think being found in bed with a man is of little consequence?" he ground out.

"N-no, Uncle, but—"

"I'll not have my chances in Washington ruined by a tainted niece." He narrowed his eyes. "Did you even consider what such a scandal would do to the Grant name? To Ulysses?"

Oh, God. Lyss. "I didn't thi—"

"You never do." He yanked a sausage-like finger at the door. "Go to your room and get dressed. You have half an hour."

Heart thudding, she fled from the room. As she raced down the hallway, the bite of reality finally sank in. Her skin crawled beneath her nightdress. Though no intimacy had passed between her and the captain, being discovered together was enough—quite enough—to force two strangers to marry.

Safely back in her hotel room, she dressed in a somber gray gown. Not exactly an appropriate wedding dress, but one that fit the occasion, as well as her mood. She ran a brush through her tangled locks and then absently coiled the mass into a bun so taut it prickled her scalp.

Sounds outside drew her to the window. The panes glistened with raindrops left from last night's storm. In the street below, people scurried mice-like, skirting puddles and dodging carriages. Shopkeepers raised their shades and opened their doors to customers who chatted happily as they moved about their business. It was a city awakening to a rain-cleansed morning.

A new thought took hold.

She could have that, too—a clean, fresh start. The idea began to grow and take form. She could have a new life free of her guardians and their constant scorn, a chance to move beyond the blame in their eyes and self-doubt in her heart—a chance to finally quell the guilt that had shaped her life.

Julia Grant had married a military man. Had Julia always been so fearless, so poised? Or had that come from being an Army wife? Callie's pulse quickened. Could she become as self-assured as Julia? Did she have the courage to take such a risk?

"Callista Louise."

She started at her aunt's shrill call.

"It's time to go." A forceful rap punctuated Eunice's words.

An unexpected, but pleasing, streak of courage steeled her spine. No one could force her to agree to this wedding.

"Callista...this minute, or your uncle will break down the door."

She pictured her rotund uncle trying to break down the solid wooden door. A tiny smile crept to her face.

"*Now, young lady!*"

Thoughts of Edward Carroll surfaced. His portly features faded and were replaced by the handsome, chiselled face of ...lordy, she didn't even know the officer's name.

"*Callista!*"

With a resigned sigh, she crossed to the door, unlocked and opened it to reveal the two people who had provided her food and shelter, but not a single thing more. A soft ache filled her chest.

"Come along," her uncle ordered. He scowled at her and then turned to waddle down the corridor.

Callie turned her attention to Eunice. The smell of beeswax and musty carpeting clung to the woman, a reminder of the Boggs' household—a clean façade hiding the dinginess underneath.

Her aunt drew in a long breath, a forewarning of the tirade to come. "Horace and I never wanted any more children after Deanna," she began. "Yet we took on the responsibility of raising you. With this marriage, I've fulfilled my promise to your father. Don't spoil it by refusing to marry the captain."

After one last piercing glare, her aunt whirled and stalked down the corridor. Callie closed her eyes and listened to the angry swish of silk fade away. She had always known she was unwanted, had known she was a family obligation. Yet hearing the words spoken aloud cut like a knife.

Soon, she'd become a duty to a stranger.

Would he think her as unworthy as her guardians did?

With a heavy heart, she forced her eyes open and her feet forward. As she descended the stairs, she surveyed the scene below. Her guardians stood at the landing, talking with two uniformed men, an older, bearded gentleman and one clutching a black bible. A small flock of family members circled nearby like waiting buzzards.

Across the lobby, a solitary figure, looking resplendent in his dress uniform, leaned against the fireplace. Broad shoulders filled the dark blue jacket, negating the need for the shoulder-enhancing gold epaulets. A vertical yellow stripe emphasized the length of blue thigh-hugging trousers and disappeared at the knees into shiny, black boots. With one arm propped on the mantel, the captain seemed to study the flames. His other hand flexed compulsively on the hilt of a curved saber, the brass scabbard winking in the firelight.

What thoughts raged in his head? Did he regret his offer to marry her? She could release him from this obligation with but a word, and yet, heaven help her, she couldn't. She may not want this marriage, but she wanted—needed—the opportunity it promised.

As if sensing her scrutiny, he jerked his head upward and focused his hard gaze upon her. He straightened and lowered his hands to his sides, his expression as cold as the steel of his sword.

Callie sucked in a breath and pulled her gaze away. Could she marry such an imposing figure? She recalled his forceful warning when Horace had lifted a hand to strike her. The captain had to possess some modicum of kindness to say such a thing. She then thought of the leering Mr. Carroll and chanced another glance at the handsome officer.

No real choice at all.

At the bottom of the stairs, she halted beside her aunt and silently prayed her trembling legs would continue to hold her upright. Horace introduced her to the chaplain and the other officer, Colonel Grierson.

The clergyman's friendly smile offered needed encouragement. "Miss Grant, are you ready to proceed with the ceremony?"

She glanced at her guardians and then her bridegroom. Was she? She didn't know this man she was about to marry. Didn't even know his name. "P-Perhaps the captain and I could have a moment alone?"

"Certainly, my dear," the minister replied. "Take as long as you need."

It was just across the lobby, but the distance from the stairs to the hearth felt like a hundred miles. Despite the chill in the room, perspiration trickled between her breasts and dampened her chemise.

"Is there a problem, Miss Grant," the captain asked as she drew next to him.

"Problem?"

"A moment ago, we were gathering for the proceedings, and now..." He motioned to the group waiting at the bottom of the steps.

Ill-at-ease, she couldn't bring herself to look him in the eye. "I-It occurred to me—"

"I'm up here, Miss Grant."

"Pardon?"

"You're addressing my buttons. Speak to me."

Callie looked up. To her relief, his expression was not nearly as angry as she expected. She cleared her throat and started again. "It occurred to me, Captain...I don't even know your name."

"A bit late for a proper introduction, don't you think?" He sighed heavily. "Chase. Chase Brooks."

"Callista Louise Grant." She extended her hand and forced a smile, trying to relieve the awkwardness. "Callie, to my friends and family."

"Yes, I know," he said as he took her hand. "The President's cousin."

"Third cousin, actually."

"An imposing family connection all the same." He gave her hand a gentle squeeze and released it.

"And your name? Chase. I-Is it a family name?"

His eyes hardened to stone. "I never knew my family."

"Not at all?"

"No."

He gathered himself, closing off from her, retreating behind a fortification she knew all too well. He was alone, like her. His sharp tone told her he didn't need anyone. Yet, he couldn't hide the sadness that flickered briefly in his eyes.

She felt the connection right through to her heart.

"I'm so sorry," she replied. "I was only five when I was orphaned. Perhaps we have that in common?"

He peered down at her, his gaze now cold and unreadable.

"Miss Grant. Captain," the chaplain's voice broke in. "If you're ready, we need to get started."

Her stomach flipped as she and Captain Brooks turned to face the minister. Surprisingly, she felt steadied by her bridegroom's aura of power and strength.

"Captain Chase Brooks, do you take this woman..."

She absently listened to the chaplain as he recited the marriage service. The captain said he never knew his family. What had happened to them? Had he lost them at a young age as she had?

His deep voice drifted over her. "I do."

"Callista Louise Grant," the minister continued. "Do you take this man..."

Did she? What type of man was her husband-to-be? His reluctance to give up his commission spoke of his dedication to the Army. An admirable trait. Yet, he seemed to be a puzzling mixture of rigidity and gentleness.

The chaplain gave her an encouraging smile. "Do you, Miss Grant?"

She cut a glance at her bridegroom. He was exceedingly handsome. Not that appearances should matter. But it did help. She gave a brief nod. "I do."

"Excellent." The chaplain beamed and handed the captain a ring. "This belonged to Miss Grant's mother and was thoughtfully provided for this happy occasion by Mrs. Boggs."

Mrs. Boggs did *what*? Callie twisted her head and regarded her aunt with startled disbelief. Eunice gave her a tiny nod.

Tears burned in Callie's eyes. Her aunt must truly be pleased at finally being rid of her burden to part with such a valuable item. With an aching heart, she turned back to the minister.

"Captain," the chaplain continued. "Place the ring on Miss Grant's finger and repeat after me."

The captain slid the ring onto her finger and, to her surprise, continued to hold her hand as he stated his vows. His grip was firm and oddly reassuring. Hope blossomed in her chest, dousing her sadness. She could make this work. She would be a good wife to this man. He would not regret having married her.

"I now pronounce you man and wife. Captain, you may kiss your bride."

Kiss? Ice filled her veins. She had never been kissed before. The Boggses made certain she led a sheltered life. And now, kiss a stranger? In front of all these people?

The captain hesitated only a second, then lowered his head. Firm lips covered hers. He tasted of brandy and comfort. Her head reeled drunkenly as it had the night before. She locked her knees to keep from swaying. The chatter in the room faded, until all she heard was the rapid beat of her heart.

Seconds passed. Or was it hours?

He lifted his head, ending the kiss. Gray eyes, once hard as granite, were now strangely molten and held hers for a brief moment before he looked away.

Dear God. Never in all her life did she dream...

She resisted touching fingertips to lips that tingled and burned. No need to telegraph her reaction to all and sundry. Her throat tightened, and she struggled to swallow. Was that how all kisses felt?

"Congratulations, Captain." Colonel Grierson stepped forward and shook hands with her husband. He then turned to her. "Mrs. Brooks. You have no need to worry. The Captain will take very good care of you."

"Th-thank you, Colonel." Her voice was a tiny croak of a sound.

Mrs. Brooks. Callista Grant Brooks. Callie Brooks. The name sounded strange to her ears. She cut a glance at the captain's chiselled jaw. Mrs. *Chase* Brooks. Fluttering wings of panic beat inside her chest and threatened to send her fleeing for her hotel room. Dear, sweet Jesus, what had she done?

"If you'll excuse us, Colonel," the captain said. "I'd like a moment alone with my wife." He cupped her elbow and guided her to a secluded corner of the lobby. A solid blue wall of chest and arms and thighs, he stopped and faced her.

With the memory of their kiss still lingering,

thoughts of the night to come nearly strangled her. She focused on the potted fern behind him and worked to bring her breathing under control by taking several deep breaths.

"I'm leaving tomorrow," he told her. "Headed back to the Indian territories."

"I-Is that where you're stationed?" she managed to ask.

"Yes, I'm assigned to Fort Arbuckle."

"We'll be living at this Fort Arbuckle, then?"

"I'm going back alone."

What? She yanked her gaze to his rigid face. "Y-you're leaving me?"

"Yes. I understand from Mr. Boggs that your father left a trust available upon your marriage. I intend to turn those funds back over to your uncle. You are to stay here and live with your guardians."

Her breath caught in her throat. He was leaving her with *them*. This couldn't be happening. "I don't understand. Wh-Why can't I go with you?"

"Because the territories are harsh and unrelenting. It's no place for a young lady like you."

"But—"

"No buts. You're not coming with me." His expression was firm and unyielding, one she'd seen cross her uncle's face many times in the past. She knew it would be useless to argue. He would not be swayed from his decision.

"I'll be in my room, number *six*, if you have any questions," he added, placing a distinct emphasis on the word six.

"That explains..." her voice trailed away as she pictured the dangling numeral.

"Yes, you used that trick of fate to your advantage quite well, my dear."

"I didn't—"

"It's over and done with. Enjoy your life. I intend to enjoy mine." With that, he spun around and strode away from her, his boot heels clicking loudly on the wood floor.

Through a haze of tears, she watched him climb the staircase, taking her dreams of a new life with him.

****

The smell of wet, burning wood drifted up from the

23

hearth. A log shifted, an ember popped, and then silence returned. Chase twirled the glass of whiskey he'd been nursing. Amber liquid sloshed inside the tumbler. Much as he wanted to get blind drunk, he knew it wouldn't help. The images would return. They always did. A month of sleepless nights hadn't tamed them at all.

He saw that day as though it had happened only yesterday. Jammed and useless rifles littering the churned-up ground. Wounded and dying men writhing in their own blood. Bodies stacked alongside the arrow-riddled wagons they'd been sent to protect. Senseless death and destruction that could have been prevented.

Anger replaced the anguish burning in his chest. He hated being stuck in Washington, forced to remain polite to the politicians he wanted to punch in the face. Bigotry and hatred kept his Negro troopers from getting the equipment and horses they needed. And they *would* need them. He'd received word that the Kiowa were getting restless in the Eureka Valley. Damn, he hoped he could get back to Arbuckle before the Indians began a full-scale rebellion.

A faint rap on his hotel door yanked him from the dark memories. He grimaced. Christ, who could that be? If it was that smiling Chinese bellboy with another trunk...

The man spoke little English. Therefore, Chase had been forced to accept the delivery, despite his attempts to have the damn thing sent to Callie's room where it belonged.

"Go away," he shouted and then took another swallow of whiskey.

The knocking persisted.

Damnation. Chase set his glass on the bureau and rose with a frustrated grunt from the comfortable chair. He crossed to the door, tugged it open, and nearly staggered back at the sight that greeted him.

Satchel in hand, his new wife stared up at him with large, brown, doe-eyes. Her faded gown hugged curves he'd fought all day to forget.

"What the hell are you doing here?" he bit out.

Her face turned ashen and he wondered if she would flee. He'd set many a man to trembling in their boots with the glare he trained on her. Yet, to his surprise, she stood before him like a brave little trooper, willing to take whatever he threw at her.

She moistened her lips. "M-May I come in? I-I wish to speak with you."

He stared at her glistening lips and then tugged his gaze upward. "I don't think—"

"Please. I won't take up much of your time." Soft, pleading eyes tunneled into him.

He ran a hand through his hair, then gave a reluctant nod. His gut churned around the whiskey as she brushed past him, leaving a rosy scent in her wake.

You're making a big mistake, Brooks. You shouldn't have let her in. He ground his teeth around a curse, shoved the door shut, and turned to face her. Like a wraith, she stood near the hearth, her smooth skin glowing in the firelight. She parted her pretty lips as though preparing to speak then, just as quickly, clamped her mouth shut without uttering a word. Her eyes filled with unshed tears.

Chase steeled himself against her misery. He'd seen enough women's tears to know they usually came hand-in-hand with some type of ploy. He didn't intend to get caught in any emotional trap. "Why the tears?"

"Our marriage...I-I don't...that is, I..."

Was she having second thoughts? It was a little too late for regrets. "You had the chance to dispute your uncle's accusations." Anger and resentment flooded his voice. "Yet you remained silent."

"You don't understand—"

"Oh, but I do understand. Marriage to me was a convenient way to escape betrothal to another man, a would-be senator, according to your pompous uncle."

She bowed her head. "You're right. I did marry you to escape an unwanted betrothal. I-I apologize for entangling you in my affairs."

"Well, you got what you wanted. Why are you here?"

Her lips trembled. The same luscious lips he'd enjoyed earlier that morning. Fire shot into his loins, and he stiffened against the desire to pull her into arms and taste her again. What had happened to his battle-hardened control? He acted like some pimple-faced

25

private, fresh off a long, lonely patrol. He forced his focus away from her tempting mouth.

"I cannot stay with them," she whispered.

He had to strain to hear her, even in the quiet room. "With whom? Your aunt and uncle? From what I've seen, they aren't ideal guardians, but—"

A faint sob escaped her lips and she whirled away from him. Her slender shoulders rose and fell as she struggled for control.

Ebony tendrils had escaped from her bun and now curled in tantalizing twirls around her neck. Would those wavy tresses feel as soft and satiny as they looked? He took one step forward and halted, lowering the hand he'd unconsciously lifted. He wanted to touch her, wanted to comfort her, yet he didn't dare. Not the way his body burned for her.

"Please take me with you."

Her desperate tone mule-kicked him in the gut. He inhaled a ragged breath. "I can't. As I said before, an outpost in the middle of the Indian territories is no place for a young lady." Besides, if he took her with him, she'd make demands of him. Become an added burden to his already time-consuming commitment to his troops.

She turned slowly and faced him once again. Sandwiched between long, wet lashes, her desolate eyes pierced him as effectively as any arrow. "Other women live at your outpost, do they not?"

Yes, but none as soft and angelic as you. He fisted his hands at his sides. "You weren't raised to endure such a life."

She lifted her chin. "I can learn. I've read extensively, and—"

He snorted. "You can't learn what you need to know out there from a book."

She squeezed her satchel tightly, her knuckles turning white with the effort. "You must allow me to come with you."

"Why? What could possibly compel you to risk your life in the untamed west?"

"I'd much rather face dangerous lands than to continue living with my guardians. I cannot go back to that cold, empty existence."

Cold and empty. Like his. He couldn't hold back a soft moan. "Callie, I—"

She stepped forward and placed a trembling hand on his arm. "Please, I'd be a good wife to you." Her gaze flitted to the bed and back to him. She shivered as though blasted by a cold draft. "In every way," she whispered.

Icy dread coursed through his veins. He couldn't permit his marriage to be consummated. If he allowed her that close, he risked becoming emotionally involved. He wouldn't give any woman that much control over him again. Ever. He'd endured enough pain to last a lifetime.

Chase yanked his arm away from her scalding touch. "No," he ground out. "I don't need a wife, or the trappings that come with one."

First her face fell, then her shoulders. Something bumped his shin. He glanced at the satchel dangling from her limp fingers. Its presence finally registered in his lust-addled brain. "Why the traveling bag?" he asked.

"I had to bring my things with me."

"Had to? Why?"

Her cheeks flamed an enchanting pink. "U-Uncle checked me out of my hotel room. He assumed I'd spend my wedding night with my husband and refused to pay for an empty suite." She nodded at the trunk sitting against the far wall. "I-I thought you knew since he had all my other belongings sent to your room as well."

Christ Almighty. There was no way in hell she was staying the night with him. "I'll go down to the lobby and see to getting your room back."

She stared at him with those luminous eyes. "I-I've tried to do just that. Unfortunately, the hotel has already rented out my room, and...and there are no others available."

Dammit to hell. Chase ran a hand through sweat-dampened hair and glanced furtively about the room. The walls pressed in on him, heavy and suffocating. Much as he wanted to send her on her way, he couldn't. He was her husband and he had a duty to protect her. "Very well. I'll make a pallet on the floor. You can sleep in the bed."

Tension went out of her face. Her lips crept into a tiny smile that sent a thunderbolt of pleasure jabbing into his chest.

27

He groaned inwardly. God help him, but he faced a long, sleepless night.

****

Callie flipped onto her back and stared at the darkened ceiling. Her face still flamed from the intimate sounds of the captain undressing, the thud of his boots hitting the floor, the soft whisper of his body sliding onto the makeshift pallet, and his faint grunt as he settled in for the night.

He'd left earlier, giving her welcome privacy to undress and fortify herself in the huge bed. When he'd returned, she feigned sleep, unable to face him in such a familiar setting.

But she still had a mission to accomplish. And hiding beneath the counterpane wouldn't achieve her goal.

She strained to hear his soft breaths. He was only a few feet away, lying—unclothed—on the floor. Her mouth went dry at the memory of waking beside him, his bare, muscular back gleaming in the early morning sunlight. She swallowed hard and whispered into the darkness. "Captain, ar-are you awake?"

Silence.

"Captain?"

He blew out a long puff of air before answering. "Yes, I'm awake."

"It was kind of you to allow me to stay in your room. I-I'm sorry you have to sleep on the hard floor."

"I've slept on worse."

"I can't even begin to imagine what you've experienced." She heaved an exaggerated sigh of longing. "What is it like to live in the untamed lands?"

"You're not coming with me."

Undaunted by his curt remark, she pressed forward. "I've read many books about the vast flatlands of Kansas, and to the south, hills that roll right up to glorious mountains."

"The books are right, the mountains are glorious. But you're still not coming."

Oh, God. How could he be so stubborn? Could he not hear how desperate she was? In other circumstances, she'd be mortified by her frantic tone. She bunched the quilt in her fisted hands. "Have you ever wanted

28

something so badly, you'd do anything to get it?"

He gave a soft snort. "Never. I'd rather do without."

"I want this opportunity, Captain." Her words came out in a breathless tumble. "I want it with every beat of my heart. A new life. A fresh start. The chance to make something of myself." Despite her efforts to remain strong, a sob caught in her throat.

He groaned and shifted on his pallet. "I understand better than you think I do."

"Then you understand why I can't stay behind. Why I must persist in asking you to take me with you."

"I just can't do it, Callie."

Tears stung her eyes. He wouldn't back down, no matter how much she pleaded. His heart was as hard as the floor he slept on. How would she endure the cold, lonely life that loomed ahead of her?

The downy counterpane grew too hot, almost stifling. Breathing became difficult. Letting go of her caged sob, she tossed aside the covers and leapt from the suffocating bed. She stopped beside the hearth, tears streaming down her face as she stared at the orange embers glowing in the grate.

Footsteps thudded behind her. A second later, the captain's strong hands cupped her arms. "Callie, don't cry," he murmured.

"I-I'm not cr-crying."

"Yes, you are. I can hear the tears in every breath you take."

He tightened his grip and spun her around. For a few breath-robbing seconds he stared down at her and then slid a finger across her cheek to swipe away the wetness.

Callie closed her eyes and savored the tenderness she might never feel again. A thought suddenly bloomed. Her husband might not want the physical closeness of marriage, but perhaps he might need other, non-emotional facets of the union.

Hopeful, she opened her eyes and looked up into his unreadable face. "I could be a good wife to you in other ways," she said, unable to keep a warble of desperation out of her voice. "I could cook and clean for you. Mend your clothes. Do your laundry."

"My striker takes care of those things."

"Please, Captain. I'll do anything you want."

"Going west means that much to you?" he asked softly.

"It means everything. I've never had an opportunity to take control my life. I want the freedom to choose my own friends, to decide what clothes I will wear, to have a home of my own."

"You make the west sound like a fairy tale. It's not."

"I've seen Julia Grant and the effect marrying a military man had on her. She's poised and confident, able to make her own decisions. I believe life at an Army garrison will give me the things I desire most."

He grew silent as though pondering her words. After what seemed like hours, he heaved a ragged sigh. "Very well. Against my better judgment, I'll take you with me."

Her heart took flight, soaring like a freed bird. Sweet, sweet Jesus. He was going to take her! "Oh, Captain, you don't know—"

He placed a finger over her lips, silencing her outburst. "I want to make one thing perfectly clear." He narrowed his eyes. "Are you listening?"

She nodded and he removed his finger.

"Ours will remain a marriage in name only," he continued. "And if I deem you are incapable of the handling the harsh conditions, I *will* send you back."

"Thank you, Captain, thank you," she gushed. "I accept your terms. And I promise. I'll quickly become accustomed to life on the outpost. You won't regret this."

He grunted. "Go back to bed and get some sleep. We have a long train ride ahead of us."

Pulse thrumming, she hurried to the bed and slid under the quilt. She shivered, not from the cold, but the realization her life was about to change. She would become an Army wife, responsible for the care of a home and her husband's needs. Callie hugged herself, unable to believe her good fortune. Her dreams were about to come true.

She lifted her eyes heavenward. *Thank you, God. Please, help me be strong. Help me be the wife this wonderful man deserves.*

THREE

Callie stood on the boarding platform and stared at the railcar in front of her. The open doorway beckoned, yet she hesitated. Once she climbed those steps, there'd be no turning back. At the far end of the platform, the huge locomotive belched a billowing cloud of steam. A sudden gust pushed the acrid fumes over the platform. Men shouted and surged in and out of the haze as they prepared the iron engine for its trek westward.

A loud, whistle pierced the air. Callie flinched and swallowed a nervous gulp. What awaited her halfway across the continent? Her husband had warned her of dangerous, untamed lands. She'd even read newspaper accounts of the brutality of the wild Indians.

She tossed a frantic glance at the pair standing near the edge of the platform. Steeped in shadows, her guardians watched with arms crossed, backs rigid, ready to ensure their charge boarded the train. Callie doubted if even the Indians could be so merciless.

A warm body brushed her arm. She turned and met narrowed, stormy eyes.

"It's not too late to change your mind."

Her heart slammed against her ribs. "But...I-I don't wish to change my mind."

The captain snorted and shook his head. "God knows I should change it for you. The west is filled with all sorts of dangers, dangers a lady like you shouldn't have to face."

But she would face them. Willingly. If it meant being far from her aunt and uncle. "I understand and accept the risks, Captain."

She found herself unable to call him by his name. It would imply an intimacy, something they didn't share. Would never share, based on the condition he'd made in allowing her to accompany him. Much to her relief. Even though she'd offered, the thought of enduring such an unfamiliar and frightening closeness scared her.

He raised an eyebrow. "And do you understand that once we reach Leavenworth, there won't be any fancy carriages to ride in, or feather beds to sleep on? We'll be on horseback, riding through unpredictable weather, eating sparse rations, and sleeping on pallets on the hard ground."

She stuffed down an unladylike snort. As if her life had been a bed of roses with the Boggses. "I won't complain."

"You will when you're hungry, wet, cold, and miserable."

Her pulse skipped. Had he changed his mind about taking her with him? She tightened her grip on the solid satchel handle to bolster her courage. "Please don't force me to stay in Washington."

He regarded her with steely eyes. "I should. I have the right as your husband."

Though her insides writhed like a barrel of eels, she met his gaze. "Please, Captain. I want this. I need it."

He studied her for an agonizing moment and then peered beyond her. "The Colonel is coming. If you're that determined to go, let's board the train."

Callie released the breath she didn't realize she'd been holding and quickly made her way up the boarding stairs before he had a chance to rethink his decision.

"Those seats there," he said, pointing to two facing, unoccupied benches.

She eased onto the leather upholstered seat and scooted to the far side. Outside the window, the capital city loomed in the distance—the last sight she'd see of the East and her family—of Lyss and Julia.

Tears filled her eyes and she dashed them away with an impatient jerk of her hand. No, she wouldn't cry. She could certainly leave her old life behind without any tears. A new home, a new life awaited her. There was no reason to be sad.

A warm, muscular thigh pressed against hers. Calmness drifted over her like a fog enveloping a still lake. It was strange how her husband evoked equal parts dread and trust in her at the same time.

The coach lurched and began to roll forward, gaining momentum as it moved. Colonel Grierson settled onto the opposite bench and gave her a wide, encouraging smile. "Well, we're on our way, Mrs. Brooks."

She nodded and returned his smile. "Yes, we're on our way."

****

After a week of enduring the incessant click-clack of iron wheels, broken only by a barge trip across the Mississippi, Callie heaved a sigh of relief when the train crossed the Missouri River and pulled into their final destination at Leavenworth City, Kansas. She'd had enough of the noise, hard bench seats, and doing her best to avoid her husband's notice. Not that she would even consider voicing a complaint. She didn't want to give the captain any reason, no matter how inconsequential, to send her back East.

They debarked and were met by two uniformed Negroes, one tall with shoulders as wide as a hawk's wing-span, the other shorter and lighter skinned. She recalled Colonel Grierson mentioning that his Tenth Cavalry was comprised of mostly black troopers commanded by white officers. The only Negroes she'd ever met had been servants.

The newcomers snapped brisk salutes. "Colonel Grierson. Captain Brooks," the taller one said. "Your mounts are on the west side of the depot along wif a wagon, as your telegram instructed."

"Thank you, Sergeant." The captain returned their salutes and then handed the trooper several brass baggage checks. "Take Private White with you to the baggage car and retrieve our luggage. Be sure to fetch my wife's trunk as well."

The sergeant shifted widened eyes in her direction before schooling his face into an expressionless mask and looking away. He gave the officers another salute, spun on his heels, and then marched down the platform, followed closely by the other trooper.

Callie shifted uneasily. Her presence had surprised the sergeant. She suspected that would be the case with many of the people she met. How would they greet the captain's unexpected new wife? With reserved politeness, as the sergeant had, or with open disdain?

She had little time to reflect on those thoughts as the captain hurried her to the waiting wagon and handed her onto the seat. The two troopers soon joined them, and the procession headed down the crowded streets of Leavenworth with Colonel Grierson and the captain riding ahead on prancing steeds.

A short time later, they halted in front of a large, four-story building. *Planter's Hotel*, the bold lettering painted atop the establishment's doorway proclaimed.

"Captain Brooks," Colonel Grierson called out. "As soon as you've settled your wife, meet me at post headquarters."

The captain snapped a brisk salute before dismounting. He handed his mount's reins to one of the troopers and instructed another to retrieve her trunk and escort her inside. A few seconds later, he disappeared through the hotel doorway

With the help of a trooper, Callie alit from the wagon and crossed the dirt-packed street to the hotel entrance. Once inside, she paused to survey the large, well-lit foyer. Rich, gilt-framed pictures lined the paneled walls. Colorful carpet runners stretched the length of the gleaming, pine floor and ended at a massive, stone fireplace occupying the far wall. Not what she expected in a frontier city, but quite pleasant nonetheless.

Several buckskin-clad men stood around the blazing fire—lean, dangerous-looking men, most likely hardened by the untamed land they lived in. They ogled her with sweeping stares. One even gave her a leering, hungry grin.

Ill-at-ease, she averted her gaze and crossed to the front desk where the captain was concluding her registration. He turned and glanced at her, before giving the foyer an assessing sweep. He directed a fierce glare of warning at the threesome near the hearth and returned his attention to her.

Callie pursed her lips. Goodness, her husband didn't seem to miss anything, much like a bird of prey watching over his territory. Though strangely pleased by his possessiveness, she couldn't stop the worry from surfacing. Would he consider her too much of a burden to let her stay?

A tall, uniformed officer strode into the lobby, drawing her attention. He carried himself with an air of confidence, shoulders back and head held high. The captain gave a low groan and formed his face into a rigid mask—an expression he usually reserved for her.

The newcomer stopped before them and swept off his hat, revealing shoulder-length, gold curls. "Captain Brooks, what a surprise," he said. "I thought you'd been assigned to Fort Arbuckle."

The captain pulled his body into a taut line and executed a brisk salute. "Colonel Custer, sir, you were not mistaken. I'm just returning from Washington and will be heading back to Arbuckle in a day or so."

Custer returned the captain's salute and moved his gaze to her. "Ah, and who might this enchanting creature be? Surely not your wife."

"Yes, sir, she is. We were married in Washington. Callie, this is Colonel Custer."

The colonel grasped her outstretched hand in a firm grip. "I'm delighted to meet you, ma'am." Deep-set, blue eyes flashed as he grazed her gloved fingers with his lips.

"Colonel," she murmured. Heat climbed into her face as she withdrew her hand from his long-held grasp. What a gallant officer. Similar to her husband in height and breadth, yet so different. A flamboyant peacock compared to the fierce golden eagle she'd married.

"You surprise me, yet again, Captain," the colonel said. "Last time I saw you, you were doing your best to avoid my wife's match-making attempts. And here you show up married."

"Some things are out of our control, sir," the captain replied tightly.

"Yes, they certainly are. Much like those ornery animals we rode in the mule race this past summer." The colonel's glittering gaze swept her face. "I imagine the captain hasn't regaled you with that particular tale, has he?"

Not sure how to take the colorful officer, she shook her head and risked a glance at her husband. A twitching jaw muscle revealed his barely controlled annoyance. Was it the topic being discussed or the tale-teller that had him on edge?

Custer chuckled and began removing his yellow gauntlets. "This past summer, the officers of Leavenworth held a mile-long mule race. The last one to finish was actually the winner of a fifty-dollar purse." He gave a roguish grin. "Of course, no one wanted that distinction, so it was a hard-ridden race, or as fast as you can get a stubborn freighter mule to run."

"And did you lose, or should I say win, Colonel?" she felt compelled to ask.

"Unfortunately, no. My mule, Hyankedank, put forth a gallant effort. So did the captain's mule. Your husband nearly won the race, or as you say, lost it."

The captain cleared his throat and stepped forward, placing a hand at the small of her back as he moved. "Excuse me, Colonel, I hate to interrupt, but I really must see my wife to our room. Colonel Grierson is expecting me at post headquarters."

"Very well, you don't want to keep Benjamin waiting." Custer gave a slight bow. "Mrs. Brooks. Perhaps your husband will bring you by for a visit. Libbie would love to hear all the latest gossip from the East."

Gossip? Mrs. Custer would learn very little from her. She did her best to stay away from Eunice's daily sessions of tittle-tattle. "Perhaps," she said before nodding to the officer. "It was a pleasure to meet you, Colonel. Good day."

Responding to the pressure on her back, she set off for the staircase, trying to ignore the tingles spreading down her spine. Though pleasant, she knew she shouldn't react so unseemly to her husband's touch. The captain expected a platonic relationship, and that's what she intended to give him.

At the top of the stairs, Chase steered Callie toward their room and then removed his hand from her back, now confident his possessive display would deter the threesome lurking in the lobby. Thank God. He didn't know how much longer he could endure the heat scalding his palm.

As they walked down the hallway, he fisted his hand at his side and worked to push aside his annoyance. Callie seemed to draw male attention like a flame beckoned a moth. And the way that brassy Custer had hovered over her hand...

"You don't like him, do you?" she asked.

"Who?"

"Colonel Custer."

"I have little respect for the man, colonel or not."

"Why is that?"

"He refused command of our sister regiment, the Ninth."

Her brow creased into delicate lines. "Why would he do that?"

"Because he didn't want to lead Negro troops."

She deepened her frown. "That's quite narrow-minded of him. What regiment does he command?"

"The Seventh, poor sods."

"You make him sound so dreadful."

"He is. George Custer is a brash, careless leader, more concerned with his own self-importance than the safety of his men. Mark my words, one of these days, his troopers will pay for his recklessness."

She shuddered and drew her cloak closer around her. Chase frowned. Perhaps he shouldn't have been so open with his harsh criticism. But around his new wife, words seemed to slip out of his mouth before he could stop them.

At room eleven, he stopped, unlocked the door, and then stepped aside to allow Callie to enter. She swept past him, leaving a rosy scent in her wake. The aroma invaded his senses, reminding him just how long it had been since he'd enjoyed the sweetness of a woman. A sweetness that could just as quickly turn to poison. He steeled himself against her allure and joined her in the room.

The sparsely furnished chamber contained a quilt-covered bed and a mirrored bureau. A single, wooden chair sat beneath a curtain-draped window. Faded, flowery wallpaper covered the walls. Not as nice as he'd hoped, but it would have to do. At least she had a plump mattress to sleep on after enduring the hard railcar bench.

Private Davis entered the room and deposited Callie's trunk on the floor near the bed.

"Thank you, Private," Chase said. "I'll be down shortly." He returned the trooper's salute and then moved farther into the room.

Callie slid her cloak off her shoulders and he reached to take the garment from her. He fingered the material and grimaced. Much too thin. Damn tightfisted guardians. Couldn't even properly clothe their ward. He tossed the cape across the bed. "Lift your skirt," he told her.

Her doe eyes widened. "Wh-What?"

"For God's sake, lift the hem of your skirt so I can see your boots," he ground out.

Without meeting his gaze, she hiked up her gown and bared worn, leather boots that encased slender, shapely ankles. He tried not to imagine those legs wrapped around his thighs as he hovered over her in the bed.

"Just as I thought," he growled. "You'll need sturdier footwear as well as a thicker, woolen cloak. There should be a woman's clothier somewhere in this overcrowded city. We'll look for one tomorrow."

She drew in a sharp breath and shoved down her skirt. "We-we're going shopping? T-together?" she stammered on a breathless exhale.

"Yes, is there a problem?"

She clutched a hand to her chest. "No...It's just...I've never..." Her face turned a lovely shade of pink. She moistened her lips before speaking. "I've only shopped with Aunt Eunice. Never with a man. Not even Uncle Horace."

The sight of her moist tongue flicking over pale, plump lips sent fire shooting through his groin. He slapped his hat against his thigh as though he could douse the flames. "You need proper clothing," he stated. "And it's too dangerous for you to shop alone. We'll go together tomorrow."

She ducked her head, red still staining her cheeks. "As you wish."

"I have to meet with Colonel Grierson," he added. "Don't leave this room for any reason. Do you understand?"

She gave him a slight nod. "I understand."

"I'll have dinner sent up to you. I probably won't be back until late tonight as I need to coordinate preparations for our trip."

"I'll be fine, Captain. Go make your preparations."

He nodded and headed for the door, doing his best to ignore the lure of the enticing four-poster. He'd not succumb to the bliss of sleep or any other pleasures that bed would hold.

Not now.

Not ever.

****

Grierson's striker shoved a hunk of wood into the pot belly stove and closed the door. Standing on the other side of the room, Chase shifted uneasily. He and the colonel had completed their discussion of departure plans, yet Grierson had asked him to remain. Needed to speak with him on a private matter, he'd said. Despite the warmth of the office, icy dread coated his insides. Instinct told him he wasn't going to like this *private matter*.

Seated at a massive desk near the corner of the room, Colonel Grierson scratched pen to paper and then looked up at his striker. "Private Moore."

The trooper crossed to the desk and stood stiffly at attention. "Yes, sir."

Grierson folded the paper and handed it to Moore. "Take this requisition to the Quartermaster. Posthaste."

The private gave a brisk salute and took the missive. "Sir, yes, sir. Right away, sir." He pivoted in a squelch of boot leather and set off for the door.

As the trooper disappeared through the doorway, Grierson set his pen aside and motioned to the chair facing the desk. "Sorry for the delay, Chase. Please, have a seat."

Please. This didn't bode well. He eased onto the wooden seat and resisted the urge to drum impatient fingers on the armrests. "What was it you wanted to discuss, sir?"

Grierson regarded him across the paper-strewn desktop. "We've known each other long enough that I feel we can be candid with one another."

He shifted in the hard wooden chair. Where was this going? "Yes, sir. We can."

"Good." The colonel thinned his lips. "What I have to say regards your wife."

"My wife? What about her?"

"I'm sorry, Chase, but I don't think you should've let Callie believe you were taking her all the way to Fort Arbuckle with you."

Damn. A bit more candid than he'd like. Chase sat a little straighter. "Callie will be just fine here in Leavenworth, sir. She'll be able to live quite comfortably with the trust her father left her."

"Comfortably, yes. But happily? She has no family or friends in the city."

"Living here will give her the opportunity she says she wants," he replied. "Without the dangers of a remote outpost." *And give me an opportunity to escape her pull.*

Grierson leaned forward and regarded him over the rim of his spectacles. "Leavenworth can be just as dangerous as Arbuckle, Chase. It's still a frontier city, full of riffraff and lawless men."

"I'll set her up with servants who will see to her safety."

"Finding loyal servants takes time. Time we don't have. I just don't think it's a wise idea."

Unease rifled through his gut. Chase rose from his chair and crossed to the window. He stared out at the soldiers marching in precise formation on the parade ground. A barked command rang out and the platoon halted as one. Orderliness and obedience. The only life he'd ever known. The only life that made him feel safe. Throwing a beautiful, unwanted wife into the mix was pure chaos.

He faced his frowning commander. "Colonel, I appreciate your concern. But it would be irresponsible of me to take Callie to Arbuckle if she cannot handle the conditions." And foolish of him to think he could have a typical marriage.

"But to leave her here, alone and friendless..."

"She'll make friends."

"Callie is a sweet girl. But with her severe shyness, I doubt she'll make many friends."

"She has her books. Perhaps she won't want to socialize."

Grierson tapped his fingers on the edge of the desk. A second later, his expression softened. A smile snuck to his lips. "I have an idea."

Chase stifled a groan. He knew that look. And he knew he wouldn't like the colonel's *idea.*

"Why don't you allow Callie to continue on to Fort Gibson with us?" Grierson held up a hand when Chase opened his mouth to argue. "Let me finish."

He snapped his mouth shut and ground his teeth. Christ, what had he gotten himself into? Perhaps he ought to rethink the benefits of having a friend in his commander.

Grierson removed his spectacles. "Along the way, you can take stock of Callie's ability to handle herself." He folded the glasses in his palm and leaned back in his chair. "If you're still inclined to leave her behind, she can stay with Alice and me at Gibson."

Chase shook his head. "I couldn't ask you and Mrs. Grierson to take on a permanent guest, Colonel."

"You're not asking. I'm offering. Alice would love the companionship. And it would give Callie a chance to adjust to life as a military wife, with Alice's guidance."

Chase ran a hand through his hair. "I appreciate your suggestion, sir. But I've already made up my mind."

Grierson frowned. "You're sure?"

"Very sure." He straightened and squared his shoulders, returning to the comfort of military correctness. "If you'll excuse me, sir, I need to see to preparations for our departure."

"Fine. I'll not pressure you further, Chase. Just think about what I've said."

He nodded and set off across the room. He'd think about the colonel's offer. But only as far as the office door.

****

Callie strolled along the boardwalk, passing door after door of quaint, inviting shops.

Colorful fabrics, shiny footwear, and glinting jewelry filled the display windows. A vendor stood in a doorway, smiling and hawking his leather goods. Another held open his door, allowing the heady aroma of freshly baked bread to escape. Most anything one desired could be found in Leavenworth.

Callie slowed to avoid a passing couple. An elbow brushed her arm. The offender mumbled a brief pardon.

She grimaced. Anything one desired—provided one had the fortitude to navigate the loud, fast-moving mob.

The figure walking beside her angled closer. She glanced at her imposing husband and felt safe and protected. Her only nagging worry was how she would endure the intimate task of shopping with a man without flaming into a bonfire of embarrassment.

"Why, Captain Brooks," came a gushing female voice. "What a pleasure it is to see you again."

Just ahead of them, a petite brunette stood on the boardwalk, twirling a fringed parasol over her head. She looked the perfect, stylish lady in her emerald green silk with matching shoes and bonnet. Beside her, a taller blonde dressed in a frothy pink confection of ruffles tilted her head and devoured the captain with gleaming, cat-like eyes.

The captain bowed and tipped his hat to each of the ladies. "Miss Stephens. Miss Dandridge."

The brunette snapped her parasol shut and stepped forward. Her long eyelashes fluttered seductively. "Libbie told us you were in town." She cut green eyes in Callie's direction, throwing daggers before her lips puckered into a pout. "She said you had gotten married. Tell us it isn't true, Captain."

"Yes, *please* tell us it isn't true," Miss Dandridge purred.

The captain cleared his throat. "You were informed correctly, ladies. I did get married in Washington. May I introduce my wife Callie?"

Two pairs of eyes sliced into her. Callie suppressed the urge to step back, away from their menacing stares. Despite the cool day, perspiration dampened her chemise.

"Mrs. Brooks," the two snapped in unison, bouncing brisk curtsies of clearly unwelcome greetings.

"Ladies," Callie murmured.

Miss Stephens scrunched her brow into a frown. "Are you in mourning, Mrs. Brooks?" she asked, her voice tinted more with sarcasm than concern.

She blinked in confusion. "N-no. Why do you ask?"

"I just assumed...with all that black...well..."

Callie glanced down at her faded black traveling ensemble. Compared to their colorful plumage, she must look like a drab little cowbird. "I—"

The captain's warm hand pressed into her back. "If you ladies will excuse us," he announced. "My wife and I have a few errands to take care of before daylight runs out." He gave her a gentle nudge forward.

Blonde eyebrows snapped together. "But, Captain—"

"Good day, ladies." He guided her past the two scowling women.

Miffed exclamations followed them down the boardwalk. Callie glanced at her husband. She couldn't blame the two ladies for resenting her. With his wide-brimmed hat pulled low and a uniform that hugged his strapping form, he cut quite a dashing figure, a handsome officer who would make any woman's heart flutter.

She knew hers did.

Her gaze drifted to firm lips now thinned into a taut, annoyed line. Her heart lurched. Was he angry at being forced to marry her when he could have his pick of lovely women like Miss Dandridge or Miss Stevens?

Her thoughts scattered as a protruding plank caught her boot heel. The boardwalk pitched beneath her. She flailed the air like a wind-tossed windmill. Her fist connected with the captain's mid-section, and he expelled a pained grunt.

As she regained her footing, heat scorched her cheeks at her clumsiness. She reached for the captain, and then, thinking better of it, fisted her hand at her side. "I-I'm so sorry. Ar-Are you all right?"

"Yes," he hissed through clenched teeth. "I'm fine." His hand closed around a nearby doorknob. "I believe the ladies' mercantile is in here."

As she darted inside, a knot formed in her belly. Dear God. How could he possibly want to stay married to a dreary, clumsy urchin like her?

FOUR

Muted chatter and the clatter of silverware filled the hotel dining room. A single candle flicked light onto the tabletop and the accumulation of dishes and glassware. Chase leaned back in his chair and took a sip of brandy, enjoying the slow burn as the spirits slipped down his throat and settled in his stomach. His gaze drifted to the nearby window. A brisk wind tossed snow flurries against the panes and managed to shove a cool draft through the sash. The candle flame sputtered and then flared back to life.

He grimaced. They would have a cold start to their journey in the morning. Though he was accustomed to the bitter weather, his raven-haired dinner partner wasn't. He regarded Callie over the rim of his glass. A healthy pink had replaced the ashen tone of her skin. Her cheeks glowed with contentment. He deepened his frown. Would the harsh trail conditions rob her of that glow? The thick, wool cape, gloves, and sturdy boots he'd insisted she purchase ought to help. But he knew from experience she would need more than warm clothing. The untamed southwest required grit and determination.

Callie dabbed at the corner of her pretty mouth and lowered her napkin. Her lips crept into the tiniest of smiles as she stared at him with those doe-eyes that would haunt him until the day he died. "Thank you for such a lovely dinner," she said. "It was delicious."

He returned her smile. "I hope you enjoyed it. That's the last good meal you'll have for a while."

"I would have been just as content with a plate of beans."

Yes, he imagined she would. Callie was the most unassuming woman he'd ever met. Was it any wonder he found himself drawn to her?

"Do you want anything else? A slice of pie? Cake?"

She shook her head. "No. Thank you. This was plenty."

A waiter approached to clear away their plates and refresh Callie's wine glass. She took a sip and when she lowered her glass, moisture glistened on her rosy lips. The urge to savor her slammed into him. Hard. He stuffed down a groan. Those warm, pliable lips haunted his dreams and often invaded his waking thoughts. Like now, when he should be enjoying the last taste of good brandy he'd have for a while, all he could think about was tugging her into his arms and making a meal of her lips.

She glanced around the room until her gaze found him again. Their eyes met and held. A current passed between them like the jolt from a lightning bolt. He knew he should break the connection, but couldn't summon the willpower.

Callie flushed a charming shade of pink and fidgeted with the cuff of her sleeve. "I-I want to thank you again for purchasing this gown for me, Captain. Though, it was totally unnecessary."

Captain. Would she ever feel comfortable enough to call him by his name? His insides twisted at the thought that she wouldn't. "Do you like the dress?" His gaze slid over the butter yellow creation that clung to every enticing curve. He certainly did.

Her face lit up like a sun-drenched meadow. "Oh, yes. I've never had anything so beautiful."

"Then it was necessary."

Her radiance was near blinding, a complete contrast to her earlier crestfallen expression when the snobbish Miss Stephens had looked down her nose and criticized her clothing. Anger filled him at the memory. He tightened his grip on his brandy glass. Callie hadn't deserved such treatment. If that snooty cow had been a man...

At that moment, he'd known he couldn't leave Callie in Leavenworth. Not with vultures like Miss Dandridge and Miss Stephens hovering about. His shy, timid wife wouldn't begin to know how to protect herself against such women. She'd be miserable. He couldn't do that to her.

He'd decided to accept the colonel's suggestion of allowing Callie to travel with them to Fort Gibson. Alice Grierson would be a much better companion, helping the timid girl fit into military life with friendly, caring guidance. Callie would be able to achieve the things she wanted out of life. And he found he wanted her to have them.

He grimaced inwardly. Dammit, when had he started to care?

****

"You doin' okay, Missus Brooks?" Private Jackson asked. His concern-filled gaze swept over her face.

Callie forced an answering smile. "Yes. Thank you for asking."

"Trail ridin' can be awful hard on a body if'n you're not used to it."

She merely nodded and tried not to squirm in the rock hard side-saddle. After three days of riding, her entire body throbbed like a bad tooth. She'd ridden for pleasure many times in the past, but never anything like this—hours and hours of bone-jarring plodding with only a brief respite at noon for water and a hastily consumed biscuit. She never expected the conditions to be so harsh.

But she wouldn't admit such a thing to anyone. The captain mustn't learn of her difficulties with the demanding journey. His threat to send her back East stuck in her mind like a fly caught in molasses.

Ignoring the pain, she focused on staying upright in the saddle. Sandwiched in the center of the formation, her well-mannered mare followed the horses in front of her with little guidance. Which was good, because Callie doubted her frozen fingers could do much controlling.

The captain and Colonel Grierson trotted in the lead, their steeds blowing puffs of steam as they plowed through the ankle-deep snow. Behind the two officers, six troopers rode two-abreast, their short overcoat capes flapping in the brisk wind. Eight more troopers trailed behind her in the same formation, the last two leading the pack mules.

Over her right shoulder, the sun sank toward the horizon. She heaved a soft sigh. Surely, they'd stop soon.

As though he'd read her thoughts, the captain raised

46

his hand and called a halt near a large copse of cottonwood trees growing along a half-frozen stream. Tufts of brown grass poked through the snow-blanketed earth and whipped in the wind. A quaint setting, but not charming enough to take her mind off her misery.

Her mare stopped with the rest of the horses, but Callie remained in the saddle, gathering the courage to climb off. There was only one way down. And it was going to be painful.

All around her, troopers dismounted and led their weary mounts to the creek. Her mare shifted and chomped on the bit. Poor thing, she needed a rest, too.

Callie clenched her teeth and slid slowly from the saddle. As her feet hit the frozen ground, every muscle in her body cried out in agony. Her knees wobbled and threatened to buckle. With a groan, she gripped the stirrup strap for support and closed her eyes, willing away the pain.

Her husband would *not* see how unsuited she was for this type of travel.

An anxious voice penetrated her agony. "Missus Brooks? I need to take yo mare to the creek."

Callie opened her eyes to find Private Jackson standing near the horse's head. A troubled frown lined his forehead. Her stomach knotted. He mustn't see how weak she was. As the captain's striker, he might feel obligated to tell his commander about her condition.

She locked her knees to keep from falling, released the stirrup, and gave him a nod. "Thank you, Private. You may take her now."

He hesitated, and she thought for one frantic moment he might question her. Instead, he gave her a friendly smile, and then turned to lead the mare and his own mount toward the stream.

Callie glanced at the glittering water and ran her tongue over dry, cracked lips. A cool, refreshing drink sounded wonderful. Her gaze drifted to the troopers rushing around her, setting up tents and running picket-lines for the horses. She frowned. Perhaps it'd be best if she went herself. The captain might disapprove of her taking his men from their work.

Steeling herself, she set off for the creek, taking slow,

short steps to avoid slipping on the slick snow. Sounds from the campsite faded as she threaded her way through the thicket to a denser, more secluded spot.

Unable to take another step, she sank to her knees at the edge of the burbling, crystal-clear creek. She removed her gloves, broke through the ice with her fist, and scooped up a handful of water. Soothing, icy liquid slid down her parched throat as she drank.

Ah, Heaven. Just as she expected.

She downed several more handfuls and then wet the hem of her gown. She scrubbed away the accumulation of dust and grime until her checks and hands tingled. Her impromptu bath complete, she pulled on her gloves and leaned back on her outstretched arms to rest before attempting the arduous task of returning to camp.

Exhaustion settled over her like a blanket. She closed her eyes and tilted her face to the faint rays filtering through the bare branches. So peaceful, so—

The crack of twig pierced the air. Startled, she snapped open her eyes and twisted toward the sound. The captain stood a few feet way, arms crossed over his chest, eyes narrowed and stormy.

Her pulse leapt. Uh-oh. That expression didn't bode well. She sucked in a gulp of frosty air. "I-Is something wrong, Captain?"

He uncrossed his arms and moved closer. "Yes, there is. I don't want you to wander off on your own. We're moving into hostile land where danger can come up on you quickly."

"H-Hostile land?" She cast a furtive glance around the dense copse. She'd been so caught up in her misery that she hadn't even considered the danger.

"I've posted sentries," he added. "But I want you to stay closer to camp from now on."

"I-I will." She licked her lips. "Do you think we'll see any..." she swallowed hard, "...Indians?"

"In these parts, you never know. Many tribes are not happy with the handling of the treaty agreements. Renegade war parties have been known to leave the reservation and attack unprotected settlements."

Sweet Mary. The thought of an Indian attack scared her more than she would admit. What if savages had come upon her alone by the creek? A shiver coursed through her.

He held a hand out to her. "If you're done, let's return to camp."

Callie slipped her hand into his and silently prayed her aching legs wouldn't betray her. She rose, took a step forward, and—to her dismay—promptly stumbled on the frozen, uneven ground.

The captain curled a muscular arm around her waist and pulled her against him. Heat flared inside her at the contact, warming every nook and cranny in her body. She tensed at the pleasure. She'd never felt such an overpowering attraction. It frightened and excited her at the same time. And was most definitely a reaction her husband would frown upon.

She steadied herself and pushed away. "Thank you. I can manage on my own now." She headed for the campsite as fast as her stiff, protesting legs would allow and hoped he would attribute her awkward gait to the slippery trail.

Seemingly an eternity later, the path opened onto the bustling camp. A moss-covered log lying near the campfire beckoned to her. She crossed the clearing and gingerly planted her throbbing bottom on the make-shift bench. Once settled, she glanced up, surprised and a little disappointed to find her husband no longer followed her.

Private Jackson approached, toting a tin of steaming coffee and a mess kit heaped with fried salt-pork and corn-mush. "Suppa, Missus Brooks?"

"Thank you, Private." She took the proffered items and nodded at the log. "Won't you join me?"

"I'd love to, soon as I get my rations." Moments later, he returned and sat beside her, heaving a contented, but clearly weary sigh, as he settled on the log. "We sho did cover a lot of ground today. Close to thirty-five miles."

She gave him a wry smile, wanting to acknowledge that her backside had suffered every jolt of those thirty-five miles. But she didn't dare. She didn't know the captain's striker well enough to trust him.

"How much further to Fort Gibson?" she asked instead.

"Bout seven mo days, if'n the weather holds out. And another five days to Arbuckle."

She groaned softly. How in the world was she going to survive another twelve days in the saddle? The thought made her aches throb harder.

Determined to keep up her strength, she shoveled a spoonful of corn mush into her mouth. The bland gruel basted her tongue and stuck in her throat. She grimaced and reached for her coffee.

"Add some of this to it first," a deep voice sounded behind her.

Turning, she spied the captain holding a silver flask in his outstretched hand. "What is it?"

"Whiskey."

"Whiskey!" she blurted. "I don't drink hard spirits."

"I didn't say you did. But a shot will help ease your saddle-sore muscles."

She opened her mouth to argue, then snapped it shut with a click of her teeth. He mentioned her saddle-sores. He knew. Her heart skipped a beat. Would he pronounce her unfit to continue on the trip?

Private Jackson reached for the flask. "I'll take care of it, Cap'n." He poured a generous dash of whiskey into her coffee and handed her the mug. "Try it, Missus. Brooks," he urged. "As the Cap'n says, it'll help ease your aches."

Callie risked another glance at her frowning husband. Perhaps if she drank the stuff, he would see that she was making an effort and wouldn't send her back East. She lifted the tin to her lips and took a cautious sip. Fiery liquid scorched a trail down her throat. She couldn't contain a gasp.

"The first swallow is the worst," the captain said. "Make sure you drink all of it." He then spun around and strode away.

Callie struggled for breath. Even if she wanted to reply to his cryptic command, she couldn't. She could barely suck in a gulp of air, much less talk.

The flames in her mouth soon abated and she managed to resume eating. In between bites of food, she cautiously sipped more of the alleged tonic and discovered, as the captain said, each subsequent swallow was easier to handle.

When she finished her meal, Private Jackson took

her dinnerware and headed for the stream. She slumped with weariness and closed her eyes, amazed to find her soreness had indeed lessened, leaving her weak and sluggish as a newborn kitten with a bellyful of milk.

"Taps for you, my dear."

Taps? Whatever did that mean? Callie opened her eyes and looked up at her husband. His hovering figure wavered. She blinked to clear her vision. It didn't help. The captain and the copse tilted. Her stomach flipped at the odd sensation. She groaned and gripped the log to brace herself.

The captain gave a soft curse and scooped her into his arms. The captivating scent of wood-smoke, horse, and man invaded her senses. She steeled herself against the urge to cuddle deeper into his embrace, a gesture that would definitely be unwelcome.

She rocked against his solid chest as he carried her across the clearing. Pleasant warmth that had nothing to do with the whiskey spread through her. Callie stiffened. She shouldn't be having such strong reactions to her husband. It just wouldn't do. He'd made his position quite clear in allowing her to come with him.

Seemingly hours later, he set her on her feet outside their tent. Head spinning, she stumbled into the canvas shelter and collapsed onto a furry pallet. She snuggled into the nest, ready to succumb to the blissful oblivion of sleep.

The captain's gentle hands curled around her waist and hefted her to a sitting position. She groaned at the intrusion and focused on his handsome face burnished gold by the firelight filtering through the cloth walls. Through a haze, she watched as he slid off her cloak and then moved to her boots.

It was such a sweet, tender gesture.

A wistful ache filled her. *Chase.* How she wanted to call out his name, burrow back into his arms and feel the closeness that had been missing in her life. But she couldn't. It wasn't what he wanted from her. Regret thickened in her throat. If only they'd met under different circumstances. Perhaps he would be more trustful of her, more accepting.

His task complete, he looked up and met her

gaze."You'll need to apply some liniment to those saddle-sores, or you won't last another day on the trail."

Liniment? "I don't understand..." She shook her head and then wished she hadn't. Bile burned in her throat and supper threatened to make a second, less appetizing, appearance. She moaned and braced a hand on the floor. "Oh, God...please stop the spinning."

He reached for her. "Callie—"

"I-I think I'm going to be sick."

"Shhhh...Lie down, then." He gently pushed her onto the pallet.

She relaxed and closed her eyes. Sleep. That's what she needed. A long night of blissful...

A faint rustling sounded beside her. Without warning, he lifted her skirt. A cool rush of air swirled around her bared bottom. She gasped and attempted to rise.

"Stay still." He pressed her back down onto the pallet. "I'm not going to hurt you."

Her pulse pounded in her ears. Dear God, despite his vow not to, her husband intended to have her. Here. *Now.*

She tensed and squeezed her eyes shut, recalling Eunice's words to remain still and endure the pain. Her books had detailed what would transpire, and she hoped the event would be over quickly, just as her aunt said it would.

Despite the icy fear coursing through her, a pleasant throb flowered between her legs. She waited with indrawn breath, wondering if perhaps Eunice had been mistaken about how unpleasant joining with a man could be.

Sweat beaded on Chase's forehead as he stared at Callie's exposed flesh. A groan slipped from his throat. He couldn't do it. Couldn't touch her silky thighs and not have her. He was already growing thick and hard with want.

He thought he had himself under control, thought he'd be able to ease her discomfort with the liniment. Lord knew she needed it. The pain slicing her lovely face had driven him to retrieve the salve. He hadn't intended to apply the damn stuff himself, but in her drunken state, he knew she'd have a difficult time doing it herself. She could barely sit up, much less twist to reach her backside.

Yet, the sight of her creamy skin was more than he had bargained for.

"No way in hell," he muttered. With a jerk of his hand, he yanked her skirt over the enticing view. Her musky scent wafted upward, making him throb all the harder.

Callie rolled upright and stared at him with wide, luminous eyes. Rosy lips were parted in innocent invitation. Her breasts rose and fell enticingly as she inhaled rapid gulps of air.

He groaned again and shoved the liniment jar into her hand. "You'll have to do this yourself," he snapped.

She blinked and looked down at the tin pot. "Wh-what is it?"

"It's liniment."

"Liniment?"

"Yes. An old, Indian remedy we carry for saddle-sore recruits. Rub it on your...um...it takes away the pain."

"Oh," she murmured and then lifted widened eyes to his face. "That's what you were...er..." She tugged her bottom lip between her teeth and averted her gaze.

He stared at her pink flesh clenched between those pearly teeth. Sweat dampened his shirt. Christ, lusting after his wife was the last thing he needed. "I have to check on the sentries." He began backing out of the tent, away from her alluring pull, away from temptation.

Once outside, he drew in a gut-deep draught of air. Good God, what in hell had he been thinking? He might as well crook a finger at the devil as look upon Callie's tantalizing flesh.

Her gagging gasp drifted through the tent walls. "This smells worse than an untended chamber pot."

A smile crept to his lips. She'd opened the tin. He knew very well how bad the ointment smelled. The fumes could tarnish steel. "You'll appreciate the results despite its unusual odor," he told her.

Callie remained silent as though she hadn't expected him to still be outside the tent. "But I'll reek," she finally replied in an anxious tone.

"We're all accustomed to the smell. Apply the ointment as best you can, then get some sleep. We have another long day ahead of us."

And I have a long night ahead of me—stuffed against the tent wall, listening to your soft breaths and trying not to remember the sight of your smooth, sleek thighs.

FIVE

For the next few days, the detail continued southward, crossing numerous shallow rivers and burbling creeks before reaching the clear waters of the Grand. They forded the swiftly flowing river and then followed well-defined buffalo trails etched into the hard-packed earth. With the help of the stomach-turning salve and a hardened resolve, Callie found the demanding journey easier to handle. She looked forward to seeing what the next bend in the trail would reveal.

Her excitement was only dampened by her husband's behavior. Ever since he'd given her the liniment, he'd barely spoken a dozen words to her. He kept his distance, letting Private Jackson tend to her needs. Her heart ached to rekindle the tenderness Chase had shown her that night in their tent. *Chase.* Even if she couldn't say his name, just thinking it made her feel closer to him.

One night, with supper over and darkness moving in, Callie settled on a log near the campfire. She absently watched a group of troopers seated around a blanket they'd tossed on the ground. Coins clinked as the men pitched money into a growing pile. Soft laughter and the shuffle of cards filled the air.

After a few hands, Private Jackson chucked his cards onto the blanket and stood. "That's enough fo me. You fellas done cleaned me out."

As he drew next to the log, Callie looked up at him. "I read about this game. It's called poker, is it not?"

"Yes'm. We was playin' five card stud."

"Why don't you take Moz's place, Missus Brooks?" asked one of the troopers.

She shifted uneasily. Play cards? With the men? Though the idea was intriguing, she couldn't imagine engaging in such an unfamiliar activity. Was such a thing allowed, anyhow?

"Th-thank you for your offer, but I-I don't know how to play," she stammered, not knowing what else to say.

"That's all right," Private Brown stated. "We can teach you."

She gave a tiny shrug. "I-I'm afraid I don't have any money."

"Yes, you do," came a deep voice behind her.

Turning, she looked up into Chase's expressionless face. Her heart skipped a beat. How long had he been standing there?

He held out a fisted hand. "If you want to play, here are some coins."

She bit down on her bottom lip. He didn't seem angry at the idea of her playing cards. Yet, with Chase, she never could be sure *what* he was thinking. "I-It's alright, if I do?"

"Not many women know how to play poker," he said. "But if you want to learn, I see no reason why you can't."

Her stomach fluttered. He actually spoke to her, encouraging her to play. Perhaps she could attempt it. Wasn't that why she'd insisted on going west in the first place? Here was a perfect opportunity to conquer her fears and experience something new.

Determined to at least try, she accepted the coins and moved to the blanket. She sank to the ground and did her best to return each of the troopers' welcoming smiles. Despite her efforts to relax, perspiration dampened her palms.

"We'll play blackjack," Private White announced. "Moses can hep you with the first few hands 'til you catch on, Missus Brooks."

Callie nodded and swiped her palms on her skirt.

Private Jackson squatted beside her, his deep voice gentle and comforting as he explained the game. "The object is to reach a total of twenty-one without goin' over. That's a bust. The ace can either count as one or eleven. Kings, queens and jacks are ten points each."

That seemed easy enough to remember. She nodded again and focused on the dealer.

Private White's slender fingers deftly flipped through the cards as he shuffled and re-shuffled the pack. He clamped the stub of an unlit cigar between his teeth and began to distribute the cards—two faced up and one faced down—to each player.

She'd been dealt a six of hearts and a two of clubs.

Moses tapped her stack with his finger. "That one flipped under is a hole card. Take a peek, but don't turn it over jus' yet."

She carefully lifted a corner of the down-turned card. A jack of clubs. Hmmm...eighteen total. Was that good or bad?

Moses inclined his head toward the blanket. "Toss a nickel into the pot. You're betting that your hand will win."

Must be good. She did as he instructed. The faint tinkle of coins rang out as the other players did the same.

Private White pulled the cigar stub from his mouth. "Hit or stay, Missus Brooks?"

Hit or stay? So many strange terms. She looked in confusion at Moses.

The trooper made a slashing motion with his hand. "You stay. Anything over seventeen, keep what you got. Don't take no more cards."

"I'll stay then," she said.

Private White nodded and queried each of the other players. More coins plunked onto the blanket. "Okay Martin, you got eleven showin'," the dealer stated. "Is you staying on that?"

Private Davis bit the side of his lip. "Umm...no, hit me."

"You sho?" Private White asked, lifting a skeptical eyebrow.

"Yes, hit me." The young trooper rolled his eyes heavenward. "Come on all you angels, no face-cards."

Private White stopped mid-deal. "You shouldn't be calling on *all* the angels in Heaven, Martin."

The trooper frowned. "Why not?"

"Didn't you hear 'bout that cavalry officer?"

"No. What about him?"

Private White fingered his cigar stub. "Weeeell, I heard tell there was this cavalry officer galloping away from a band of chargin' Injuns. His horse stumbled and pitched him to the ground and he broke his leg. He prayed for *all* the angels to help him back on his horse." Private White paused and glanced around at his captive audience.

"Lordy, George," Private Brown exclaimed, "don't leave us a hanging."

"Yeah," another muttered. "Finish the story."

Callie leaned forward. *Yes, George, what they said.*

Private White grinned and continued. "With extra-*ordinary* effort, the officer leapt onto his horse and promptly fell off the other side. Once agin lying on the ground, he looked up to the Heavens and said, 'All right, jus' half of you this time.'"

The troopers gawked at the smiling dealer, each looking like a child robbed of a promised peppermint stick. Callie ducked her head and stifled a giggle. Out of the corner of her eye, she saw Private Jackson shake his head.

"Do you jus' lie in your bunk thinkin' up these stupid stories, George?" Moses scoffed.

"You laugh at most of my jokes, Moz," Private White replied, his voice rising in playful indignation.

Another trooper snorted. "George, that one was so dumb, it was funny."

He smiled. "I'm glad you liked it, Henry."

"Jus' deal the card to Martin," Private Jackson muttered with a roll of his eyes.

"Fine." Private White tossed a card onto Martin's pile.

It was a five of diamonds. A wide smile dimpled the trooper's baby-smooth face. Callie bit her lip to keep from laughing. Private Davis would need to work on his "poker face" a bit.

"Okay genelmen, let's see 'em," George called out.

Private Brown dug an elbow into the dealer's gut, evoking a pained grunt.

George grimaced and rubbed his ribs. "Whadja you do that for, Henry?"

"Ladies, too."

Private White glanced in her direction. "Sorry, ma'am, ladies, too."

Callie smiled and flipped over her card, watching as the others did the same. Private Davis issued a hoot of laughter and scooped up the pile of coins he'd won.

"Lucky scamp," George grumbled.

The trooper grinned. "Must've been *half* them angels this time."

Callie's smile spread to her heart. Why had she been afraid? These men were the friendliest, funniest bunch she'd ever encountered. How lucky she was to be included in their game.

A strange euphoria enveloped her. She finally felt a part of something. Accepted. And she owed it all to one man. Callie could sense his presence behind her, watchful and intimidating. How was it that after only a short while in their jovial company, she felt more comfortable around his men than she did around their commander?

Chase stood behind the group ringing the blanket, his eyes riveted on his wife's slender back. Firelight tossed golden streaks onto her ebony locks. He fisted his hands against the urge to move closer and run his fingers through the silky strands. After nearly losing control of himself during the liniment debacle, he'd vowed to stay clear of her, put temptation out of his reach.

Yet, time and again, he found himself drawn to her. Like now. He should leave. Check on the sentries. Check on the horses. Anything, but remain by the campfire and his tempting wife. However, he couldn't move. It was as though shackles held his feet chained to the ground. He wondered for the hundredth time why he'd agreed to bring her with him.

Hand cupped to his mouth, Private Jackson leaned toward Callie, yet Chase could still hear the trooper's whispered remark. "If'n George don't have a nine in his hole, you kin probably win this hand."

"But he can't have one of those cards." She waved her hand over the blanket. "They're all either showing or were used in the previous hands."

"What!" Private White exclaimed around the cigar stub clenched between his teeth. "Moses, did you teach her to count the cards?"

"Course I didn't," Moses huffed.

Chase smothered a grin. In addition to being a beauty, Callie was a quick study. His men didn't stand a chance against her. Neither did he, it seemed. He cleared his throat. "Unless you men want to be cleaned out by a pretty card shark, you'd best fold up for the night."

Moses chuckled. "I think you have the right of it, Cap'n." The trooper pointed at the cards lying on the blanket. "What you got, George?"

Private White thinned his lips and flipped his hole card to expose a seven of clubs, not enough to beat Callie's hand.

With a loud guffaw, Private Jackson swept the coins into her hands. "Don't you mind George none, Missus Brooks," the trooper told her. "He's just a sore loser."

On the other side of the blanket, Private Brown shook his head and groaned as he climbed to his feet. "I don't know 'bout ya'll, but I'm wif the Cap'n. I'm goin' to call it a night."

The others murmured in agreement and began to rise.

Chase extended his hand to Callie. Supple fingers slid into his palm, sending fireworks shooting up his arm. He stifled a groan.

She rose, steadied herself, and then thankfully pulled out of his grasp. "Here are your coins, plus a few extra." She held her fisted hand out to him. "Thank you for the use of them."

"Keep the money," he said. "The troopers may want a chance to win it back."

She gave him a hesitant smile. "All of your men are so kind and friendly. They make me feel quite welcome."

"You make it easy for them to welcome you. Most white women refuse to come within ten feet of a Negro."

She lifted her chin. "I would never treat them like that."

Chase glanced at his retreating troopers, glad they had accepted Callie into their fold. She needed their friendship. He wouldn't allow himself to get that close to her. He couldn't.

His tattered heart wouldn't survive another betrayal.

****

As her mare traversed the backbone of a small knoll, Callie glanced at the billowing clouds streaming like horses' tails across the blue sky. The winds had shifted overnight, bringing warmer air into the region and melting the snow. Green shoots had popped their heads through the soggy earth, eager to greet the life-giving sun.

She likened herself to those tender sprouts, stretching toward the unknown, eager to welcome her new life. She'd already made a good start by overcoming her fear and socializing with Chase's men. At this moment, she believed she could tackle any obstacle.

A splash of white flashed in the brush beside her. Startled, she jerked her head around and spotted a long-eared rabbit racing across the meadow.

"Jackass rabbit," Private White announced behind her.

She twisted to face him. "Why are they called that?"

"Them hares got ears longer than a mule's. They make a mighty fine stew, too. Shame we can't hunt none."

"Oh? Why not?"

"Rifle fire might draw any hostile Indians in the area down on us."

Hostile Indians. A fearful shudder rattled through her. She pulled her cloak tighter.

"You know what goes good with rabbit stew, Missus Brooks?" the trooper added.

She shook her head.

"Wild prune pie, that's what. You eva had wild prune pie?" His toothy grin held the promise of another witty yarn.

She smiled. "No, I can't say that I have."

He looked past her. His grin fell into a disturbed frown, and he reached for his rifle. "Hostiles," he shouted. "Ridin' hard from the west."

Her heart leapt into her throat and she turned her head with the others. In the distance, a large band of mounted Indians swarmed down a hill and raced toward them. Piercing yips and pulse-stopping howls filled the air. All around her, the scrape of withdrawn rifles sounded, followed by the ominous click of cocked triggers.

Her stomach seized. *An Indian attack! Sweet Mary, please let this be a dream.*

"Into that ravine ahead," Chase commanded.

Callie leaned forward as her mount surged forward with the rest of the horses. The mare's pounding hooves matched the thud in her chest. She swallowed the last bit of moisture in her mouth and grimaced. Grit and fear clogged her throat. This was no dream. It was a nightmare.

Minutes later, the detail roared to a stop in a wide gulch. Troopers dismounted and rushed to position themselves along the rim. Callie slid from her saddle and stood in the middle of the melee, looking around in bewilderment.

A muscular arm clamped around her waist and tugged her toward one side of the steep-walled ravine. Hovering over her, her rescuer forced her against the dirt wall and then gently pushed her into a squatting position. "Stay down," he ordered.

Chase. Even if she wanted to reply, she couldn't. A deafening barrage of gunfire blasted out as the troopers fired at the approaching Indians. The bone-rattling sound reverberated down her spine. Her vision clouded as memories of a long-ago day burst into her mind.

Cannon-fire. A loud explosion. Smoke and choking dust. Bile climbed in her throat. A celebration turned ugly and painful.

The thud of pounding hooves penetrated her fog.

She blinked to clear her eyes and gaped in horror as a painted Indian galloped into the gully. Arrows spurted from his bow like bullets from a gun. One projectile zinged inches from her head and lodged in the dirt wall beside her. The feathered rod quivered from the impact.

Her skin crawled with goose-bumps. She wanted to scream, wanted to burrow into the ravine wall. But the most she could manage was a tiny squeak and a fistful of soil.

Troopers fired at the attacking warrior. The Indian's mount stumbled, righted itself, and then plunged to the ground, squealing in agony. The unhorsed brave rolled to his feet and gave a hair-raising yelp. With his brightly decorated face contorted in rage, he lifted his bow to resume shooting.

Gunfire blasted out. Red exploded on the warrior's chest. He jerked from the force of the bullets and one sickening second later, fell across the now still and silent carcass of his horse.

"Sergeant Greaves," Colonel Grierson shouted over the din. "Check and make sure that heathen is dead."

The sergeant raced toward the fallen brave. Using his rifle barrel, he flipped the Indian onto his back and then stuck the tip against a blood-smeared temple.

Callie shuddered and averted her gaze from the horrid sight. An agonized scream sliced the air to her left, and she jerked her head toward the sound. With pain contorting his baby-smooth face, Private Davis collapsed against the ravine wall, a hand pressed to his bloodied shoulder.

Her heart lurched. Dear God. She should go to him. Give him whatever aide she could. But, heaven help her, she couldn't. Her trembling legs refused to move.

Callie watched helplessly as the trooper slid to the ground and the dark stain on his jacket grew larger. Images from that long ago day returned. The endless streams of blood. The agonized screams and the mangled, unmoving bodies. She'd been just as powerless to help that day as she was now.

An eternity later, the rifle fire dwindled and stopped. Chase stepped away from her and looked down, his expression tense with concern. "Are you all right?" he asked.

She nodded, unable to speak past her fear constricted throat.

"Good. Stay here." He spun around and signaled to his men with a jerk of his hand. "Sergeant Greaves, watch for them to regroup. The rest of you tend to the wounded while you can."

He then crossed to Private Davis and knelt beside the injured trooper. Chase gently pushed aside Martin's blood-caked hand. Fresh blood surged from the ragged bullet hole.

Callie tensed. Dear God, that bleeding had to be stopped or Private Davis would die. *Put pressure on it.*

Chase glanced over at her. "What did you say?"

She blinked. Had she spoken aloud? "P-put pressure on the wound," she repeated. "It'll help stop the bleeding.

Chase stared at her with glittering, unreadable eyes and then yanked off his yellow neckerchief. He stuffed the makeshift bandage against the wound and pressed down with the heel of his hand. Martin groaned, but remained still.

When Private Brown arrived to take over the trooper's care, Chase rose and strode toward her. "How did you know to apply pressure to stop the bleeding?"

"I read an article written by Doctor Atkinson. Th-That's what he recommended for heavily bleeding wounds."

"Private Davis is fortunate you've read extensively."

"Yes, well, I...wish...I-I wanted to help, but..."

"Combat is not easy to bear. Even the bravest of men cower at times. You did well for your first encounter."

His encouraging words failed to comfort her. She should have helped when Martin fell. He was so young and innocent, not a day over sixteen, at best. Callie fisted her hands, digging fingernails into her palms. She would never forgive herself if he died because she couldn't force herself to move.

Colonel Grierson approached and nodded to Chase. "What's our situation, Captain?"

"It appears the Kiowa are done for the day, sir," Chase replied. "We'll make camp here tonight and try to move-out in the morning. As for the men, we've got four wounded, one pretty seriously." He glanced at Martin. "Private Davis took a bullet in the shoulder and bled extensively before it was staunched. We need to get him to Gibson as soon as possible."

Grierson frowned. "They were Satanta's warriors, were they not?"

"Yes, sir. I'm hoping it was just a hit and run tactic, and he'll head back to the sanctuary of the reservation."

The colonel grunted in agreement and shifted his gaze to her. "Mrs. Brooks, I'm glad to see you are unharmed. As I said before, your husband will take good care of you."

"Yes. He did. Thank you, Colonel."

He looked back at Chase. "Let me know if you need me, Captain."

As the colonel strode away, Callie studied her husband's rigid profile. He stood like a statue, stiff and unmoving, as he peered beyond the ravine at the distant hills. His face barely betrayed the weariness she knew he must feel after such an intense battle.

She managed to rise on shaky legs and glanced at the

churned-up meadow. Lifeless bodies, human and animal, littered the ground. Her gaze drifted to Private Davis and her stomach sank.

Another sad day that would forever haunt her thoughts.

SIX

Callie reined her mare closer to Private Brown. "How's he doing?"

Holding the limp body of Martin Davis before him on the saddle, Henry frowned and shook his head. "Not so well, Missus Brooks. He stopped moanin' hours ago."

Worry gnawed at her insides. That didn't sound good. Not good at all. "The captain says we should be nearing Fort Gibson soon."

"Yes, ma'am. Just over that rise of hills ahead."

She glanced at the swell of grassy knolls in the distance. "Hang on, Martin," she murmured. "It's not much further."

The patrol soon topped the hillock overlooking Fort Gibson. An American flag fluttered from a pole set in the middle of a large parade ground. Soldiers marched in formation across the dirt-packed field, kicking up dust as they moved. Dozens of wood-hewn buildings dotted the enclosure.

As the detail entered the garrison, Private Brown peeled away and followed a well-worn path leading west, most likely toward the hospital where Martin would get the aid he needed. Callie sent a silent plea heavenward, praying the Army doctors would be able to help the wounded trooper.

Chase reined in beside her and nodded at the teeming parade ground. "Almost half the regiment is here preparing for the move to Camp Wichita," he said. "Unfortunately, that means all available quarters are occupied. Colonel Grierson insists you stay with them while we rest and re-supply."

And where will you stay, she wanted to ask. She nodded instead. "That will be fine, Captain."

The patrol halted in front of a clay-and-mud-chinked

cabin set at the far end of a long row of similar buildings. As Colonel Grierson dismounted, an older, dark-haired woman pushed through the front door and raced down the porch steps. "Benjamin," she cried out as she rushed into the commander's arms. Behind her, four children poured onto the veranda, their excited yelps filling the air.

Callie looked away from the intimate greeting. Her gaze landed on Chase, who now stood next to her knee. He raised his arms, offering to assist her off the mare. Panic surged through her at the thought of him touching her, of making her body react in that strange, uncontrollable way it always did. Yet, she couldn't refuse his help. Not in front of his men.

Steeling herself, she unhooked her leg from the pommel and slid into his arms. As he lowered her to the ground, her breasts skimmed his hard, muscular chest. Despite her attempt to keep her reactions in check, a pleasant ache surged through her. She wanted so badly to mold against him, to feel his warmth, feel...

Dear God, this had to stop. She moved out of his embrace and concentrated on brushing away the imbedded trail dirt. Where was a bucket of water when you needed one? Her skirt and unwanted desires needed a good dousing.

Chase cleared his throat, drawing her attention upward. The colonel and his wife stood before them, smiling patiently. Heat suffused her face at getting caught unawares.

"Mrs. Grierson." Chase swept off his hat and inclined his head. "I'd like to introduce my wife, Callie."

"It's so nice to meet you, Mrs. Brooks." Mrs. Grierson glanced at her prancing, howling brood and smiled. "Benjamin says you'll be staying with us for a few days. I hope you won't mind living with four noisy children. I'm afraid they're quite excited to see their father."

"Please, call me Callie." She smiled as well, relieved by the woman's warm greeting. "The children won't be a bother at all. Thank you for allowing me to stay with you."

"It'll be nice having another woman in the house. Captain, have one of the men bring her things inside."

"Yes, ma'am." Chase tugged on his hat. "Callie, if you should need me, I'm billeting with the men outside the parade area."

So that's where he'd be staying. She should be glad to have a few days respite from his disturbing presence, yet she wasn't. Though she'd slept huddled against one side of their tent, with him on the other, she'd miss the odd intimacy, the comfort of knowing he was only an arm's length away.

Alice Grierson's sweet voice intruded on her thoughts. "Callie, how about a nice cup of tea? I have some wonderful English teas Benjamin brought me last summer."

"That sounds wonderful." Callie gave Chase one last, lingering look, and then joined the cheerful pack entering the cabin. Her heart lightened as Colonel Grierson tossed a giggling toddler high in the air. With such enjoyable distractions, perhaps her stay without Chase wouldn't be so bad.

Besides, it would give her a chance to tame her reactions to him.

****

The next afternoon, Alice and her four children escorted Callie on a tour of the garrison. They passed the bakery, a kitchen, and a large mess hall. The fort swarmed with uniformed men, who entered and exited the massive barracks and nearby officers' quarters like bees in a hive.

The eldest Grierson boy drew next to her, his chest puffed out like a bantam rooster. "I'm going to West Point just like my father," the fourteen-year-old boasted.

"How wonderful, Charlie," she replied. "Have you ever traveled to the East?"

"Only as far as Illinois. That's where our family is from. I'm going back this fall to continue my education."

"I'm going to be a doctor," Robert asserted as he stepped between Callie and his brother.

Charlie frowned and gave the younger boy a shove. "Go 'way, Robbie. I was talking to her first."

"You just want to talk with her 'cause you think she's pretty. Captain Brooks wouldn't like you sparkin' his wife."

With a cub-like growl, Charlie charged his brother and tossed him to the ground. Arms and legs flailed as the

68

two tussled on the roadway, kicking up a large cloud of dust.

Callie pressed a hand to her chest and took a step back. Good Heavens. Was this normal behavior for young men? Tutored alone at her guardians' home, she hadn't been around many young males while growing up, especially ones prone to brawling.

"Charles Henry Grierson," Alice scolded as she bent and snatched a handful of shirt collar. "Get off your brother this instant."

Charlie grunted and rolled to his feet. Young Robert spat on the ground and then jerked upright. The two continued to glare at each other like a pair of bristling dogs.

Alice placed fisted hands on her hips. "Such behavior in front of a guest, you ought to be ashamed of yourselves. Both of you go back to the house and wait for us to return."

The twosome hung their dirt-streaked heads. "Yes, ma'am. Sorry, Mrs. Brooks," they responded in unison before turning and heading home.

Alice gave Callie a wan smile. "Please excuse the boys. This is a hard life for them, moving from place to place, living in tents for most of the year."

"I understand." She glanced at the pair. "Will they be all right?"

"Oh yes." Alice waved a dismissive hand. "They'll soon be best friends again and plotting new misadventures to undertake."

"Oh, well, I'm glad...I guess."

Alice nodded and grasped Callie's elbow. "Let's continue on, shall we?"

A feeling of contentment washed over her as she fell into step beside the friendly woman. In the space of one day, she had come to admire the colonel's gracious wife. Self-confident and poised, Alice reminded her of Julia Grant. Military life must surely create such women. Hope blossomed at the thought—one day—she might become just like them.

They reached a long, rectangular building. Alice stopped at the foot of the stairs and snagged Harry's arm. "Here's the hospital," she said. "You mentioned that you wanted to check on Private Davis?"

Callie nodded.

"Then, I'll wait out here with Harry and Edie," Alice continued. "I'm afraid they'll disturb the men if I take them inside."

"I won't be long, then."

"Please, take all the time you need."

Callie mounted the stairs and walked through an open doorway into a large chamber. Dozens of cots, some occupied and some empty, lined both sides of a central walkway. The room smelled surprisingly clean and well-aired. She hadn't expected to find a Territorial medical facility following the innovative healing methods she'd read about. Private Davis was clearly in good hands.

"Can I help you, ma'am?"

Turning at the sound of the deep, masculine voice, she gazed up into two glittering sapphires, the bluest, brightest, most disconcerting eyes she'd seen since meeting Chase Brooks. "I-I'm looking for Private Martin Davis," she managed to say.

He studied her for a moment, then pointed to the far end of the room. "He's over there," he answered in a quiet, formal tone. "If you'll follow me..."

She trailed him down the aisle until he stopped at the foot of an occupied cot. Covered to his shoulders with a fresh, white sheet, Private Martin seemed to be sleeping quite peacefully. His breathing appeared normal and the grayish pallor was gone from his face.

Relief flooded her at finding him looking so well. "Thank the Lord," she murmured.

"Private Davis is very fortunate," her escort replied. "He lost a lot of blood before he arrived. I didn't think he'd make it through the night, but he fooled me."

"Yes, he's very strong and courageous. Are you his doctor?"

He smiled. "Yes, ma'am. William Giles."

"Pleased to meet you, Doctor Giles." She couldn't help but return his smile. He reminded her of the doctors in Philadelphia. The reserved, professional bearing, the comforting warmth one would expect to find in a good physician. And he was very handsome.

"I'm Mrs. Brooks," she explained. "Thank you for

taking such good care of Private Davis. It was a terrible battle. I'm just thankful so few were injured."

"You were there, ma'am?"

"Yes, my husband's men were ambush—"

"Brooks, did you say?" He cut her off, puzzled. "The only Brooks I know is—" The jeweled eyes widened. "Mrs. Brooks, as in, *wife* of Captain Chase Brooks?"

"Yes. Chase Brooks."

In an instant, the professional decorum evaporated, and William Giles let out a hoot. "I must apologize," he said with a shake of his head. "You took me by surprise. I've known Chase for quite a long time. Years, in fact. A wife is...er...the last thing I expected him to bring back from Washington."

Not what the captain expected to bring back either. She almost said it and then thought better. "It happened rather suddenly."

"Love at first sight, eh?" He was still shaking his head, delight flashing in those charming blue eyes. "Well, I'm not surprised. Chase draws women like moths to a flame."

"Really?" She bowed her head, recalling the lovely Misses Dandridge and Stephens.

"Yes, ma'am. Always has. There'll be a trail of broken-hearted women all the way from here to Arbuckle."

There must have been something in her expression, because he quickly resumed his reassuring bedside manner. "But those days are, I'm sure, now behind him." Doctor Giles grunted. "Chase would be a damn idiot..."

The comment trailed off. Callie looked up, anxious to hear the remainder of his thoughts. But the doctor no longer looked at her.

"Well now, speak of the devil," he exclaimed. "Chase, you ole hound dog, did you expect to keep a wife as pretty as this a secret?"

"From a self-proclaimed lady's man like you, Will? Absolutely."

Callie wheeled around and froze. Chase's gait was easy and relaxed. He was laughing. In fact, he grinned like a fool. For a moment, she wasn't sure this man was her husband. Well, at least she knew he *could* smile.

Something else was different about him as well...Ah, he'd shaven. For the first time, she realized he had dimples. Darling, enchanting dimples tucked into the corners of his smile. It nearly took her breath away.

Chase stopped beside her and extended a hand to Doctor Giles. "Good to see you, my friend. I see you've met my wife." He placed a hand at the small of her back, a subtle yet oddly possessive gesture. "Callie, this is an old friend of mine, Lieutenant William Giles."

"Yes, we've met," she said. The warmth of Chase's touch radiated down her spine in pleasing waves.

"Callie, is it?" the doctor asked. "What's your given name?"

"Callista," she replied.

"Ah, Callista. A late Latin name derived from Greek word *kallistosa*, meaning 'most beautiful.' Very appropriate."

"You read Greek, Doctor Giles?"

"I read anything I can get my hands on," he stated. "And by all means, call me Will." He flashed a devastating smile.

Warmth crept up her throat and into her face.

"And you, Callie?" he added. "Do you read Greek?"

"My wife," Chase said before she could so much as draw a breath, "is quite well read."

"An educated woman...out here." Will gave Chase a wink. "You're full of surprises, my friend. Perhaps she can teach you a thing or two."

"At least I'm smart enough to learn," Chase bit back.

"Really? I'd like to see—"

"I have a small library," she interrupted. They were beginning to remind her of the squabbling Grierson boys. "A modest collection, but I'm quite proud of it."

"Here? With you at Fort Gibson?" the doctor asked.

"Yes. Would you like to see it?"

"Truly?" His blue eyes sparkled. He clasped her hand and pressed it to his heart. "I will promise you anything, madam, if you will share your books."

Chase groaned out loud. "You're flirting with my wife, Giles."

"She's offered me books. I may have to steal her away from you."

"Be careful. I may just let you have her." Chase turned and abruptly changed the subject with a wave toward the sleeping trooper. "How's Private Davis doing?"

As the two men settled deep into discussion about Martin's care, Callie stepped back, putting distance between herself and Chase. *I may just let you have her.* He was joking, of course. Yet something pinched. His tone, perhaps. The quickness of the remark, as though the thought was already formed.

Despite her attempt to shut him out, Chase's deep voice intruded. "No, that was General Sheridan's idea. Perhaps we should discuss this later, Will."

"Perhaps we should," the doctor responded. "How about this evening after mess?"

"I should be free by then. My requisition for carbines finally arrived, and I've ordered the men to test them on the firing range. I'm headed there now."

"Excellent. We can sample a bottle of Tennessee whiskey I bought off a peddler last fall."

A hand brushed her elbow. "Callie, are you ready to leave? I met Mrs. Grierson out front and told her I would escort you back. She left earlier with the children."

She faced him. "Certainly. I just wanted to check on Private Davis." She nodded to the blue-eyed physician. "Good-day, Doctor Giles."

"Good-bye, Callie. Come back and visit *any* time."

Chase heaved an exasperated sigh. "God, Will, don't you ever give up?"

"Never," the lieutenant replied with a laugh. "I'll see you this evening, Chase."

A smile crept to her face as they descended the front stairs. "You're close to Doctor Giles, aren't you?"

"He's like a brother to me."

"How long have you known him?"

"We met during the War. He helped me save a good officer and friend."

"Helped you, how?"

Chase looked past her. His gaze grew distant, almost haunted. "A fellow officer, Lieutenant Wiggins, took a mini-ball to the thigh. It was days before we could get him to the field hospital. Infection set in. Will wanted to amputate, but Matthew begged me not to allow it."

She could feel Chase's anguish plowing into her, even now, years after the War had ended. "And you stopped Doctor Giles from carrying out the procedure?"

"Yes. Despite his misgivings, Will removed the mini-ball and showed me how to care for the festering wound. He came by as often as he could to help. With a little luck and a lot of hard work, Matthew survived."

She broadened her smile. "I'm beginning to like Doctor Giles, more and more."

Chase's cloudy gaze cleared. "Yes, well, we should get going. I hope you don't mind if we stop by the firing range first. I need to check on the men."

"No, I don't mind." She tensed as his hand settled once more at the small of her back, making her body hum like an angel's harp. Would she ever become accustomed to his merest touch? It was quite disconcerting. And if Chase ever discovered her reactions...

She focused on the dirt-packed path ahead of her and tried not to think about the pleasing sensations riding her spine. As they crested a small incline, she shielded her eyes from the sunlight and surveyed the field below. Half a dozen troopers huddled around a mule-drawn wagon. Private Brown crouched in the wagon bed, attempting to pry the lid off a long, wooden crate. The men caught sight of their commander and immediately jerked to attention.

Chase waved a dismissive hand. "At ease, men. Let's get started while we still have some daylight left. Sergeant Greaves, set up targets at fifty and one hundred yards."

"Yes, suh," the sergeant replied and then directed the men to unload the wagon.

They toted a dozen sacks across the field and propped them against stakes driven into the ground. A red circle had been painted in the middle of each bag.

Chase pulled a rifle from an open crate. "You'll have to get used to this short cocking blade," he told the men gathered around him. "Spencer moved it to the left of the breech block carrier, but it should make reloading a lot quicker."

"That's music to my ears," Private White sang out in his customary jovial tone.

"Take a moment to get familiar with the firing

mechanism, then we'll start zeroing them in." Chase shifted his gaze in her direction. "Callie, stay behind the wagon where it's safe."

With the unnerving memory of the Indian attack still fresh in her mind, Callie quickly moved behind the wagon. He didn't have to tell her twice. Panic fluttered inside her at the thought of the noise to come. She locked her knees against the urge to run. If she wanted to be a good military wife, she would need to control her fear of gunfire.

Callie braced her arms across the wagon rails and watched the men. Each trooper withdrew a rifle from the crate. Private White muttered another comment. She couldn't hear his words, but judging from the grins on the other men's faces, it must've been a comic one.

"Form up," Chase commanded.

The troopers broke apart and formed a line at the edge of the field, facing the sack-targets.

"Ready," Sergeant Greaves called out.

In one fluid motion, the men lifted their weapons, barrels pointed skyward.

"Aim."

Like the rippling motion of an ocean wave, they lowered the rifles and aimed at the sacks. Callie tensed, waiting for the blast she knew would follow.

"Fire."

The loud crack of belching gunfire reverberated in her ears and rattled her teeth. Although she had been expecting the thunderous sound, she jumped. The men fired several more rounds, each blast mining holes in her skin. Her knees wobbled. She tightened her grip on the wagon to keep from swaying. Sweet Mary, how could she hope to become a competent military wife if she cowered at the sound of gunfire?

"About six inches high at fifty yards," Sergeant Greaves announced during a lull in the firing.

Chase strode behind the formation. "Good. Now try one hundred yards."

Another volley of rifle fire resounded across the meadow. Stuffing flew into the air as bullets ripped through the thick burlap.

"Four inches, Cap'n," the sergeant exclaimed

excitedly.

Chase nodded, clearly pleased. "Better than I expected. Let's test as many as we can."

The troopers returned to retrieve more rifles from the crate. With the absence of gunfire, Callie's pulse slowed. Her breathing began to even out. She heaved a relieved sigh. That wasn't so bad. At least she hadn't fainted.

Sergeant Greaves rounded the wagon and stopped next to her. He lifted his hat and swiped sweat from his brow with a faded neckerchief. "Aftanoon, Missus Brooks," he greeted. "Nice day for early spring."

"Y-yes, it is," she managed to squeak.

"Have you eva fired a rifle before, ma'am?"

She shook her head. "N-no. My Uncle Horace refused to keep firearms in the house. Said only evildoers kept such things."

He grunted and looked across the wagon. "Cap'n, might be a good idea to give Missus Brooks a quick lesson on shootin'. She ought to know how to handle a rifle in these parts."

Her heart crashed against her ribs. Her? Shoot a rifle?

Chase stared at her and then moved to the edge of the field. "Come over here, Callie."

She dug her fingernails into the wood plank and shook her head. "I-It's not necessary."

"It is necessary," Chase replied. "I want you to be able to protect yourself should you need to."

Her vision blurred. Knees she'd managed to bring under control began to tremble. She stiffened, struggling to remain upright. "I-I can't," she whispered.

Chase frowned and headed toward her. "Why can't you?" he asked, his tone edged with frustration.

"I-I just can't. Please." She looked up at him, knowing her expression held fear, but was unable to conceal it.

Chase studied her for few agonizing seconds and then nodded. "Very well, I won't force you." He turned back to the men. "Sergeant Greaves, continue testing the rifles. Set aside any that aren't working properly. I'll be back shortly."

The walk back to the Grierson's was silent and quick. As they neared the cabin, Chase pulled her to a stop beneath a tall cottonwood. He scoured her face as though wanting to memorize every feature. His gray eyes darkened and pain darted into his expression.

"Callie, there's something I have to tell you," he said, his voice strangely drawn.

Her heart plummeted to the ground. Something told her she wasn't going to like what he had to say. "Wh-what is it?" she asked, though she really didn't want to know.

He reached for her trembling hand and gave it a squeeze of reassurance. "Don't be upset. It's for the best."

Her stomach joined her heart in the dirt. She closed her eyes and battled the dread welling inside her. "What's for the best?" she managed to whisper.

"I want you to stay here with the Colonel and Mrs. Grierson."

She forced open her eyes. "Stay here?"

"Yes. I'll be going on to Arbuckle without you."

Without her. A sob caught in her throat. *No, no, no!* He didn't mean it. He couldn't. "I-I don't understand." Her constricted throat made speaking difficult. "I th-thought you had...accepted our marriage."

"Callie, you can have a wonderful life here with the Griersons. And with Alice's guidance, you can achieve the goals you've set for yourself."

Dear God. Chase didn't want her. He might as well plunge a knife into her heart as to leave without her. Tears burned in her eyes and she choked back another sob. "I-I'll learn to shoot a rifle if that's what you want."

"It's not learning to shoot or anything else. I just think you'll be safer staying here at Fort Gibson."

"But, I-I want to go with you." She drew in a shaky breath. "Please don't do this, Captain."

"Callie, I—"

The cabin door banged open, interrupting him. Footsteps clattered down the stairs, and a tiny human projectile careened into her, nearly knocking her to the ground. Chase steadied her and then reached down to ruffle Harry's copper locks. The youngster yelped and swatted at the sizeable hand attacking his head.

Callie stole a glance at her husband, surprised by the tender expression etched on his face. Did he yearn for a son? A child he could love and raise to follow in his footsteps? Yet, creating a child required intimacy, a familiarity Chase swore would never occur. And his leaving would forever seal that vow.

Harry tugged on her skirt. "Callie, come inside. Time for jack-rocks."

She peered at the boy through a watery haze. "All right, Harry, just a minute." She lifted her gaze to Chase. His stoic expression had returned.

"Good-bye, Callie," he said, his gray eyes now dark and unreadable. "I hope life here will give you what you want." He then spun around and strode down the path, taking what she feared was the only thing she wanted in her life.

SEVEN

"Of all the harebrained ideas." Will grunted and shook his head. "Have you been drinking that rotgut poison Tatum sells?"

Chase clenched his whiskey glass tighter and shifted in his chair. "No, I haven't. And the suggestion came from Colonel Grierson. I wouldn't call the man *harebrained*."

"Have you even thought this through?"

"What's to think through? There's nothing wrong with wanting to see my wife taken care of."

Will snorted. "There is, if you're not the one doing the caring."

He tossed a glare at his friend, for all the good it did. Will's ole hound dog, curled near the hearth, would've paid more heed to such a look.

"Chase, you can't just leave her here," Will admonished. "She belongs with her husband...with you."

"Callie belongs where she'll be happy and safe."

"She can have that with you at Arbuckle."

He ground his teeth and looked away from Will's knowing stare. No, she couldn't have those things with him. He'd just make a mess of this marriage, just as he'd done with his first.

"She's not Miranda," Will said softly as though reading his mind.

"God-dammit, Will, leave it be."

"No. I'll not let it be. You're my friend, and I think you're making a big mistake."

Chase turned and glared at his persistent friend. "My mistake was telling you in the first damn place."

Will thumped down his glass, sloshing liquor onto the side-table between their two chairs. "I see you're still as pig-headed as ever."

Chase grunted. What a waste of good whiskey.

Will leaned back in his chair. A moment later, he steepled his fingers under his chin and gazed at Chase through narrowed eyes. "You're starting to care for her, aren't you?"

His stomach rolled over. Christ. Why hadn't he remembered how damn shrewd Giles was? A chameleon couldn't hide from the wily bastard. He blew out a long puff of air. "I don't want to discuss this, Will." A cold bite laced his forceful tone.

Will ignored the warning. "You care."

He bounded to his feet with a growl. "I said I didn't want to discuss my wife—"

"She's breeching your walls, and it scares the hell out of you."

Chase tossed back the remainder of his drink and then slammed the glass on the side-table. Hands fisted at his side, he stalked to the window and stared out into the darkness.

Sweat pooled in his armpits and soaked into his shirt. Yes, he cared for Callie. She was a breath of fresh air in his stale, stagnant life. As much as he wanted to stay away from her, he couldn't. All along the trail he'd sought her out—wanted to be near her, wanted to keep her safe. Even now, thoughts crept unbidden into his mind, of their future, of children. Of heated, tantalizing nights.

To have those things, he needed to open up to her, trust her. He needed to let himself feel again.

A hand clamped down on his shoulder. "Chase, you can't hide behind that fortress for the rest of your life," Will said. "Sooner or later, you've got to let someone in."

Pain knifed into his chest. "I did that once, and you see what it got me."

"Don't paint all women with the same brush, Chase. What if she's the one woman who could teach you to love again?"

He faced his friend and grimaced. "Christ, Will. Now you're going all sappy on me."

"But, what if she is? That one in a million we're all looking for?" He shook his head. "I can't speak for you, but I don't plan to spend my whole life in the Army. Someday I want to leave this behind me. Settle down with a good woman, have a family, die an old man in my own bed in my wife's arms. If the right woman came along...well I'd hate to think I missed the chance at happiness because I was too pigheaded, or scared, or just plain stupid."

Chase drew in a ragged breath. "What if she's not *the woman?*"

"You'll never know if you leave her here." Will gave his shoulder a gentle squeeze. "From what little I've seen of her, Callie seems to be a sweet, young lady. And, she's accepted your decree of no intimacy...though, how you can turn away from a woman as beautiful as she is..."

"*Lieutenant,*" Chase growled in warning.

Will slid his hand away. "Take her with you, Chase. Take life one day at a time. Let things develop slowly, naturally. Who knows what the future holds."

"Besides," he added, his chin thrust up in challenge. "The Chase Brooks I know would never run from a fight. Isn't your own life worth fighting for?"

Chase fisted his hands at his sides. He'd rather battle a horde of renegade Indians than put his heart back out there to be stomped on. What he wouldn't give to have one of those peyote-induced visions foretelling the future. Then again, with his rotten luck, all he'd see was Callie in another man's embrace.

****

Twenty-four hours later, Chase tied Zeus to the picket line, gave his mount an appreciative slap on the rump, and headed toward camp. They'd made good time today, crossing the Arkansas at noon, and then pushing further south at a good enough clip to get here and set up camp before sundown. Weather permitting, they'd reach Arbuckle within the week.

As he entered a small clearing, his gaze immediately found the captivating creature perched on a log near the fire. Radiance lit her face that had nothing to do with the firelight. It began that morning. Her cheeks had flushed with obvious delight when he told her he'd changed his mind about bringing her along. Even through the hard ride her glow remained. She'd stayed bright as a candle all day.

She glanced up, caught his look, and smiled. She lifted her hand to her throat and then higher to tuck a loose curl behind her ear. It was an utterly feminine gesture—one that filled him with a sudden, fierce joy. A joy that just as quickly dulled to dread.

Not long ago, Miranda had smiled at him, too. Patted her hair like that. Tilted her head and batted her lashes and used all the typical female tricks to wrap him around her finger and tie him up in knots. He'd spent a great deal of time since then hardening himself to such illusions until finally he could look at a woman—have a woman—but not give any of himself away.

Yet unlike his first wife's smile, Callie's bloomed first in her eyes. It was warm, sincere, heartfelt, and he knew it was coming even before those soft, full lips began to curl. Looking at that mouth now, Chase wasn't surprised at the pull in his groin. Christ, he was a man after all, and a man who hadn't had a woman in his bed for longer than he cared to recall.

Of course, he noticed those whiskey-colored eyes, the raven sheen of her hair, the promise in that lush body. But he also noticed the protective instincts she brought out in him. His satisfaction in pleasing her and both the pride and jealousy he felt when other men looked her way. In the back of his mind, he saw the firm rein on his control slide another notch.

Callie turned back toward the fire, and Chase blew out a breath he hadn't meant to hold. Giles suggested letting things develop slowly, naturally. Had almost made it a dare. Chase cursed himself for rising to Will's bait, though in his heart he knew that wasn't really why he'd relented. His friend had been right—Callie was getting to him, a fact made more compelling because in her innocence, she was completely unaware of doing it. Every moment, she crept deeper into places he swore no one would ever reach again. He had no idea how to stop it—was no longer sure he wanted to try.

Private Jackson bobbed a nod at the sizzling skillet he held over the flames. "Suppa's 'bout ready, Cap'n. Why don't you grab a tin and eat with your wife?"

Chase frowned. There was no way he'd be able to keep his body from betraying him. "I have to check on the sentries," he replied. "I'll eat later."

He plunged into the copse, forcing his mind away

from Callie and onto his duties. After a brief conversation with Corporal Dunn and the other pickets, he returned to camp, taking care to remain a good distance from his alluring wife. He accepted a tin of beans from Moses and settled at the thicket's edge. Despite his efforts, his gaze strayed to the campfire where Callie held court over a handful of troopers.

"How's about a game of poker?" Private White invited.

Henry Brown shook his head. "Naw, my eyes is too tired to look at a hand of cards."

The others nodded in agreement.

George leaned against his saddle and tucked his hands behind his head. "What? Ain't you feeling lucky on yo birthday, Henry?"

"I told you not to say anythin'," Private Brown huffed. "I don't want a big fuss made 'bout it."

George snorted. "Not much fuss we kin make out heah."

Callie's mouth lifted into a heart-stopping smile. "Do you know how the custom of celebrating birthdays started, Private Brown?"

Her sweet, tantalizing voice called to Chase like a siren summoning a lost sailor. He stilled his fork and leaned forward, wondering what amazing tidbit she would dispense.

"No ma'am, I sho don't," the trooper replied.

"Well, the custom started in Europe a long time ago. To protect the birthday person from evil spirits, friends and family would gather around, bringing gifts and good wishes."

Henry raised a dark eyebrow. "No foolin'?"

"It's true," Callie added. "There are many rituals associated with birthdays. In Germany, if a man reaches the age of thirty unmarried, he has to clean the steps of city hall. All of his friends throw rubble for him to sweep."

Private White gave a laughing bark. "Henry, you'd best buy you a good, sturdy broom."

Chase hid his smile with a forkful of beans. George White was in the wrong profession. The clown should've joined a traveling circus. He shook his head and returned his gaze to Callie's animated face. She was enjoying herself. Even her ever-present stammer was gone. She interacted with his troopers just like the perfect officer's wife, friendly and respectful. His heart crow-hopped. No wonder he couldn't leave her with the Griersons.

He prayed he hadn't made the wrong choice.

"The sweeping is said to show all the maidens how well the man cleans house," Callie continued. "Perhaps even gain him a sweetheart."

Private Brown grimaced and rubbed the scar on the side of his face. "Good sweeper or not, it'd be hard for a marked man like me to spark a woman."

Her smile faded. "How did it happen, Henry?"

Chase tensed, wondering if his men would keep the tale toned down. He didn't want them frightening her with the gory details of Henry's injury.

"Some dam—" Private White broke off and tossed a sheepish glance at Callie. "Oh, 'scuse me, ma'am." He cleared his throat and began again. "Some fool Irish infantryman wearin' drinkin' jewelry caught Henry with a right hook."

"Drinking jewelry?" she asked.

"Yes'm. They's horseshoe nails bent into a ring with the nail heads pointin' up. Worn on the fingers, they's nasty little buggers in a fight."

Chase frowned and watched his wife intently. She didn't seem distressed by the brutal description. In fact, her expression softened, and she placed a comforting hand on Henry's shoulder.

"Well, Private Brown," she murmured. "That scar actually makes you look quite intriguing, like a dangerous, seafaring pirate. Were you back East, I've no doubt the women would fall at your feet."

Private White smirked. "Yeah, laughing."

"George!" Callie admonished, adding a "tsk-tsk" of annoyance to her scolding.

The abashed trooper ducked his head. "Sorry, ma'am."

Chase swallowed a gulp of coffee. His diminutive wife had his sometimes difficult troopers eating right out of her hand.

He'd best be careful, or else he might find himself doing the same. He was willing to let his relationship with her develop slowly, just not blindly.

****

For the next few days, Chase pushed the detail as much as he dared. He had three recuperating troopers and a wagon loaded with rifles to consider. Not to mention a wife unused to riding over such grueling terrain.

On the evening of the fourth day, he stopped the patrol on the north bank of the Canadian River. He watered Zeus and then led the steed to the picket line. After removing the saddle and sweat-soaked blanket, he rubbed the horse's dampened coat with a cloth rag.

Private Jackson approached and placed an arm across the stallion's rump. "You sho you don't want me to do that, Cap'n?"

He shook his head. "No. I'll take care of him tonight."

"All right then. I found a spot in the river where there might be a school of papermouths. Think I'll see about catching some fo suppa."

Chase's mouth watered as the trooper disappeared into the brush. Flame-kissed crappie sounded awful good, much more appetizing than the hardtack and beans they had been eating. Anticipating the tasty meal, he resumed the ritual of grooming his mount. He usually delegated the task to Moses. But just now, the chore took his mind off other more distracting thoughts.

Faint footsteps approached. Chase tensed and halted his movements. A quiver trotted down his spine. Only one person could tread so delicately, could torment him so effortlessly.

Callie's sweet voice drifted over him. "Zeus looks like he's about to fall asleep."

Heat shot through his veins. Chase shifted the rub-rag to his other hand, refusing to look at his wife's entrancing face. "He's always a pussycat when getting brushed."

"I can sympathize with him. A good cleaning sounds like heaven. I'd like to bathe in the river if that's all right."

Chase suppressed a groan at the image of her in the river, water sluicing around her bared flesh. He recalled the smooth whiteness of her thighs and knew the rest of her would look just as silky.

"Captain?" she persisted.

He sucked in a steadying breath and turned his head. Even with her face streaked with dirt and her hair disheveled, she looked like an angel. He nodded in the direction of the river. "There's a shallow bend about fifty yards down river you can use. Don't go any further," he warned, knowing his sentries guarded the camp within that distance.

She gave a quick nod, pivoted, and headed for the river. He knew he shouldn't, but he just plain couldn't help himself. He watched her glide through the tall grass, her backside swaying provocatively. Flames licked at his loins. He ached to have her—there, now—on a soft mattress of grass.

Zeus stomped his hoof, jarring Chase back to reality.

He gave the horse a pat. "Thanks for the reminder, ole boy." He had to keep his thoughts away from his wife's comely attributes. He would not consummate his marriage, no matter how much he desired Callie. She hadn't proven herself to him. And they were headed for a garrison filled with hundreds of men, any one of whom could entice his new bride away from him.

Sergeant Greaves emerged from the underbrush. "Double sentries are posted as directed, Cap'n."

Chase looked up from his task. "Good. I hate to burden the men with extra duty, but we can't allow our cargo to fall into enemy hands." *Neither the guns, nor Callie.*

"Satanta won't get his filthy hands on our rifles," Julius replied. "I already warned the men to keep a sharp eye out. Private Brown spotted unshod pony tracks on the west bank. The prints looked to be a little over a day old, but we can't take any chances."

"Be sure to—"

A woman's scream sliced the air.

Pulse thrumming, Chase withdrew his revolver and bolted toward the river with Sergeant Greaves and several other troopers pounding behind him. On the other side of a tight bend, they came upon Callie standing near the water's edge. Unbound hair shrouded her wet, shift-clad body. Her face was ashen and tight with fear.

Chase scanned the area for danger and seeing none,

rushed toward her. "What is it?" he asked as he pulled her into his arms. "Why did you scream?"

She shuddered and tucked her head against his chest. "O-Over by that thicket..." she paused and swallowed. "A-A rotted body...floating in the shallows."

"Check it out, Sergeant."

As Julius trotted toward the shallows, Chase pulled in several slow, deep breaths and worked to slow his racing pulse. God, she had scared the hell out of him with that scream. He wouldn't be surprised to find a few gray hairs under his hat.

"Found the body, Cap'n," Julius called out. "And it looks like it might be Private Samuels. There's a mail pouch still strapped to his back."

"Damn," Chase muttered. Robert Samuels had been missing ever since the green recruit had left on a mail run to Gibson in February. The hapless trooper had been listed as a deserter. Yet clearly he'd given his life in the performance of his duty.

Callie's shudder drew Chase back to the present. She didn't need to see a rotted corpse fished out of the river. One look had apparently been quite enough.

"Retrieve the pouch and assign a burial detail, Sergeant." He eased Callie away from him and began unbuttoning his jacket. Her widened eyes pierced into him as he slipped out of his coat and flipped it around her shoulders.

"Come on." He grasped her elbow. "You can finish dressing in our tent."

Her fingers trembled as she clutched his coat tighter around her. "I-I'm sorry my scream caused such a panic."

He wanted to reach out and caress her pale face, but restrained the impulse. He didn't want to encourage her with thoughts that he might care. "No need to apologize," he said instead, guiding her along the path. "It was a natural reaction."

Callie ducked her head. "I hope...I mean, I don't want..." She drew in a long breath and then looked up, her luminous eyes clear and no longer troubled. "I hope you don't regret changing your mind about bringing me with you."

He hoped not either. "You should get out of those wet

clothes before you take ill."

Upon reaching the tent, she slipped out of his coat and handed it back to him. She then ducked through the tent flap, revealing a well-rounded bottom, perfectly outlined by the wet, clinging shift.

His loins tightened and he sucked in a deep breath. Now *he* needed a dip in the icy river.

****

The next morning, the detail forded the Canadian River. Recalling Private Samuels' swollen body, Chase maneuvered his mount next to Callie's to ensure her safe crossing. It was his duty, after all, to protect her, no matter how much she affected him.

Zeus climbed the embankment and pranced through the grass on the other side. Cool air swirled around Chase's sodden legs. He pulled his overcoat tighter and glanced upward. Dark clouds hung low in the sky, promising an icy, wet ride on the last day of their journey.

Just after the midday halt, the rain began, a fine, misty shower that further dampened their clothes and their spirits. Chase reined up and allowed the detail to pass. As Callie's horse drew near, he shifted Zeus into formation beside her.

Though her face was hidden beneath a hooded cloak, Callie had to be miserable in her saturated clothing. His own wool uniform chafed annoyingly with each stride Zeus took. "We should reach Arbuckle in another four hours," he told her. "Can you handle the weather, or do we need to stop?"

"I can manage," she replied, her voice dripping with weariness. "Let's keep going."

"Very well. Inform Private Jackson if you need to rest." He nudged Zeus into a gallop and headed back to the front of the column. Callie responded much as he'd expected. He was coming to admire her grit and fortitude, traits he never would have credited to her in Washington. Day by day, the harsh land they traversed had molded her. A different woman than the one he'd married was emerging.

A woman he wasn't certain he could continue to avoid.

Near dusk, Zeus crested the peak of a steep hill.

Below them, nestled in a rolling meadow, stood the rain-darkened buildings of Fort Arbuckle. Chase blew out a relieved breath. He feared he would return one day and find the structure reduced to ashes from an Indian raid.

As if realizing a warm stall and fresh oats awaited him, Zeus picked up his pace. Chase looked forward to dry quarters and a comfortable bed as well. Except, his lodgings only had one bed, and a wife trailed behind him. Perhaps they could share the bed—they'd done so once before. Besides, his weary body wouldn't know a tantalizing woman slept next to him.

Hah, fat chance of that happening.

The detail soon plodded through the garrison entrance. Chase called a halt near Officers' Row and dismounted. He tossed Zeus' reins to a waiting trooper and directed Sergeant Greaves to secure the wagonload of rifles and Private Jackson to escort Callie to their quarters.

As his men scurried to carry out his orders, Chase strode through the pelting rain towards the Commanding Officer's cabin, a short distance away. He vaulted onto the veranda, knocked mud off his boots, and then rapped on the door. He removed his hat and fidgeted impatiently with the sodden brim while he waited. He'd much rather help Callie settle in than meet with the Major. But orders were orders.

The door opened and faint yellow light spilled onto the porch. Major James Roy, Commander of the Sixth Infantry and Post Commander of Fort Arbuckle, stepped into the doorway. "You're late, Brooks. I thought you'd lost your patrol." He grunted. "Come inside and give your report."

Chase quashed his rising anger at the major's words. He wouldn't give the man the satisfaction of knowing his spiteful jab had succeeded. Stepping through the entry, he followed his commander into a large sitting room. A blast of heat greeted him, and he resisted the urge to pull impolitely at his chafing collar. No need to provide Roy any more ammunition than necessary.

Chase tucked his hands behind his back, gave his report, and then fell silent. Mrs. Roy's soft humming as she sat near the hearth was the only sound to break the quiet.

"Satanta, you say," the major finally replied. He frowned and tugged on his thick mustache. "That far east?"

"Yes, sir. Took me by surprise, too."

"I'll have Ben Baker ride out to the Antelope Hill reservation and investigate. Anything else?"

Chase tensed. When facing a rattlesnake, one had to be on guard. "There's one other thing, sir."

"Yes, what is it?" As usual, the major's tone sounded irritated.

"I brought someone back from Washington with me, sir. A wife, to be exact."

"A what?"

"A wife."

The commander snorted and leaned back in his chair. "Got caught with your pants down, did you?"

"James," Mrs. Roy admonished.

"Sorry, dear." The major regarded him through narrowed eyes. "Will your quarters suffice, Captain?"

"Yes, sir. They should be just fine," he responded tightly. No way in hell would he ask for preferential treatment. Not that he'd get it anyway.

"Good. Get your report of the skirmish with Satanta in writing to me tomorrow. You may go."

Chase brought his feet together with a click and gave the major a brisk salute. He then headed for the front door, glad to have that task over and done with.

Sarah Roy's haughty voice pulled him to a stop. "Oh, Captain Brooks…"

He stifled a groan. "Yes, Mrs. Roy?"

"Please ask your wife to have tea with me tomorrow after drill call," she replied, the invite clearly more of an order than a friendly request.

"Yes, ma'am, I'll do that." He tugged open the door and stepped into the damp night air.

Before he could close the door behind him, the major's harsh words sliced through the opening. "A wife, he says. What type of woman would marry a low-life like Captain Brooks? Surely not one you would want to invite to tea, my dear."

Chase pulled the door closed with a jerk of his hand.

Pompous bastard. God help anyone who treated Callie with anything other than respect. With fury heating his insides, he shoved on his hat and trotted across the muddy expanse between the two buildings. Upon reaching the door to his quarters, he pushed inside and glanced around the lamp-lit room. Disappointment flooded him at finding his striker the sole occupant.

"Missus Brooks done already ate and gone to bed, Cap'n," Private Jackson announced. "She was plum tuckered out."

"Thank you, Private." He shrugged out of his dripping overcoat and hung it and his hat on a wall peg. "I appreciate you looking after her."

"Jus' doing my duty, sir." The trooper dipped his head at the plate of steaming food on the table. "Here's your suppa. Good evening, sir."

"Good evening, Private."

Moses left the cabin and pulled the door shut behind him, leaving Chase alone with his thoughts, alone with his wife. He ran a hand through his damp hair and stared at the bedroom door. His wife slept beyond that door, nestled in his bed, snuggled against his pillows. He closed his eyes and tried not to picture her warm body writhing beneath the sheets...beneath him.

His sodden uniform felt suddenly too tight, too chafing.

Despite his efforts to remain unaffected, the bedroom and his wife's innocent pull beckoned. Chase strode across the floor and halted in front of the closed door. He hesitated, his hand hovering over the knob. He couldn't have been more terrified if the fires of hell awaited him on the other side.

Damn weakling. With a soft growl, he grabbed the knob, shoved open the door, and stepped into the darkened room.

A faint, feminine moan drifted across the room.

He froze. Faint light illuminated the figure in his bed and the ebony hair spilling across the pillow. His pillow. A deep groan escaped his lips.

He faced a long, sleepless night.

EIGHT

"*No!*" she wanted to scream, but couldn't force the word out of her mouth.

Painted with garish colors and mounted on fierce war ponies, a band of red-skinned Indians circled her. She tried to run, but her rag doll legs refused to cooperate. She stumbled and fell. One brave leapt on her and wrapped his muscular arm around her waist.

Callie opened her eyes and stared at the planked ceiling. Her heart thundered like a stampeding herd of cattle. Damp with sweat, she fought to quell the horror of her dream. It had been so vivid, so real.

She slowly became aware of the warm weight of an arm lying across her stomach and the comforting heat of a body stretched next to her. She turned her head to the side. Early dawn light filtered through the window, bathing her husband's handsome face in a faint, rosy glow. His ever-present scowl was gone, replaced by a vulnerable boyish expression.

The terror of her dream faded, chased away by the pleasant stirrings in her lower belly. Chase had never been so close before, his body touching hers so intimately. She itched to trail her fingers over his arm and feel his smoothness, his strength.

Warmth suffused her at the thought of him doing the same to her, probing places that throbbed for his touch. Callie groaned softly and fisted her hands. She had to get such thoughts out of her head. Chase didn't want that type of relationship. She'd only torment herself, if she continued to imagine having one.

Moving carefully, she slid from under his arm and inched out of the bed. Her bare feet hit the icy floorboards. She shuddered and hurried across the room to her trunk. Place needed rugs. Badly. Teeth chattering, she slipped out of her nightgown and into a calico day dress and stockings.

Strident trumpet notes pierced the quiet, and a deep groan rose up from the bed. Chase turned onto his back and stretched an arm across his forehead.

Callie hitched in a breath. Had he not slept well? She certainly had, at least until the horrid dream. Unwilling to be caught staring, she grabbed her boots and tiptoed from the bedroom.

Halfway into the other room, she stopped. Private Jackson crouched near the hearth, coaxing a fire to life in the fireplace. She must have made a noise because he turned toward her.

A smile lit his dark face. "Mornin', Missus Brooks."

"Good morning, Private," she greeted. "I didn't expect you to be here." The nutty aroma of brewing coffee drew her attention to the small cookstove. Her empty stomach rumbled.

"Yes'm," Private Jackson responded. "It's my duty to serve the Cap'n, married or not. Would you like a cup of coffee? There's also biscuits 'n jam on the table if'n you want somethin' to eat."

He had cooked breakfast? But that was her job.

She padded to the small table and sat on one of the wooden chairs to pull on her boots. Her insides knotted with apprehension. This was her home now. *Her* responsibility. No matter how much she liked Private Jackson, she couldn't let him perform the duties she should do—that she wanted to do.

Callie drew in a fortifying breath and planted her booted feet firmly on the floor. It was time to start taking control of her new life. "Private Jackson," she said, surprised and pleased by her composed tone. "I understand you feel it's your duty to serve Captain Brooks. However, as his wife, I should be the one to see to the household duties. I hope you understand."

Moses rose from the hearth and faced her. A perplexed frown creased his brow. "I understands, ma'am. But it's an honor and a privilege to serve you and the cap'n. You needn't worry yourself with cooking and cleaning and such."

"But I want to do those things."

93

"The other officers' wives are happy to let their husbands' strikers take care of the household duties. It gives the ladies mo' time to socialize."

"I'm not like the other officer's wives." Her voice rose an octave, despite her effort to keep it level. "I don't care to socialize."

Moses scratched his head. "Yes'm, but—"

"What's going on here?"

Her gaze flew to the doorway at the sound of Chase's voice. Dressed in a partially buttoned, white, cotton shirt, creased trousers, and a pair of suspenders flattened to his broad chest, he filled the doorway with his imposing presence. His granite-hard eyes tunneled into her.

Callie shifted uneasily. That unyielding look didn't bode well. "P-Private Jackson and I were discussing the household tasks."

Chase frowned. "It's his duty to serve us."

"I understand." She paused to swipe damp palms down the folds of her gown. "But a wife should be responsible for her husband and her home."

"A wife should obey her husband's wishes."

Her heart thumped. Yes, she should obey him. But, in this instance, the driving need to manage her life, her home, overrode his orders. She lifted her chin. "And what of my wishes?" she challenged.

"What of them?"

"I want to cook and clean and do any other task that a home or a husband requires. Please, don't take away the one thing that will make me happy."

Private Jackson cleared his throat. "Cap'n, if I might say somethin'?"

"Yes, Private?" Chase growled.

"I don't see the harm in allowin' Missus Brooks to handle the wifely tasks, such as cooking and cleaning. I can continue to attend to your military needs as per Army regulations."

Thank you, Moses. She held her breath, waiting for Chase to answer. Please, please, she silently begged him.

With his face set in an expressionless mask, he walked to the stove, poured a cup of coffee, and blew across the steaming brew. He took a sip, then another. A moment later, he lifted his gaze and regarded her with piercing eyes.

She had to force herself not to look away.

"Doing these things will make you happy?" he asked.

"Yes. Very happy."

"Then, you shall have it. From now on, meals and household duties are your responsibility. Private Jackson will see to my military needs."

A smile crept to her lips. She'd done it. She'd stood up to her husband and won. Callie glanced at Moses, surprised and pleased by his conspiratorial wink. "Thank you, Captain," she said. "Private Jackson and I will work out the details."

Moses nodded. "If you'll excuse me, Cap'n, I need to see to the horses before mess."

"Permission granted," Chase responded. "Oh, and check Zeus' front fetlock. He stumbled yesterday in the rain and may have clipped it. Don't want him coming up lame on me."

"Yes, suh, Cap'n." The private glanced at her. "Good day, Missus Brooks."

She gave her new best friend a wide smile. "Good day, Private."

As the door clicked shut behind the trooper, Chase strode across the room to the sideboard where Moses had neatly arranged shaving soap, a straight razor, and a basin of water. A task that would become hers from now on.

Callie watched, mesmerized, as he began the task of shaving. The smell of sandalwood, the faint scrape of razor on skin, and the splash of water invaded the quiet room. Memories blossomed—of her childhood and the many mornings she'd sat on a foot stool and watched her father perform the same ritual, making the same swishing, scratching noises. They were the sounds of home.

Chase picked up a towel and wiped away the soapy remnants, revealing a clean-shaven profile. Her pulse quickened. Would his skin feel as smooth and satiny as it looked?

He turned and caught her staring.

Heat rushed up her neck and into her face. She quickly averted her gaze. What was wrong with her? She was playing with fire, and if she wasn't careful, she was apt to get burned.

"The post commander's wife Sarah Roy invited you to tea after drill call this morning," he said as he shrugged into his uniform jacket. "The CO's living quarters are in the next building."

Drill call? Which one of the two dozen bugle calls was that? She ran through the litany of tunes in her head. Sweet Mary, they all sounded alike.

"Drill call is at ten o'clock," he added in a clipped tone, as if he'd noticed her confusion. Without another word, he crossed to the door, slid on his hat, and left. Only the click of his boot heels said farewell.

With a heavy heart, she sank onto a chair. Her husband was obviously having a difficult time accepting her presence in his life. She didn't know how much more unobtrusive she could be, but she would certainly try.

****

As the last notes of *drill call* faded away, Callie hesitated at the front door. Would Major Roy's wife be as friendly and gracious as Alice Grierson? God, she hoped so. Just the thought of meeting a stranger filled her with dread.

Yet, as the wife of an officer, it was her duty to socialize with the post commander's wife. Callie squared her shoulders and pushed aside her unease. She could manage a simple tea with Mrs. Roy. She'd endured much worse with Eunice and her cronies.

Once outside, she gave the fort a quick glance. She hadn't been able to see much the night before in the darkness. Not as large as Gibson, Arbuckle contained the same split-log buildings surrounding a huge central parade ground. A breeze swept across the arena, fluttering the American flag hanging from a tall pole.

Reminded of her duty, Callie tugged her cloak tighter and set off at a brisk pace for the post commander's residence. It would be ill-mannered of her to be late for her first social event.

She passed door after door as she traversed the veranda. Officers' Row was a large, multi-family dwelling, which housed the officers posted at the garrison. How many had wives living with them? She supposed she'd find out soon enough.

Upon reaching the end of the porch, Callie carefully picked her way across wood planks set over the muddy ground between Officer's Row and the CO's quarters. She climbed the stairs to the Roy's cabin, knocked on the door, and then absently fussed with her skirt while she waited.

The door swept open, and a pleasant-looking woman dressed in a gown of royal blue sateen smiled at her from the threshold. "You must be Mrs. Brooks," she said. "I'm Sarah Roy. Please, come in and join us."

Us? She only managed a nod before the woman whirled around. Callie smothered her rising panic and rubbed a hand down the front of her yellow, silk gown. Thank goodness Chase had insisted she purchase the dress. Though she felt like a complete mess on the inside, at least she looked presentable.

The faint hum of conversation filled the cabin as she followed her hostess down a narrow hallway and into a sitting room. Instant silence descended.

"Ladies," Mrs. Roy called out. "This is Captain Brooks' new wife."

A dozen pairs of eyes drilled into her. Her chest tightened in a familiar response, and she struggled to keep her feet from doing an about face. She could do this. She had to. Chase expected it of her.

Mrs. Roy introduced her to each of the women. Callie returned their greetings with a smile, doing her best to act as gracious as Julia or Alice would have.

Sarah pointed to a wing-back chair. "Mrs. Brooks, please have a seat while I prepare tea."

Callie nodded and eased into the chair, wishing she could disappear into the colorful chintz fabric.

"Are you from Washington, dear?" asked the older, red-haired woman seated beside her—Mary Peters, if she remembered correctly.

"No, ma'am," she replied. "I'm from Philadelphia. We were in Washington attending General Grant's Inauguration."

"Oh, is your family connected to the President in some way?"

"Actually, the President is my cousin."

Gasps of surprise resounded in the room.

"Your cousin?" Mary exclaimed.

"Yes, on my father's side. My maiden name is Grant."

Mrs. Roy stopped in front of Callie and held out a pretty china cup and saucer. "Well, James will be interested to learn of the captain's clever choice of a wife."

Clever choice? Whatever did that mean? Callie managed a smile and accepted the tea.

Frances Yates, a slender, slightly buck-toothed brunette, heaved an envious sigh. "Was the Inauguration a grand affair? I imagine the ball gowns were simply gorgeous."

Callie nodded. "Yes, they were quite stunning." She pictured her own drab, high-necked gown. *Well, at least most of them were.*

"You know...mmmfff," Mrs. Peters mumbled around a bite of scone. "Those cockade hats from Paris...are the latest trend in the East. My sister wrote..."

The conversation drifted to talk of gowns and accessories, allowing Callie an opportunity to study the women. Her gaze strayed to the pretty blonde seated next to Francis Yates on the other side of the room. Betsy Alvis' Dresden looks would surely turn any man's head.

Betsy pursed her rosy lips. "Did you see that dress Amanda wore? I've seen better clothes on a whore."

"Betsy," Frances admonished.

"Well, it's true. Amanda wouldn't know fashion if it jumped up and bit her. That foul-mouthed, Southern huss—"

"We all know how you feel about Amanda Forsythe," Sarah Roy interrupted. "Let's not spoil our lovely tea with talk of Rebel trash."

Callie stiffened. Their remarks reminded her of the spiteful chatter that had often spilled from Eunice Boggs and her cronies. Her heart went out to the vilified Amanda, whoever she was.

"Can't fault Amanda for telling the truth," Mary Peters mumbled under her breath as the other women prattled on.

"Pardon?" Callie said.

Mary leaned closer and whispered, "Betsy Alvis has roaming eyes and roving hands, if you get my meaning."

"I thought she was married."

"That doesn't stop her. When Lieutenant Forsythe became her next target, Amanda called her out." Mary chuckled softly. "You never heard such colorful phrases and dire warnings as the ones Amanda heaped on Betsy. They worked, too. Betsy gives Tom Forsythe a wide berth these days."

Callie smiled inwardly. The more she heard about this Amanda Forsythe, the more she liked the woman.

Betsy's shrill voice pierced her musings. "Mrs. Brooks, you must tell us how you managed to capture the elusive captain in such a short period of time."

Warmth flamed in her face. She wanted so badly to give the brazen woman a scathing retort, but she couldn't find the words, or the courage, to do so.

"Now, Betsy, don't press the girl," Sarah Roy admonished.

The feeble rebuke did little to stop the mouthy blonde. Betsy tipped her pert nose upward. "Well, knowing Chase as I do, it just seems unlike him to marry so suddenly."

Chase? A fist clamped around Callie's throat, tightening like a hangman's noose at the familiar use of her husband's name. She struggled to draw in a breath. Just how well did this pretentious blonde know Chase?

"Let her be, Betsy," Frances cautioned. "The poor dear has enough to contend with, considering her husband commands Negro soldiers." The woman gave a dramatic shudder and clutched her shawl tighter around her shoulders.

Sarah Roy focused an unwavering gaze in Callie's direction. "They'll not bother you if you keep your distance from them."

What? Callie blinked in disbelief. Had she heard correctly? Did these women expect her to treat her husband's troopers, her friends, like some sort of trash? She'd rather keep her distance from these pompous, self-righteous peahens.

A baby's wail drifted into the room. Sarah broke off her unnerving stare and rose from her chair. Callie shuddered inwardly as the image of Eunice Boggs crossed the floor and disappeared from view.

"She's right, you know," Mary Peters said. "You

should keep your distance from the black soldiers. They carry all sorts of parasites and diseases."

Callie opened her mouth to deny such an ugly accusation, but was interrupted by the return of Mrs. Roy carrying her infant son. As though they had been discussing nothing more inconsequential than the weather, the women abandoned their talk of the Negro troopers and rushed to exclaim over the child.

Yet, Callie couldn't dismiss the topic so easily. It gnawed at her like a hungry bedbug. How could anyone believe such drivel? Well, she—for one—had heard enough rubbish for one day.

She set aside her tea cup and rose to her feet. "Mrs. Roy, thank you kindly for inviting me to tea, however, I really must be going. As you can expect, I have much to do to make my quarters livable."

"Of course, dear," Mrs. Roy said. "We're so glad you came. If you need anything at all, please let me know."

Callie pasted on a smile and nodded. "I will. Thank you again. Goodbye, ladies." She managed a sedate exit, despite the fury bubbling in her veins.

Outside the cabin, she paused on the veranda and inhaled a deep, refreshing breath. She had expected awkwardness at the tea, but not such open censure. It seemed some women were the same no matter where they lived.

As she started across the makeshift walkway, the muffled thud of boots drew her attention to the parade ground. Dozens of men marched in formation, their movements coordinated by Sergeant Greaves' bellowed commands. She spotted Private Jackson and several of the other troopers from E Company. She couldn't imagine snubbing such friendly, caring men.

"Horrid women," she muttered as she climbed the short stairs to Officers' Row.

"You must've met Mrs. Roy and company."

At the sound of the feminine drawl, Callie jerked up her head. An auburn-haired woman stood in the end doorway, her hazel eyes gleaming with delight. Dressed in a plain, sage-green muslin gown with matching covered buttons that trailed to the hem of her pleated skirt, the young woman nodded. "Hello, I'm Amanda Forsythe."

Ah, the disparaged Amanda. A smile crept to Callie's lips. The woman's choice of clothing looked perfectly acceptable to her. "Callie Brooks," she replied.

"Brooks? Are you—"

Callie smothered a chuckle at the woman's wide-eyed expression. "Yes, I'm the wife of Captain Chase Brooks."

"Oh, how wonderful," Mrs. Forsythe exclaimed. "I assume you met the captain in Washington. My husband Tom commanded E Company while Chase was away. Oh dear, where are my manners? Won't you come inside and have lunch?"

Callie blinked and tried to keep up with the rush of words. "I just finished tea with Mrs. Roy..."

"Oh, do come in. I have fresh bread and a delicious ball of cheese."

"Well, I suppose—"

Mrs. Forsythe snagged her elbow and pulled her through the doorway and into quarters very much like Chase's. Two chairs and a settee faced the nearby hearth, while a cookstove, a wooden table, and four chairs occupied the other end of the main room.

"Please have a seat at the table," her hostess urged.

Callie followed the woman across the room and eased onto one of the high-backed chairs. She watched while Mrs. Forsythe served tea and lunch as swiftly as she dispensed chatter.

"So, did you meet Captain Brooks in Washington?"

Callie nodded and stirred a sugar cube into her tea. "Yes, I was attending my cousin's Inauguration."

"Your cousin? As in President Grant?"

"One and the same. Ulysses is from my father's side of the family."

Auburn curls bounced with Amanda's nod. "And I thought being related to General Edward Alexander was impressive. Of course, he was a *Confederate* commander. Not much of an advantage in this Army nowadays."

Callie recalled Sarah Roy's ugly words. *Rebel trash.* She grimaced inwardly. Bigotry of all types seemed to flourish at Arbuckle. "I've always wanted to journey south," she admitted. "Where are you from, Mrs. Forsythe?"

"Please call me Amanda. Mrs. Forsythe sounds so

101

stuffy. Reminds me of my mother-in-law." She smiled and broke off a hunk of bread. "I'm Georgia born and bred. Although we weren't your typical Southerners. Father abhorred slavery. I imagine that's the reason I detest the narrow-minded women at Arbuckle."

Amen to that. Callie gave a soft sigh. The more she talked with Amanda Forsythe, the more she liked the vibrant, no-nonsense, young woman. "Is your husband from Georgia, as well?" she asked.

"Heavens, no. He was a Union officer stationed in Atlanta. Swept this little ole Southern girl right off her feet. Just as I imagine the captain did to you."

Callie forced a smile to her lips. She hoped Amanda would move on to other, safer topics. She wasn't ready to discuss the details of her loveless marriage.

****

By the time the afternoon light waned, Callie's head reeled from Amanda's deluge of advice and humorous tales. She had enjoyed every minute of their chat and wished she could stay longer, but she had to see to Chase's supper. She couldn't very well renege on the responsibility after fighting so hard for it.

As she rose to take her leave, the front door crashed open and a handsome, uniformed officer dashed into the room. "Amanda, you absolutely will not believe the news—" He stopped abruptly and swept off his hat. "I'm sorry. I didn't realize you had company."

A wide grin dimpled Amanda's face. "Tom, I'd like to introduce you to Callie, Captain Brooks' new wife."

He shook his head. "I should'a known you'd find out first, Amanda." He turned and gave her a slight bow. "Lieutenant Tom Forsythe, Mrs. Brooks. It's a pleasure to meet you, ma'am."

"Lieutenant." Callie nodded to the officer before turning to her newfound friend. "I had a lovely afternoon, Amanda. Thank you for lunch and the wonderful tips on settling in."

"I enjoyed our lunch, as well." Amanda gave her arm a gentle squeeze. "I'm so glad we met, Callie. I think we're going to get along famously."

She returned Amanda's smile. "I think so, too. Good day to you both." Callie eased past the grinning officer and stepped through the doorway onto the veranda. As she headed toward her quarters, she suppressed the urge to break into a girlish skip. She'd found a friend, a real friend. Not one of those phony, backstabbing women with Mrs. Roy. Yes, she and Amanda would most certainly get along.

Harried shouts rang out, startling her. She slowed and glanced at the parade ground. Half a dozen soldiers raced toward the enlisted barracks, brandishing rifles and handguns.

Her heart tripped. Not another Indian attack.

A moment later she spotted the cause of the uproar. A large, gray wolf emerged from the back side of the barracks. It loped through the puddled rainwater, head down, saliva dripping from its lolling tongue.

Callie clutched a hand to her chest. Next to renegade Indians, wild animals rated a solid second on her list of things to avoid.

The wolf abruptly reversed its course and headed straight for her. She froze, unable to pull her gaze from yellow eyes that glowed with irrational intensity. The sound of gunfire blasted the sudden stillness. Bullets thudded into the mud near the wolf's paws. Seemingly oblivious to the threat, the animal continued its unfaltering trek—right at her.

An errant bullet whizzed past her head and lodged in the wall behind her. Yet she stood immobile. She knew she should run, flee to the safety of her quarters. But the only movement she could manage was a quick blink.

An ear-splitting gunshot reverberated along Officers' Row. The wolf stumbled, righted itself, took several more steps, and then toppled onto its side, a mere arm's length in front of her. A shriek lodged in her throat, its force nearly choking her.

Footsteps pounded toward her. Someone spoke, but she couldn't make out the words. Her vision clouded and without warning, her knees buckled.

A pair of muscular arms curled around her and hefted her against a solid chest. The scent of sandalwood pierced the fog in her head. She knew that smell. Knew it very well. She looked up into familiar stormy eyes.

"Are you all right?" Chase asked, his voice strangely

103

hoarse. "Did they hit you?"

She blinked in confusion. "Hit me?"

"Did a bullet strike you?"

"N-no. I don't think so." The only pain she felt was the soft ache to snuggle deeper into the comfort of his arms. A gesture she knew would be inappropriate and unappreciated.

"Here, Captain," she heard Amanda call out. "I've opened the door for you."

Chase carried her into their quarters and eased her onto a chair. His concerned gaze combed her face and then moved over the rest of her.

Embarrassed by her collapse and Chase's intimate perusal, she closed her eyes and leaned her head against the chair back. Her first day at Arbuckle was quickly turning into a disaster.

Boot heels clicked across the floor. "Is she all right?" Lieutenant Forsythe asked.

"Yes, I believe she is," Amanda replied. "Just a bit shaken up. And it's no wonder, what with all those bullets flying about."

"Those damn fool infantrymen," Chase bit out. "They could've killed her with the pot shots they were taking. Thank God, you were able to get a clean shot, Tom."

Callie opened her eyes and lifted her spinning head. "There's no reason for all the fuss. I'm fine." She forced a reassuring smile to her lips. "Truly."

"I'll stay with her, if you'd like, Captain," Amanda said.

Chase shook his head. "Thank you for the offer, Mrs. Forsythe, but that's not necessary. I was just going off-duty when the ruckus started."

"Very well, Captain. Send for me, if you need any help."

"I will." He rose and walked to the door with the Forsythes. "Lieutenant, assign a detail to haul that rabid carcass outside the garrison and burn it."

Callie suppressed a shudder. Another experience to add to her growing list. What else did this strange, new life have in store for her?

Chase closed the door and crossed to the sideboard. He poured a shot of whiskey into a tumbler and carried the drink to her. "Here, this will help calm your nerves."

She shook her head. "No. Thank you, but I don't need it. I'm fine." She gripped the armrests and prepared to stand. "I should see to supper."

He placed a gentle hand on her shoulder, stopping her. "I'll see to supper."

"But—"

"No buts." He pulled the padded footstool closer and situated her feet on it. "You sit right there and rest. I'm perfectly capable of cooking a meal."

"You?"

He lifted an amused eyebrow. "I wasn't always a pampered officer."

Heat flamed in her cheeks at her *faux pax*. She ducked her head. "No, I suppose not."

He patted her foot and stood. "You had a disturbing experience. Just relax. I'll see to supper tonight."

Though she appreciated his solicitous attention, her stomach still knotted with unease. She should be the one cooking supper. Not him. Would she ever overcome her weaknesses and become the wife he deserved?

NINE

Callie stepped off the veranda and did her best to ignore the dried blood soaked into the ground a few feet away. She wouldn't let yesterday's wolf incident mar such a beautiful day. Southerly winds had brought warmer air into the region, and she intended to enjoy the unexpected change.

She soon arrived at her destination and eased through the open doorway and into the stables. She'd seen a large contingent of men and horses gathered on the parade ground and figured it was a good time to visit her faithful mare.

The heady smell of leather, horses, and straw wafted around her as she walked along the dirt-packed aisle. As far down as she could see, stalls lined both sides of the long, central corridor.

"Keep still, I said," a distraught voice rang out, breaking the stillness.

Callie moved toward the sound. A trooper stood inside one of the stalls, attempting to saddle a leggy sorrel. With his back turned to her, the man bent, slipped a trembling hand beneath the horse's belly, and grabbed the cinch dangling on the other side. He jerked upright and wagged his head at the horse. "Now don't you be trying to take no chunks outta my hide," he warned.

As he began fastening the cinch, the uncooperative gelding flattened its ears and twisted around, baring its teeth. The trooper gave a nervous shriek and jumped out of the animal's reach.

"Private Johnson," a deep, irritated voice bellowed from the stable entrance. "Get your yellow-bellied ass onto the parade ground. *Now*."

"Coming, Sergeant," Private Johnson replied, his high-pitched voice wavering with obvious distress.

Callie's heart went out to the miserable trooper. Poor fellow. Some horses were more difficult than others. And Private Johnson seemed to have found a prickly one. She reached into her pocket and pulled out a sugar cube.

"Why don't you distract him with this treat?" she offered.

The trooper whirled around. His nostrils flared as he drew in a deep breath. "You give it to him. I ain't getting near those chompers."

"If you hold the cube like this..." She extended her hand, palm upward, toward the horse. "He can't bite you." The gelding arched his neck and lipped the treat from her palm. Callie nodded to the trooper. "Now, finish tightening the cinch."

His mouth set in a grim line, Private Johnson did as she instructed. The treat-distracted horse didn't even bat an eyelash. Callie smiled in satisfaction. She'd learned that trick with one of Uncle Horace's ornery mares.

His task completed, Private Johnson snagged the reins and led the horse forward. "Thank you, ma'am. I'm fine once I git on him. It's just down here that I can't stomach."

"You're welcome, Private. I'm glad I could help." She stepped back to allow the trooper and his horse to pass.

As the pair disappeared through the main doors, Callie resumed her trek, content to amble along in the quiet warmth of the stable. A familiar reddish-brown head appeared and leaned over a stall door.

Callie smiled and angled toward the horse. "Hello, Hera," she whispered as she rubbed the mare's forehead.

Hera nickered a soft greeting. Callie dug into her pocket and retrieved another sugar cube. As moist lips grazed her outstretched palm, a snort sounded from the next stall. A second later, a larger, reddish-brown head came into view. Zeus bounced his head up and down, sending his black mane slapping against his neck.

Callie laughed and stepped closer to the impudent steed. "Jealous?" She reached up and scratched his muzzle.

Zeus lowered his head and gently butted her with his nose.

"Yes, I brought you a treat, as well." She palmed

another sugar cube. Like a gentleman, the huge destrier took the sweet without even touching her hand.

"I see you found Zeus' Achilles heel."

She whirled and met Chase's smoky gaze. Her heart skipped. He was so close. She could feel his warmth crashing into her like waves on the shore.

"Private Johnson mentioned a lady had helped him with his horse."

Oh dear. Was he upset with her? His unreadable expression and even tone revealed little of his mood. She swallowed hard. "I-I needed some fresh air and decided to visit Hera. The private was having a difficult time with his saddling."

Chase glanced at the mare. "You call her Hera?"

"It seemed appropriate. Zeus and Hera. From Greek mythology."

His eyes gleamed like molten silver. "Yes, I know. Very appropriate."

"Cap'n?" A trooper called out from the stable entrance. "Corporal Hayworth's detail just arrived with the new remuda."

"Thank you, Private," Chase responded. "I'll be right there."

Remuda? Before she could open her mouth to ask what that was, a nudge from behind shoved her into Chase's rock hard chest. He exhaled a hiss of air and wrapped his arms around her. His heat spread beneath her fingertips and warmed her breasts. A pleasing tremor coursed through her. Sweet Mary, how she ached to melt against him, to yield to her screaming need to be more to him.

But she couldn't. He didn't want any physical or emotional attachments. He'd made that quite clear. She'd best move out of his embrace before he realized how deeply he affected her. Her future depended on keeping her marriage in name only.

She tried to push away. To her surprise, he tugged her closer, refusing her the freedom she sought. She tensed. Had he changed his mind about their relationship? Callie tilted her head and peered into smoldering, gray eyes. Heat unfurled in her belly, sending a clipper ship of desire and anticipation sailing through her.

Chase released a long, slow exhale. His warm breath caressed her face and skidded down her neck. Like a bee seeking nectar, she moved her gaze to his slightly parted lips. Would his kiss feel as wonderful as it had on her wedding day?

Male laughter and the thud of boots intruded.

With a curse, Chase thrust her away and stepped back. His jaw muscles twitched in obvious displeasure.

Displeasure with her or with the interruption?

Heated blood coursed through her, building in intensity rather than abating. Disconcerted, Callie edged backwards and collided with Zeus' stall. She spun around and faced the perpetrator of the disturbing incident. The stallion arched his neck and wagged his head in a defiant gesture.

Bad horse. No more sugar cubes for you.

"Keep that up, and I'll replace you with a more complacent nag from the remuda," Chase told the horse, his voice controlled and even—a complete contrast to her raging inner turbulence.

Zeus snorted and tossed his head, nickering loudly as if he'd understood what his master said and highly disagreed.

"Mule," Chase muttered.

Callie absently reached up and scratched the stallion behind his ear. She needed time to compose herself before she faced Chase again. "What exactly is a remuda?" she asked, hoping her voice sounded as unaffected as his.

"It's the herd used by the cavalry," he said. "We haven't been able to give the horses a good rest between patrols, so a detail was sent into Texas to acquire additional mounts."

"I see." She relaxed her taut shoulders, thankful her heartbeat was returning to normal, the heat in her body subsiding to a mere smolder.

"If you're finished with your visit, I'll walk you back to our quarters."

She drew in a calming breath and turned. His blazing eyes pierced into her.

He stepped closer and plucked a piece of straw from her hair. "You shouldn't come to the stables unescorted," he warned softly. "Bedlam can sometimes erupt, making it much too dangerous for you to wander about alone."

"I understand," she said. Her stomach fluttered uneasily. "I'll have Private Jackson accompany me in the future."

His emotionless mask slipped back into place. "Good." He lifted his arm to her. "Ready then?"

She placed her hand in the crook of his elbow. Disappointment enfolded her in a suffocating embrace. For a brief moment, she thought there might be something more between them, something her lonely heart yearned for. But Chase had shut himself off, retreated back into his fortress.

She wished she had the courage to ask why. But, she feared confronting him, feared his answer, his dry assurance that he was capable of loving someone—just not her.

****

O Captain! My Captain! Our fearful trip is done. The ship has weather'd every rack. The prize we sought is—

Callie lowered her book and sniffed. Something smelled strange, almost like—

Sweet Mary, supper! She tossed Whitman to the table, sprang to her feet, and raced for the kitchen. Gray smoke streamed from the pot sitting atop the stove. She grabbed a cloth rag and moved the sizzling pan off the flame. As she fanned away the acrid haze, her heart fell at the sight of the blackened ash crusted in the pot. She'd ruined supper. Had she not been so involved in her book-

A knock sounded on the door followed by the screech of hinges. She turned, surprised to see Private Jackson poking his head through the doorway.

"Everythin' all right, Missus. Brooks?" he asked. "I smelled something burnin' and...Oh, I see."

Heat scorched her face and seared her ears as she recalled how strongly she'd fought him for the right to cook for Chase. And here she'd gone and bungled a meal. What a goose she must appear.

Private Jackson stepped into the room, the captain's freshly polished saber clutched in his hand. "No need to fret none, ma'am. I's burned many a meal on that cantankerous cookstove."

What a sweet man, blaming the stove for her mistake instead of criticizing her efforts. "I expect I can salvage a small portion that isn't burned," she said with a shrug.

Moses hung Chase's saber on a wall peg near the door, then faced her. "You'll only be needin' enough for yourself. Cap'n Brooks asked me to tell you he won't be home for suppa. Paperwork's keeping him busy again, I 'spect."

Again? He hadn't joined her for supper the night before, either. She sighed and bowed her head. "Oh, well, I wasn't hungry, anyway."

"Still upset over that rabid wolf?"

She nodded, not wanting him to know that Chase's absence—not the wolf—caused her lack of appetite. Ever since the episode in the stable, her husband seemed to be avoiding her. He stayed away until the wee hours of the morning, then rose early the next day and slipped away before she woke.

Nearly lost in her musings, she remembered Private Jackson and looked up. He stood by the door, fingering his short-brimmed kepi hat. He opened his mouth and then shut it without saying a word.

"Is there anything else, Moses?" she asked.

He bowed his head. "Yes'm, there is."

Her own misery would have to wait. Moses needed her. "What is it?"

"I'll understand if you say no..."

"I never say no to my friends, Moses. I'd do anything for you, you know that."

"If'n it's not too much trouble...I-I's wonderin' if you'd be so kind as to read me a letter from my wife Daisy?"

"Why, I'd love to read your letter to you. Let's sit by the fire." She settled into a wingback chair and waited for him to follow.

After a moment, he stepped forward and extracted a folded letter from his pocket. He handed her the missive, one that he'd obviously handled many times as evidenced by the numerous creases and smudges on the white parchment.

She unfolded the letter and glanced up. Moses stood by the other chair, shifting his weight from foot to foot. "Please have a seat," she urged.

His gaze shot to the front door and back to her.

"It's perfectly acceptable for you to sit with me while I read your letter," she told him.

A rabbit's dash of hesitation crossed his face before he lowered himself onto the padded chair. He perched close to the edge as though anticipating a hasty retreat.

She cleared her throat and began to read the personal missive aloud. Although written in childish sentences with many words misspelled, the letter conveyed the love and adoration Daisy felt for Moses. Callie caught a glimpse into a world she barely remembered as the woman detailed her family's Christmas holiday and New Year's celebration. How wonderful to have such a close-knit family. It was something she'd dreamed of having again. Tears filled her eyes as she passed the letter back to Moses.

He rose, wiping away his own tears as he stood. "My Daisy sho can write a fine letter. I 'preciate you taking the time to read it to me, ma'am."

She shook her head. "It was little enough after all you've done for me."

Her head whirled with a new thought. Moses couldn't read and most likely couldn't write either. Were the other troopers as illiterate as he? She had extensive book knowledge. Why not lend a hand with their education? She owed them that much after they had accepted her so readily into their midst. Besides, it might help keep her mind off Chase and her loneliness.

"Moses, how many troopers are unable to read or write?" she asked.

"Most all of us. Before the chaplain took sick, he gave us lessons each evening after mess."

She tapped a finger to her lips. Her self-adopted brothers needed her. To be able to write to their loved ones and read the answering letters, what a wonderful gift that would be. But could she overcome her shyness and face a room full of men?

She squared her shoulders. She had to, one way or another.

The time had come to fully conquer her timidity and become a woman she could be proud of—a wife Chase might come to admire.

****

Callie woke alone in the empty bed. Sunlight poured through the window, painting the walls in brightness. She tilted her head. No noise sounded from the kitchen. She frowned. Had she slept through reveille? She'd wanted to get up early, prepare Chase a nice breakfast, and then broach the subject of teaching the troopers.

Sighing in dismay, she rose and donned her stockings and day gown. She reached for her boots, but they weren't beside the wardrobe where she'd left them. Puzzled, she padded into the kitchen. An empty coffee mug sat on the table. Well, at least she knew her husband had come home at some point during the night. She'd waited up for him until exhaustion had sent her crawling into their bed—alone.

She took a step forward and spied her boots propped beside the sideboard, gleaming from a fresh polishing. "Moses," she murmured, knowing it had been the thoughtful trooper who had cleaned the ever present mud from her boots.

Fierce determination filled her. No more dithering. If Chase couldn't see fit to come home at a decent hour, then she had no choice but to continue ahead, with or without his permission. Moses and the other troopers needed her.

After slipping on her boots, she retrieved her wrap from the wall peg and set off for the hospital. A small cluster of soldiers looked up from their duties at the edge of the parade ground. Though they remained silent, their stares cut holes into her resolve. She averted her gaze and forced her feet forward, ignoring the niggling worry that she probably shouldn't be traipsing around the fort unescorted. She had a mission to accomplish, and she wouldn't let anything, or anyone, distract her.

Upon reaching the hospital, she drew in a steadying breath and entered the huge building. Cots lined both sides of a wide aisle, much like the infirmary at Fort Gibson. Thoughts of the friendly Doctor Giles calmed her.

A uniformed officer emerged from the other end of the room, wiping his hands on his apron as he approached. "Can I help you, ma'am?"

She smiled. "Yes. I'd like to speak with the chaplain if he's well enough to have company."

"Certainly, right this way." The doctor retreated in the direction from which he'd come and stopped next to a cot mid-way into the room.

Reclined against a stack of pillows, a balding man rested with his hands folded over his bulging belly. His wrinkled face sagged with heavy jowls, reminding her of an English bulldog she'd once seen. She hoped he was as friendly as the dog had been.

The doctor gently shook the man's shoulder. "Chaplain. Chaplain, you have a visitor."

The sleeping clergyman snorted once, twitched, and then opened his eyes. He moved his bewildered gaze from the doctor to her. "Oh, so sorry," he murmured. "I must have dozed off."

"If you'll excuse me," the physician stated. "I have a patient to check on."

As the doctor departed, the chaplain tilted his head to the side and regarded her with kindly eyes. "Well, then, what can I do for you, young lady?"

Despite her resolve, her knees trembled, threatening to knock together like a child's silly noisemaker. She locked them tight and smiled at the clergyman. "Good morning, Chaplain. My name is Mrs. Brooks."

"Brooks? The new wife of Captain Chase Brooks?"

Why did everyone stare at her in amazement when they learned who her husband was? It was quite disconcerting. "Yes," she said. "I'm sorry to disturb you, sir, but I have something I need to discuss with you."

"Ahhhh," the clergyman responded. "And what do you need to discuss, my dear? Problems with your marriage?"

Heat crept into her face. Good Lord, that was the last thing she'd discuss with anyone, including a man of God. "Oh, no, sir. It's nothing like that." She drew in another calming breath. "I understand you've been teaching the illiterate troopers to read and write. I want to volunteer to help with their instruction."

There, she'd done it. No stammering, no stuttering, just a plain, straightforward request. She almost danced a jig at her accomplishment.

"Well, I must say, this is the first time anyone's volunteered to help." He grimaced and shifted his weight on the tiny bed. "Unfortunately, I've had to put their instruction on hold while I recover from this infernal episode of gout."

She bent and tucked a stray edge of his sheet back into place. "If you'll just give me the particulars, I'd be happy to step in while you're convalescing."

The clergyman pursed his lips. "You're not afraid of colored men? Most officers' wives usually are."

She shook her head. "Of course not, many of the troopers are my friends. That's why I'm here. I want to help them."

"And you've discussed this with your husband?"

Warmth drained from her face. No, she hadn't. Would Chase object? She really had no way of knowing. He kept such a tight rein on his emotions, she couldn't begin to fathom his reaction.

The chaplain gave her a wide, encouraging smile. "Well, knowing the captain's dedication to his troopers, I doubt he would oppose your helping his men. I'll inform the troop leaders that instruction will resume tonight in the mess hall. Classes are Tuesday and Thursday evenings after supper. Is that suitable?"

"Yes, that will be just fine." She backed away from the bed. "I'll leave you to get some rest, Chaplain. Thank you for allowing me to help."

"No, *thank you,* Mrs. Brooks. And congratulations on your marriage."

She headed back down the aisle, excitedly formulating lesson plans in her mind. Once outside, she glanced skyward and smiled. She would now be able to give something back to the wonderful men who had befriended her.

Was it her imagination, or was the sun suddenly shining brighter?

****

The soothing call of the night insects filled the air. Chase shouldered against the porch post and let his thoughts wander to Callie. The past few nights, he'd come home well after she'd fallen asleep, crawling into bed and letting exhaustion override any lustful thoughts he might have. And he did have them, in his dreams and even during the day, images that clouded his mind and interfered with his duties.

Just the other day, while on maneuvers outside the garrison, he'd almost been bitten by a rattler sunning itself on a boulder. Leading Zeus through a rocky gulch, he'd paid little attention to his surroundings. He'd been too occupied with thoughts of his wife and her soft, enticing body. Lucky for him, Zeus had been alert. The steed had yanked on the reins, saving one or both of them from a nasty snake bite.

Chase glanced across the darkened expanse at Officers' Row. Pale lamplight glowed from the windows lining the building. Callie occupied one of those rooms, alone and possibly hurt by his inattention. A pang stabbed into his gut. Hell, he could control himself for one night.

He tucked on his hat and with a grunt, set off across the parade ground. Upon reaching his quarters, he pushed through the door and entered the unoccupied front room. Dying embers glowed orange in the fireplace, a clear sign the fire hadn't been tended in a while.

Chase frowned. Had Callie turned in already? It wasn't that late, only an hour or so since the bugler had sounded *mess*.

He moved into the bedroom and froze at the sight of the undisturbed bed. Where the hell was she? Heart thudding like a Kiowa war drum, he spun around and strode back into the front room, scouring the table, the cupboard, and then the sideboard, looking for a note Callie may have left him.

Nothing. Dammit to hell, where had she gone?

Unbidden, old torments surfaced, reminding him of another's betrayal. He ground his teeth and forced away the ugly images. He wouldn't let such thoughts torture him.

Think, he admonished himself. *Think. Think. Forsythe.* Yes. Callie had probably decided to spend the evening with Amanda.

He left his quarters and marched down the veranda to the lieutenant's door. Once there, he gave a quick rap and then stepped back. Gut churning, Chase lifted his hat and swiped at the sweat trickling down his brow. She had to be here. His mind wouldn't accept any other alternative.

The door swung open, and Tom frowned at him from the entryway. "Captain, what—"

"Is my wife here?" he snapped.

"No, sir, she isn't. Didn't she tell you?"

"Tell me what?"

"She's at the mess hall, giving the troopers reading and writing instruction."

Chase snorted. "*My* wife...teaching a room full of men?"

Amanda eased into the doorway beside Tom. "Callie spoke with the chaplain this morning, Captain. She expected to return home long before you finished your duties for the night."

Christ Almighty. What had gotten into his shy, unassuming wife? "Thank you, Mrs. Forsythe. Lieutenant." Chase rammed on his hat and wheeled around.

Hands fisted at his side, he crossed the parade ground, battling the urge to break into a trot. God help him, his wife wasn't with a man, just a whole room full of them. He'd received the missive advising the evening instruction for his troopers would resume. He'd assumed the chaplain had recovered from his malady and was conducting the classes. Not Callie, his timid wife, the one who avoided large crowds like the plague.

He entered the mess hall and stood at the back, scanning the room for the petite, ebony-haired woman who haunted him day and night. She wasn't hard to spot amid the dark-skinned, uniformed troopers. She leaned close to Private White and helped him form a letter on the slate.

An irrational surge of jealousy stabbed him. He wanted her hands on *him*, touching *him* with such tenderness. He crossed his arms over his chest and watched as Callie moved from trooper to trooper, giving one a pat on the shoulder and nodding her lovely head at another. Her bright smile lit the room more effectively than any lantern.

Chase shook his head. He couldn't believe this confident young woman was the same one he'd married less than a month ago. The Irish infantrymen often talked about changelings. Perhaps she was one of those.

He turned his attention to the men sitting at the string of tables. They seemed to be responding to Callie's tutelage with marked enthusiasm. Even the cantankerous Private Sanford worked with uncommon diligence on his slate. Of the hundred and fifty troopers on the post, only about two dozen had attended tonight's class. He'd bet his last dollar there'd be more the next night, and the one after that. Callie would draw them like flies to honey.

She looked up and spotted him in the doorway. The radiance drained from her face. Her pale lips formed a perfect "O", and she grasped the corner of a table for support.

Private White apparently noticed her distress and glanced in Chase's direction. Rabbit-like, the trooper bounded to his feet, snapping his body ramrod straight and calling to the other men.

Bench legs scrapped on the floor as the troopers rose and stood stiffly at attention. A textbook response to the presence of an officer. Just as he'd expected. Unlike his wife who failed to follow the simplest of orders. He unfolded his arms and commanded gruffly, "Carry on, men."

The troopers cast furtive glances at Callie as they returned to their seats. With pink flushing her cheeks, she squared her shoulders and marched toward him. Brown eyes flashed with fierce determination.

Chase stiffened. God, she was lovely, even with her mouth pulled into a pencil-thin line. He ached to pull her into his arms and pounce on those enticing, rosy lips.

She halted before him and cupped trembling hands on her hips. "I know why you're here," she stated, her unwavering tone surprising him.

"Oh. And why is that?"

"To stop me from helping these men."

"Should I stop you?"

"No. They need me."

"You cannot just act on a whim, Callie. The Army has specific procedures that must be followed. I've told you this before."

She tilted her chin upward. "I spoke with the chaplain, and he accepted my offer to help."

"And when were you going to inform me?"

She blanched. "I fully intended to tell you, whenever you decided to grace me with your presence." She ran a pink tongue over her bottom lip. "No matter what you say, I won't give up this *whim*."

Chase lifted his eyebrows at her bold statement. By God, his timid wife had found her backbone, and all for the cause of his troopers. How could he possibly refuse to allow her to perform a service that his men so desperately needed?

Except, she'd challenged him. He couldn't permit such blatant disobedience. No one defied his orders. No one. Besides, he still couldn't shake the tormenting image of her folded in another man's arms.

He leaned forward and addressed her in a soft, yet firm tone. "If I had so ordered it, you would *not* continue teaching. However, as these troopers are in need of instruction, I will allow you to go on with your volunteer work. With one condition..." He straightened to his full height. "Private Jackson, front and center."

The trooper rose and hurried across the room. "Suh," Moses responded as he came to a stop and stood at attention.

"Private, I'm assigning you the duty of escorting my wife to and from these evening instructions, unless I am free to do so myself. Understood?"

"Yes, suh. Understood, suh."

"Carry on."

As Moses retreated, Chase shifted his gaze back to Callie. She peered up at him with wide, confused eyes. A fleeting shadow of pain crossed her pretty face and then disappeared. His gut twisted. God, he hadn't meant to hurt her. Why couldn't he be as even-handed around her as he was with his men?

She heaved a faint sigh that sliced through him as easily as any shouted oath. "Thank you, Captain," she whispered.

Aiming to soften his harsh words, he took a step closer and stared down into her bewitching face. "I want to apologize for the long hours I've been away. I've been involved in training maneuvers as well as trying to catch up on my paperwork."

His gaze locked on luscious lips he wanted to crush beneath his own. Fire licked at his groin. He fisted his hands at his side, fighting for control. He didn't need a repeat of the disturbing episode in the stable where he'd come within a hair's breadth of kissing her, of taking her right there in the warmth of a stall. He wasn't ready for such a leap in their relationship. Not yet.

Chase sucked in a steadying breath and continued. "I realize I should've been more considerate. All of this is new to you, and it was callous of me to leave you alone for such a long period of time."

Her doe-eyes filled with tears. He struggled to keep from reaching out and stroking her smooth, flushed face. If he did, he'd be lost. Lost to his body's lust for her.

Her soft reply almost undid him. "That's the nicest thing you've ever said to me. I have missed your company, but I know I'll soon become accustomed to this new life. I've learned so much already."

"Yes, you have, and I admire your fortitude. Please, return to the men. I think they're impatient for your help." He nodded toward the troopers who had begun tossing cursory glances in their direction. Moreover, he needed time to collect himself. "I'll wait for you to finish and walk you home."

His hardened heart lurched at the sight of her lovely smile.

"I'd like that," she murmured. "We won't be much longer."

He watched her walk to the front of the room, unable to tear his gaze from the seductive sway of her hips. God, she was incredible. Beautiful, smart, and courageous. Everything he wanted in a woman. But could she be trusted?

A short time later, she ended the lesson and joined him at the door. Once outside, she tucked her hand in his arm and gazed up at the stars. "It's a beautiful night, isn't it?"

"Yes, very beautiful." *Just like you.*

Her tinkling laugh played jack-rocks with his heart. "The moon reminds me of the yarn Private White spun this evening. He's such a jokester. How do you keep a straight face around him?"

"It's not easy," he replied, surprised by his admission. What was it about this woman that made him divulge things he never would reveal to anyone else?

She turned her captivating smile on him and nearly took his breath away. Chase suppressed a moan of frustration. He wished he had the capacity to make her smile more often, to give her the love she deserved. But he couldn't. The painful memory of Miranda wouldn't allow him to commit more of himself than a guarded friendship.

TEN

The aroma of bubbling stew and the sounds of Chase's soft whistling filled the room. Sitting before the hearth with a torn gown draped across her lap, Callie smiled, her heart humming along with the music. Her husband had finally begun to relax around her, a gift worth more than a sack full of gold.

Chase halted his whistling and grunted. "Crazy Quakers don't know what they're getting into."

She looked up from her mending. "Why is that?"

"Those peace-loving reformers are volunteering for the President's new Indian Policy." He shuffled the papers he'd been reading into a stack on the table. "They want to supervise the Indian Agencies. Take over the role of tribe agent."

"Isn't that a good thing?"

"Not necessarily. I don't believe the Kiowa or Comanche will behave any better under the Quaker's genteel control than they do now. It's actually going to make things worse."

She frowned. "Worse, how?"

"This new policy places the agents in full control. The military can only assist if called upon. Our hands will be tied if the reservation Indians misbehave."

"What of the Indians not on reservations?"

"That's different. Those renegades will be regarded as hostile. We'll be allowed to make all attempts to capture them."

All attempts. She shuddered. That didn't sound good. "I know you've been training the men hard. Are they ready to face hostile Indians?"

"God, I hope so." He looked away, his eyes turning dark with anguish. "I don't ever want to fill as many graves as I did last fall."

"You really do care for them, don't you?"

"They're the only family I've ever known. To lose one, is to lose a friend, a brother."

She blinked in amazement. She couldn't believe he was opening up to her, trusting her with something so personal. Did he now regard her as part of his family as well? She nearly floated to the ceiling at the heartening thought.

Unfamiliar trumpet notes blasted through her blissful fog. She frowned and tilted her head to the sound. Though she'd begun to distinguish each of the daily bugle calls, this was one tune she hadn't heard before.

Chair legs screeched on the floor, startling her. She jabbed the needle into her finger. Wincing, she looked up.

"Sorry about supper," Chase said as he rushed past her. "But I have to go."

His hurried tone prickled the hairs at the back of her neck. "What bugle call is that?" she asked. "I haven't heard it before."

"Boots and saddles." He snagged his saber and hat and yanked open the front door. "There's trouble."

Trouble! She tossed aside her sewing and jumped to her feet. Heart thudding, she raced through the open doorway and stopped on the veranda, watching as Chase joined the growing formation of horses and troopers on the parade ground.

Boot heels thudded on the wood planks. Tom Forsythe bounded to the ground in front of her. "Lieutenant," she called out. "What's going on?"

"A large band of Comanche were seen crossing the hills just west of here," he shouted over his shoulder.

Comanche. Sweet Mary. And Chase and his men were no doubt preparing to pursue them.

As if echoing her thoughts, Chase mounted Zeus, raised a yellow-gauntleted hand, and motioned the troopers forward. The patrol galloped as one brave, eager unit, thundering through the gate until they disappeared from sight.

Callie dug her fingernails into the porch post. *Oh God, please keep them safe.*

A comforting hand patted her arm. "He'll be fine, Callie."

She faced her friend. "I can't stop thinking of the danger they're riding into."

Amanda gave her a knowing smile. "You can't dwell on the dangers. You'll only eat your heart out with worry."

Not worry? How could she not worry? Chase or any of his men could be wounded—or worse. She shuddered and tried to push aside the ugly image. "How long will they be gone?" she managed to ask.

"Hard to say. Five, maybe seven days, depending on how far south the Comanche lead them."

Seven days. It would seem like an eternity. She would try to be strong. Chase would expect it of her. Callie gathered her courage and pushed away from the post. "I had stew cooking for supper. Would you like to join me?"

Amanda nodded. "Yes, that sounds like a good idea. We should keep each other company. The first few days alone are the worst."

Back to being alone. Her heart sank. She would miss Chase and their newfound, and quite welcome, companionship.

As Amanda helped her with supper, Callie half-heartedly listened to her friend's amiable chatter. Her mind kept wandering to Chase and the troopers. She didn't know what she'd do if anything happened to any of them.

Amanda's garrulous prattle penetrated her morbid thoughts. "It'll be such fun. Do you have a ball gown?"

Callie blinked in confusion. "A ball gown? Whatever for?"

"For the post commander's birthday party. Weren't you listening to me?" Amanda gave her a sympathetic smile. "Of course, not. You were thinking about the captain."

She grimaced and stirred the stew. "I was. I'm sorry. Please go on."

Amanda placed soup bowls and spoons on the table. "Next Saturday night, the officers are throwing a gala for the major's birthday."

Callie heaved a resigned sigh. Her meager collection of somber blue, gray, and black gowns would pale in comparison to many of the outfits that would be worn at the ball. She'd not needed such luxurious gowns back East, and her guardians certainly wouldn't have purchased them if she had.

"I suppose I have a dress that will do," she said.

Amanda shook her head. "Oh no, you'll not wear something that will *just do.* I have a trunk full of ball gowns that Libbie Custer left me when her husband was assigned to Fort Riley. I'm sure we can find one that will fit you."

"Custer? I met the colonel in Leavenworth. He's quite a colorful character."

"Hmmmph. He's more fastidious about his looks than Libbie is. But she adores him anyway."

A wistful smile crept to her lips. She knew all about adoring a man despite his faults.

****

Twenty-four hours after Chase's departure, Callie stood in Amanda's bedroom amid half-a-dozen dresses scattered on the floor. She knew her sweet friend had contrived this get-together to keep her from worrying over Chase. Though her heart wasn't into trying on gowns, she didn't want to hurt Amanda's feelings by being ungrateful.

Callie fingered the reddish-orange skirt cascading in ruffled rows to her feet. "What do you think of this one?"

On her knees beside a huge trunk, Amanda peered up at her with twinkling, mischievous eyes. "Honestly?"

"Yes, honestly."

"You look like an overripe tomato."

An overripe..? Callie blinked. A long-forgotten sensation tickled her throat. Then, like a volcano spewing lava, laughter surged forth, bubbling from her in waves. "A r-rotten tomato." She clutched her belly and collapsed to the floor in a heap of orange satin.

Amanda joined her, rolling onto her back and laughing until tears coursed down her cheeks.

"Holy...Moses...Amanda," Callie managed between gasps. "It's been a long...time since I laughed so...hard."

"Me, too." Amanda sat up, giggling one last time as she wiped away her tears. "Lordy, get out of that horrid contraption."

"It is horrid, isn't it?"

125

Her friend leaned over and rummaged through the massive trunk. "I know the perfect gown is in here somewhere."

Callie swiped at her own tears and slipped out of the ugly dress. Happiness enveloped her. Her life was finally beginning to come together as she'd dreamed. She had many wonderful friends and a rewarding job as a teacher. Only one thing was missing—Chase's love.

"Oh, this is it," Amanda exclaimed. She rose from the trunk, clutching a pale pink gown. "Try this one."

Callie stepped into the wide skirt and fastened it at her waist. Seven narrow, puckered rows, each a darker pink than the one before it, adorned the bottom half of the garment. She ran her fingers over the delicate black lace that formed the overskirt. Exquisite. A gown meant for a princess.

Amanda helped her into the matching bodice and then tied the laces into a tight, constricting band. Callie struggled to inhale. Why must women put themselves through such torture? Only a man could have designed such clothing.

Amanda finally stepped back. "There, let's see." She spun Callie around. "Maybe a tiny tuck on each side, but otherwise, it's a perfect fit. You look absolutely stunning. Go see for yourself."

Callie moved in front of the floor-length mirror and gazed in amazement at the gown. It was fabulous—a pink and black confection of ruffles and lace, straight from a bon-bon box. However, it did have one flaw. She grimaced and tugged on the bodice.

"Stop!" Amanda shouted. "What in heaven's name are you doing?"

"It's too low. My bosom and shoulders are exposed." Callie frowned at the image of her shamelessly bared chest.

Amanda clucked. "They're supposed to be, silly."

"But I've never worn such an indecent gown. Everyone will gawk at me."

"Of course, that's the idea. Captain Brooks won't be able to take his eyes off of you."

Callie halted her ineffectual tugging. Wasn't that what she wanted, for Chase to notice her as a woman, as his wife? Yet, it seemed to be such a brazen attempt to gain his attention. "I don't know..." she murmured.

"Hush. There'll be no more discussion. You're going to wear this gown to the gala and enjoy doing it. Now, let's see about altering that bodice and cleaning it up a bit."

As Amanda began to undo the laces, Callie closed her eyes and pictured Chase unable to resist the lure of the enticing gown. He would pull her into his arms, his body heat warming her as no fire ever could. He would touch her as a husband would touch a wife.

A tremor pulsed deep inside her, a need aching to be fed. God help her, but she wanted to be his wife in every way.

But that was not the type of marriage he wanted. Why? What kept him from opening his heart to her? Several times, she'd seen banked emotions glowing deep within his eyes, desire he'd effectively tamped down before allowing anything more to develop.

She fisted her hand in the lacy overskirt. She'd find out why he held back. Once he came home. If he came home. Her throat thickened with fear.

Please God, bring him back safely.

****

Callie walked around the mess hall, placing chalk and slates on the tabletops. Her thoughts strayed to her first night of teaching. She'd been so nervous she'd almost lost her supper. Yet, as the evening progressed and the troopers responded to her lessons with unveiled enthusiasm, she'd relaxed and enjoyed herself, even laughing at Private White's entertaining jokes.

Now, she looked forward to her evening classes and the distraction they provided. Worry over Chase and his patrol gnawed at her, despite her efforts to remain strong. She barely slept and had to force herself to eat.

The soft shuffle of feet sounded at the back of the room. She looked up, expecting to see troopers entering the mess hall. Instead, a young woman stood in the doorway, fingering the faded folds of her calico dress. Tall and willowy, with lovely, corn silk colored hair spilling from a bun atop her head, the woman cleared her throat and spoke in a soft, husky voice. "Are you Mrs. Brooks?"

"Yes, I'm Mrs. Brooks. What can I do for you?"

"I heard you were giving lessons to the troopers."

"You heard correctly." Callie put down the last slate and moved toward the stranger. "We're just about to start class. What is it that you need?"

Sad green eyes that held the haunted look of someone who had seen more of the weary world than they wanted followed her progress. "I was wondering..." The woman paused and moistened her lips. "I know it's a strange request, but I thought..." She flicked a nervous glance at the door. "Would it be possible for me to join your class?"

Callie kept her surprise at bay. She didn't want to send the wrong signals. She applauded the woman's desire to improve herself. Not many females had the courage to do so. Was she a soldier's wife? Or one of the many laundress woman who worked at the garrison?

"Why certainly you may join us," she answered, keeping her tone light and cheerful. "What's your name?"

"Rose. Rose Franklin."

"It's a pleasure to meet you, Mrs. Franklin."

"Not Missus. Rose will do just fine."

Callie gave the woman an encouraging smile. "Very well, Rose it is. Please come in and have a seat. The troopers should be arriving shortly."

"Thank you, Mrs. Brooks, thank you. You don't know what this means to me." A faint gleam of hope flashed in Rose's eyes as she eased onto one of the benches in the back row.

Callie motioned to the front of the Hall. "There's plenty of room up front."

"I think I'll just sit here."

"But you won't be able to see as well."

"It'd be best if I stay right here, ma'am."

"Well then, if this is where you feel most comfortable..." Callie trailed off, unwilling to push further. "But we're all here to learn."

"Thank you, Mrs. Brooks."

"Please, call me Callie."

Rose gave her a wan smile and nodded.

Callie returned to the other end of the room. Perhaps after Rose became better acquainted with the class routine, she'd feel more at ease and move closer.

A few minutes later, the troopers began to enter the mess hall. Odd glances flitted from Rose to her and back. A few shook their heads, others mumbled beneath their breaths.

Private Sanford moved to the front of the room. A frown furrowed his leathery face. "Mrs. Brooks, I don't think it's a good idea to have that woman here."

"Why? Is there some regulation against civilians in the mess hall?" she asked.

"No, ma'am. It's just...well, Cap'n Brooks might not like it."

Why would Chase object to Rose's presence in her class? Surely he wouldn't deny any woman the opportunity to better herself. "Well, the captain isn't here and Rose wants to learn." She tiled her head to the side. "I'm sure you understand that desire."

"Yes'm, sorry, ma'am. Whatever you think is best." As she started to turn away, the trooper spoke again. "Excuse me, ma'am. There's something else."

She turned back to find several other troopers had gathered behind him.

Private Sanford held out a paper-wrapped package. "We all wanted you to have this here piece of elk tenderloin. Private Dunn brought down a big stag early this morning."

Her heart lifted at their considerate offer. "Why, thank you, all of you. What a nice thing to do."

"It ain't much," Private Sanford said. "But we just wanted you to know how much we 'preciate you schoolin' us. Not many folks would've taken the time."

"Not many white folks, you mean," someone mumbled.

Callie pictured Mrs. Roy and her bigoted cronies. An angry quiver passed through her. Private Sanford was right about some people not wanting to help the Negro troopers. Thank God, she wasn't one of them.

****

"You've hardly touched your lunch, Callie," Amanda chided. "You don't want Chase to return to a scarecrow of a wife, now do you?

Callie swirled her fork in the mixture of beans and

bacon. "It's been six days, Amanda. The waiting is just so difficult."

Her friend sighed. "I know it is, sweetie. But you have to have faith."

"I'm trying. But I keep seeing those awful images from the Indian attack. Arrows and blood and..." She broke off with a shudder.

"You have to think positively. Chase is an exceptional commander. He'll bring himself and his patrol home safely. You'll see."

The thunder of hooves echoed into the room. Callie jerked her head upward. Was it..? Could it possibly be..?

Amanda broke into a smile that probably mirrored the one on her own face. They both sprang to their feet and rushed for the door. The two of them trying to fit through the doorway at the same time might have been comical had they not been so excited.

Pulse thrumming, Callie grabbed onto an upright post for support. A column of weary, dusty troopers trotted across parade ground, led by an unfamiliar officer riding a white-socked horse. Her heart plummeted. It wasn't Chase's patrol.

The strange officer halted and dismounted. Major Roy rushed across the arena and stopped before the shorter man, giving him an eloquent salute. After a few minutes, the newly arrived troopers dismounted and led their horses toward the stables.

"General Philip Sheridan," Amanda said. "Lieutenant General of the Army, Commander of the Division of the Missouri. Major Roy must be quite anxious about his unannounced visit."

With disappointment jabbing her like a prickly cactus burr, Callie sighed and faced her friend. "I wonder what brings him here."

Amanda shrugged. "Who knows? I'm sure we'll find out soon enough. Arbuckle's gossip line works faster than the telegraph."

Callie gave a vague nod and scanned the now empty parade ground. She had so hoped the patrol was Chase returning. Heaviness settled back on her shoulders. It seemed her taxing wait would resume.

Amanda squeezed her elbow. "I have an idea. Why

don't we go to the Sutler's store and look for those rugs you wanted to purchase?"

"I don't know..."

"Come on. It'll take your mind off the captain. Besides, I need a new pair of gloves."

Callie gave a half-hearted shrug. "Very well. I guess we can go and see what we can find."

Lunch cleared and cloaks retrieved, they set off for the small cabin located behind the quartermaster's hut. Several horses were tethered outside the store, one a lovely paint with a silky, white mane. Callie gave the sleek horse a quick pat before venturing inside.

A dank, musty smell permeated the clapboard building. Shelves and bins lined the room and contained everything from boots and gauntlets to crackers and butter. An aproned clerk stood behind a long counter, talking with a trooper.

Amanda pointed at one narrow passageway. "You go down this aisle. I'll try the other. Call out if you find anything."

Callie nodded and headed down her appointed path. She poked and prodded and moved items aside in an attempt to locate the rugs. As she eased around a small crate, a tall, bearded man stepped into the aisle in front of her. Long, unkempt locks tumbled to his broad shoulders. A trooper's overcoat covered mud-splattered buckskin trousers that were tucked into the tops of dusty, knee-length boots.

Callie halted and eyed him warily.

The man doffed his wide-brimmed hat and moved closer. "Aftanoon, ma'am. Name's Moz Milner."

"Mr. Milner," she murmured as she countered his advance with a step backward.

"You can call me Joe. California Joe. I'm a scout for General Sheridan's patrol."

She averted her gaze from his intense stare. She wasn't about to call him anything.

The scout's soft whistle sent spiders crawling down her neck. "Doggone if you ain't the prettiest little filly I done eva laid eyes on."

The inside of her mouth turned to cotton. Dear God, where was her budding self-confidence when she needed it? This audacious man deserved a dressing down for his forward behavior.

"Callie," Amanda called out. "Come here. I found the rugs."

Thank God. She whirled and retreated down the aisle. She found Amanda in the next row, standing with the apron-clad clerk.

Amanda pointed a toe at several rugs draped across the floor. "What do you think of these? The green and tan would look nice next to your hearth."

Callie glanced over her shoulder at the deserted aisle before looking down at the rugs. "They look fine to me," she responded, relieved that the obnoxious scout hadn't followed her.

"Excellent." Amanda turned to the clerk. "Put them on her husband's account."

"Husband's name?" the clerk asked, pencil poised over his ledger.

Amanda leaned closer and poked the open page. "Captain Chase Brooks. And we'll have to send someone over later to retrieve them."

A raspy voice cut in. "I'd be more'n happy to offer the services of my horse to carry yer rugs, Missus Brooks."

Heart thudding, Callie spun around. The insufferable scout stood a few feet away, one hip cocked against a wooden barrel. He stared at her with lazy, hooded eyes while slapping his hat against his leg.

"I promise to be a genelman," he added.

"Joe, you haven't a gentlemanly bone in your body," a lilting Irish voice rang out.

The scout pursed his lips as a short, slender man stepped into view. Although quite dusty, the newcomer's gray trousers and brown tweed jacket bespoke a more refined demeanor. The Irishman doffed his derby hat and bowed to her.

"Teague O'Malley, ma'am, journalist for *The Washington Weekly Chronicle*. I'm riding with the General to record his campaign against the Indians." He glanced at the scout. "I'd be happy to act as chaperone, if you wish to accept Joe's offer."

Amanda smiled. "Why thank you, Mr. O'Malley. That's mighty kind of you."

Callie leaned closer to her friend. "We don't know these men, Amanda."

"There's naught to be afraid of ma'am," Mr. O'Malley stated. "Joe will behave. I'll see to it meself."

Somehow the scrawny Irishman's chest-thumping promise failed to reassure her. Despite the chill in the room, perspiration beaded between her breasts and dampened her chemise. Callie shifted uneasily. Something inside her screamed against letting these men into her home.

Amanda gave her a reassuring smile. "It'll be all right, Callie. They'll be in and out before you know it."

Callie swallowed hard and found herself nodding.

"Wonderful." Mr. O'Malley bent over the larger rug. "Grab that end, Joe."

Before she could change her mind, the two men had her rugs packed onto Joe's horse, which just happened to be the well-groomed, paint gelding. At least the unkempt scout took care of his mount, if he didn't care for his own appearance.

As they crossed the parade ground, Amanda's garrulous chatter competed with the throb in Callie's temple. "Mr. O'Malley, did you happen to attend President Grant's Inauguration in Washington?"

"Indeed, I did. 'Twas a most grand affair, although the weather wasn't quite so agreeable."

"Mrs. Brooks was at the ceremony as well."

He raised an inquisitive eyebrow. "Was she now?"

"Absolutely. General Grant is her cousin."

"Is that so? Perhaps I should conduct an interview on the fair relative of our new President." His emerald eyes twinkled as he regarded her over the paint's rump.

Callie felt heat rush into her face at his appraisal. She shook her head. "I'm afraid your readers would find me a boring subject, Mr. O'Malley."

California Joe tugged the rug-laden horse to a halt in front of Officers' Row. "Somehow, I doubt that, darlin'," he drawled.

Her stomach lurched. What was she thinking, allowing two strange men to accompany her home? Even with Amanda present, it still seemed wrong. Chase would object. She just knew he would—most emphatically.

Despite her misgivings, she remained silent. Amanda appeared to have things under control as she directed the two men with no-nonsense authority where the rugs should go. And amazingly, the rude scout behaved himself.

A short time later, the men maneuvered the last rug through the doorway and into the front room. Amanda scooted aside the wingback chairs and pointed to the vacated spot. "Put it there."

Grunting and huffing, the pair unrolled the rug and positioned it as directed.

Amanda studied the arrangement. She frowned and wagged a finger at the fireplace. "A little closer to the hearth, I think."

The men leaned over and adjusted the rug.

"No, no, that's too much," Amanda said.

"Dang it woman, make up yer mind."

Amanda clucked. "Hush Joe, you offered to help. Now push it to the left. That's it. Perfect." She pivoted around. "What do you think, Callie?"

Callie fidgeted with a fold of her gown. "It looks lovely." She glanced at the men and then looked away. "Thank you both for your help. I believe we're all set now." She felt guilty at her lack of hospitality, but she wanted the men out of her home. Now.

Joe sucked a breath between his teeth. "How's about having a drink with us to show your 'preciation? Got a bottle of whiskey in my saddle bag."

Callie tensed and eyed the fireplace poker. She should have listened to that little voice inside her head. California Joe was trouble. With a capital T.

"Now, Joe. You promised to behave," Mr. O'Malley admonished. He grabbed a handful of Joe's overcoat and tugged the scout toward the door.

Joe frowned and dragged his feet. "Aw, Teague—"

"Good afternoon, ladies." The Irishman tipped his hat to them before yanking the much taller man onto the veranda.

Callie hurried across the room and heaved the door closed. Thank heavens they were gone. She didn't know what she would have done if Joe had insisted on staying. Though her fear of a disaster had been laid to rest, she still couldn't shake the niggling doubt that she'd made a horrible mistake in allowing those strangers into her home.

ELEVEN

"Excuse me, Mrs. Brooks?"

Callie turned to find an unfamiliar soldier standing just beyond the veranda steps. "Yes, may I help you?"

"Private Jones, ma'am." He tipped his hat to her. "I was ordered to escort you to post headquarters."

Warmth left her face. Dear God. They'd received word of Chase's patrol. Her husband was dead. Trembling knees wavered, and she braced against the doorjamb to steady herself.

Blue eyes flashed with concern, and the private took a step toward her. "Are you all right, ma'am?"

How could she be all right? She'd never hear her husband's captivating voice again, never feel his touch, never become his true wife. She swallowed around the knot in her throat. "W-will they bring his body back to Arbuckle?"

"Ma'am?"

"Major Roy wishes to inform me of...my husband's death, does he not?"

"No ma'am. We've had no word from the captain's patrol."

She locked her knees to keep from crumbling into a relieved heap. *No word.* Better than she expected. Not much. But enough to give her hope. She released her pent-up breath. "Then why am I being summoned to Post Headquarters?"

"General Sheridan wishes to speak with you, ma'am."

The General want to speak with her? She barely knew the man. Callie glanced at the blank-faced soldier and knew she wouldn't get any answers from him. She drew in a calming breath and stepped off the veranda. "Then, we mustn't keep the General waiting."

Upon reaching Post Headquarters, Private Jones

ushered her inside and down a narrow hall. The lingering smell of cigar smoke filled the corridor. At the far end, General Sheridan stepped out of an open doorway. A smile creased his well-tanned face. "Mrs. Brooks, so good of you to come." He pointed to the chamber behind him. "Please, join me."

Somewhat comforted by his calm expression, she nodded and eased past him into the small room. Flags and armaments lined the planked walls. The red, swallow-tailed Sixth Cavalry guidon stood in one corner beside an American flag. A massive wood desk occupied the far wall. Major Roy's office, then.

"Please, have a seat," the general urged.

She settled on a high-backed, wooden chair facing the desk and resisted the urge to drum her fingers unladylike on the armrests. After enduring Chase's absence for so long, she was short on manners and patience.

Sheridan sat in the desk chair and peered across the paper-strewn desktop.

Unable to contain herself, she blurted, "Why did you wish to see me, General?"

He tilted his head and regarded her with a steady gaze. "I received a telegram from President Grant. It seems he was made aware of your forced marriage to Captain Brooks."

"Oh," was all she could manage.

"He asked me to check on your welfare."

Callie shifted uneasily. She'd hoped Ulysses wouldn't learn about the circumstances surrounding her marriage. She didn't want him worrying about her. He had more important issues to occupy his time.

General Sheridan leaned forward. "Ulysses ordered me to bring you back East should I learn you were being ill-treated." Sharp, shrewd eyes tunnelled into her. "Are you unhappy with your marriage?"

Unhappy? Her marriage left her disappointed and frustrated at times. But, she was far from unhappy. She lifted her chin and gave the officer a direct look. "I'm very content with my marriage to Captain Brooks. I have no desire to return East."

Tension left his face. His smile returned and he leaned back in his chair. "I hoped as much. Captain

Brooks is a fine officer. I'll inform President Grant of your decision."

She nodded and rose from her seat. "Thank you, General. Please relay to Ulysses my appreciation for his concern."

"I'll be sure to do that, Mrs. Brooks." The general stood and walked around the desk. "However, if you ever change your mind, you only have to send word to me."

Callie bit down on her bottom lip. She wouldn't be changing her mind. Only one man had the power to send her back East. And she prayed to God he would never exercise that right.

As she left the headquarters' building, the somber notes of retreat rode the air. She paused to observe the lowering of the flag. The setting sun cast an orange glow across the parade ground and upon the men standing in formation around the flagstaff.

Her gaze wandered to the garrison entrance. Where was Chase? Were he and his men all right? Pictures of bloodied bodies draped over saddles swam before her eyes. Bile burned in her throat. She swallowed and tried to push aside the ugly images. She wanted to be strong. Wanted to be the steadfast woman Chase would be proud to call his wife. But her strength was fast deserting her.

With a heavy heart, she resumed her trek across the parade ground. She climbed the steps to Officers' Row, then paused on the veranda to give the entrance one last hopeful look. A movement caught her eye, a flutter she wasn't quite certain she'd seen. She blinked and stared at the darkening shadows.

The faint jingle of spurs rang out. She sucked in a sharp breath and clutched her chest. Could it be..? Seconds later, Chase rode into view, leading a weary column of troopers. Her heart galloped beneath her fingertips.

He was alive!

Callie watched through tear-filled eyes as he reined in beside Major Roy, dismounted, and gave a brisk salute. After a few moments, the barked command of "dismissed" echoed across the arena, triggering a mass movement of all the mustered men. Chase handed Zeus' reins to a trooper and began walking in her direction.

She stood frozen, unable to move, unable to breathe. She'd dreamed so often of this moment, she wondered if it were truly happening. She drank in the sight of him, her aching thirst seemingly unquenchable.

His boots and uniform grayed with dust, Chase stopped at the edge of the veranda and swept off his weather-beaten hat. He scoured her face as though searching for an answer to a plaguing question.

"Welcome home," she murmured, breaking the awkward silence.

"It's good to be home." His voice dragged with weariness.

"Did you locate the renegades?"

He gave a faint snort. "More like they found us. The raiding party doubled-back and attacked our patrol."

She drew in a breath and ran her gaze down his lean length, just to satisfy her lingering doubts. Though covered with dust, he seemed unharmed. But what of the others? "Was anyone hurt or..?" She couldn't bring herself to say the word aloud.

"A few minor wounds. No deaths, thank God."

"Oh, thank heavens. I prayed every day for the patrol's safety. It seems He answered my prayers."

"Him and those new rifles we finally got. After an hour of getting picked-off, the renegades withdrew and fled into Texas. We lost their trail on the Brazos, and running low on provisions, we had to return."

"Regardless, you should be proud of your success."

"I am proud of my men. They've risen above many people's expectations."

She couldn't stop the admiring smile that stole to her lips. "So has their commander."

He reached out and tugged a stray curl. "Thank you for the thoughtful compliment, though I can see from your washed-out look the waiting was hard on you. I wish I could have spared you the torment." His smoky eyes perused her face, tenderly, almost like a...

Her heart soared. Was he finally beginning to care for her? She ached to catapult into his arms and let him hug away all the pain she'd endured. But she wasn't sure enough of their relationship for such a display. She gave a tiny shrug instead. "It wasn't so bad. I had Amanda and my teaching to help me through the wait."

"I'm glad they could help." He cleared his throat and released her hair. His granite eyes returned to their usual hardness as he slipped on his hat. "I need to meet with Major Roy and give my report. With General Sheridan present, I may be a while."

She nodded. "That's fine. I'll keep your supper warm." Her body quivered with suppressed joy as he turned and headed across the parade ground. Chase was home. He was finally home. She sent a silent prayer of thanks heavenward.

As she turned to see about supper, she spotted Lieutenant Forsythe folding Amanda into an intimate embrace. A wistful sigh escaped her lips. One day, maybe Chase would trust her enough to do the same. For now, she'd just be content with slowly earning his love.

****

The wind howled outside the window, pelting the panes with rain. A bright streak of lighting lit the room, followed by a resounding crack of thunder. Chase leaned back and drained the last of his coffee. He liked storms. They always brought a little excitement into his dreary life. Much like the woman standing behind him, her soft rosy scent making him yearn for things best left unwanted.

"The venison was good," he said. "Tender and juicy."

"Y-Yes," Callie murmured. "The troopers gave me a strap of tenderloin in appreciation of m-my...teaching efforts."

He frowned at her oddly strained tone. He couldn't imagine she'd be upset by a gift. "That was nice of them."

"It was a sweet gesture." She drew next to him and held out the steaming coffee pot. "More?"

"Yes, please." He slid his cup to the edge of the table.

As she began pouring, lightning doused the room in brilliant light. A resounding boom chased the flash. Callie flinched and spilled coffee onto the tabletop. Eyes widened in alarm, she stared at the spreading puddle.

Chase lifted his cup out of the spill. Was she afraid of the storm? He hadn't noticed her jumpiness before. But then they hadn't had any squalls as violent as this since she'd come to Arbuckle.

140

Callie broke out of her trance with a shake of her head. "Heavens, l-look at what I've done." After setting the pot back on the stove, she began dabbing at the spill with a cloth rag.

Another crash of thunder rattled the dishes in the cupboard. She jerked again. This time, a startled gasp escaped her lips.

Not wanting to, but feeling as though he should, he placed a comforting hand over hers. She trembled beneath his touch. "It's just a springtime squall," he told her. "It'll be over soon."

"I-It's not the storm," she whispered.

Not the storm? He cocked his head and studied her tight face. "Then, what is it?"

"I-I...Oh, it's silly. We needn't discuss it."

He raised an eyebrow. "It's not so silly when you shake like a cornered rabbit. Tell me what has you so upset."

"I can't."

"Yes, you can. I'm your husband." His gut clenched. Where had that come from? He wasn't anywhere near to being a real husband to her.

"I suppose..."

Chase gave her an encouraging nod. "Take a deep breath. Then let it all out."

She glanced at the window and back at him. A frown furrowed into her brow. A few seconds later, her chest rose as she drew in a deep breath. "When I was a little girl, my...my parents were killed by an exploding cannon." She shuddered and closed her eyes.

"Go on," he urged softly. "It's all right."

She opened her eyes. Her tortured gaze gouged a hole in his gut. "I-I witnessed their deaths. To this day...loud noises bring back the memories."

Good God. He hadn't expected that. What should he say? Do? He knew very little about comforting a distraught woman. Miranda's hysterics had been confined to shouting tirades. He patted her hand awkwardly. "I'm sorry you had to see such a thing, Callie. And here, I thought my childhood was lousy." He managed a wry grin and then felt bad for trying to make light of her struggle.

The vein at the side of her neck pulsed unevenly. She

141

opened her pretty mouth to speak and then clamped it shut just as quickly. She deepened her frown and slid her trembling hand out of his grasp.

There was something else. Something she was afraid to tell him. "There's more to your story, isn't there?"

Callie gripped the table edge like a lifeline. "Yes," she whispered. "There's more."

"Tell me."

She remained silent, staring at him with sad, haunted eyes.

"You'll feel better if you talk about it," Chase persisted.

She swallowed hard and when she spoke, her desolate tone knifed into his heart. "I-It was a July Fourth celebration. Father had forbidden me to go near the cannons. Yet..." She crossed her arms over her chest and rubbed her upper arms as though trying to generate some warmth.

"You can do this," he said. "Finish your story."

Callie stilled her rubbing and drew in a breath. "I disobeyed my father...s-snuck closer to the cannons to get a better look. Even talked my younger cousin, Deanna Boggs, into coming with me."

"Boggs? Was she the daughter of your guardians?"

"Yes...the poor, innocent child." Tears pooled in her eyes. "She died in the explosion...along with my parents, who had come searching for me." Her anguished voice trailed off into silence.

Chase fisted his hand on the tabletop. A lot of things were starting to make sense. He gave a low growl. "That explains the Boggs' cruel treatment of you. They blame you for their daughter's death."

A sob tore from her lips. "They had every right to...to scorn me. I killed their daughter *and* my parents by disobeying. Some days, I wish..."

"What do you wish?" he asked, though he already suspected the answer.

Tears and torment stained her lovely face. "I wish I'd died along with them."

Before he knew it, he was on his feet and pulling her into his arms. Callie burrowed into him and released her grief in great, heaving sobs she must've held inside for years.

Chase returned to the chair and eased her onto his lap. "Shhhhh," he murmured, rocking her the way he'd seen Alice Grierson console little Harry. "You're not to blame for their deaths. You were only a child."

She rested her head against his chest, her warm tears soaking into his shirt. He could barely make out her words as she stammered through her sobs. "A st-stupid, w-willful child...just...hic...like Aunt Eunice always s-said."

His heart bucked. How could anyone saddle a child with such a burden? He should have strangled Horace Boggs when he had the chance. "You have to let go of the guilt, Callie," he whispered into her hair. "It was just a horrible, unfortunate accident."

She snuggled closer. As her wretched sobs tunnelled into him, he continued to rock her, wishing he could ease her pain. He knew quite well how guilt could eat at a person's soul. His own was chewed to shreds.

After a few minutes, her sobs slowed to soft hiccups. She lifted her head and pushed away from his chest. "I-I'm sorry." Her tear-stained face flushed a pretty pink. "I didn't intend—"

He couldn't stop himself from reaching up and thumbing away her tears. "It's all right. You needed to get it out. Feeling better now?"

"Y-Yes, I am. Thank you." She drew in a ragged sigh and pulled her strength around her like a cape. Her resilience was one of the things he admired about her most.

"I'm glad I could help," he said.

She wiggled upright, then wiped her face with a corner of her apron. It was then that he realized how familiarly her bottom rested on his thighs. Fire and longing shot into his loins. He ground his teeth against the pleasure. Now was not the time to desire his wife. Callie was fragile and vulnerable. Christ, making love to her was the last thing he should be thinking about.

She gave him a watery smile. "Where were you thirteen years ago when I needed you?"

He grunted. "At age twelve? Probably polishing forty pairs of boots for leaving the fort against orders."

143

She widened her smile. "We're not so different, after all, are we? Tell me about your childhood."

Chase shifted uneasily, both from her intimate position in his lap and her pointed question. "I guess you have a right to know."

"Right to know what?" Her doe eyes anchored him, bright and steady, like a beacon on a fog shrouded night.

"When we were married, I told you I never knew my parents. What I didn't tell you..." His throat tightened, clamping around on the words. God, this was harder than he thought.

"Please. Go on," she urged, her tone soft and reassuring.

Chase grimaced. Who was consoling whom now? He took a deep breath and continued. "I never knew them because the woman who gave birth to me worked at the local brothel. When she abandoned me, the troopers at Fort Smith took me in and raised me. I guess they felt sorry for the orphaned tyke dogging their every step."

Her eyes softened. "So you didn't have one father. You had dozens of them."

He nodded, surprised by her easy acceptance of a parentage that had eaten at him his whole life. "I guess I never looked at it quite that way. But yes, they were all my fathers. Once I grew old enough, the troopers schooled me on a variety of subjects. They were tough, but fair."

Chase recalled those days as if they were only yesterday—long, grueling hours on the parade ground, muscle-fatiguing maneuvers on horseback, and endless nights pouring over books and military tomes. Looking back, he wouldn't have traded one minute of it for a normal childhood.

"They taught you well," Callie murmured, bringing him back to the present.

"Yes, they did," he said. "By the time I joined the Army, I knew more than most West Point graduates."

"And thus enabling your successful rise in rank." Her enraptured smile nearly knocked him out of the chair.

"That and Colonel Grierson," he managed to say. "In sixty-one, the Colonel and I fought together in western Tennessee and northern Mississippi. When he was given command of a cavalry brigade, the colonel brought me with him."

"You admire him a lot."

"Yes, I do. Grierson is an amazing tactician. During General Grant's Vicksburg campaign, we rode south into Louisiana, operating behind enemy lines without a supply line. Only sustained twenty-four casualties the entire operation."

"Good heavens, what an accomplishment."

"It was. And our success was the main reason we were invited to your cousin's Inauguration." *And consequently bringing you into my life.*

"I'm glad you were." Her tender gaze swept over his face. Rosy lips parted in innocent invitation.

Heat once again blasted his groin. His rod thickened with longing, and he muzzled a groan. Christ, he had to get away from her—now—before he did something he'd regret. Chase set her away from him and bolted to his feet. "The storm has passed," he grunted out. "I should go and check on the guards."

A confused look passed over her face before she looked down and worked at straightening her skirts. He steeled his heart against her disappointment. She didn't understand her power over him.

And he intended to keep it that way.

****

Callie double-stepped in order to keep up with Chase's ground-eating stride. "Where are we going?"

"You'll see," he answered in a cryptic tone.

"Why are you toting a rifle?"

"No more questions, Callie. You'll find out soon enough."

She opened her mouth to question him further and then snapped it shut. Chase Brooks could be as obstinate as an ornery mule when he wanted to be. If she hadn't witnessed his tenderness the night before...

With a shake of her head, she continued onward, kicking through the dew-splashed grass as she walked. Cottony clouds drifted across the blue expanse. A raven circled overhead and then settled in a treetop, cawing shrilly to its flock mates. The idyllic day matched her own serenity. Eden couldn't be any lovelier.

They entered a rolling meadow where Sergeant

Greaves, Private White, and Private Brown waited, also armed with rifles. Beyond the threesome, sack cloths painted with red circles dotted the grass. Eden turned to Sodom in the space of a heartbeat. The men were taking target practice.

Her heart slammed against her ribs. Why had Chase brought her here? She pulled to an abrupt halt.

Chase stopped as well. "It's all right, Callie. I understand now why you're afraid of gunfire. I'm going to help you get past your fear and learn to shoot."

She fisted her trembling hands. "I-I've tried to overcome my fear. It's useless."

"It's not useless." He took her hand and gave it a gentle squeeze. "You can do this. You're a lot stronger than you think."

Her palms grew damp. She bit down on her lip and shook her head. "I c-can't."

"Yes, you can. I'll be right beside you." He tugged on her hand. "Come on."

Callie pried her feet free and followed him across the field. She wanted to be strong, wanted with all her heart to be able to put her fears behind her. But they'd been with her for so long...

"All set, Sergeant?" Chase asked as they drew next to the troopers.

"Yes, sir, Cap'n. Target's at fifty yards." Sergeant Greaves flicked a reassuring smile at her, then moved to stand with the other men.

Chase held out his rifle to her. The breath lodged in her throat. She stared at the weapon as though it were a deadly snake.

"It won't bite you," he said. "Take it."

She looked up into his encouraging eyes and then at the rifle. She didn't want to disappoint him, but God, to shoot a gun...

"It's all right." His tone was soft and reassuring.

Callie wiped damp palms down the length of her gown and drew in a calming breath. She could do this. She reached out and grasped the weapon. It was surprisingly warm.

"Good. Now, let's start with the basics." Chase launched into a brief explanation of the gun's mechanics.

Callie blinked and tried to focus on his instructions. Cocking lever, breech loader, sights—strange words, made stranger by her inability to concentrate. All she could think about was the noise the thing made.

"Aim it at the target and shoot the way I told you," Chase said.

She swallowed around the sawdust in her mouth and faced the sacks. She lifted the rifle and settled the butt end against her shoulder as he'd instructed. Though it weighed little more than a broom, the long weapon wavered in her awkward grasp. Memories of the exploding cannon echoed in her head. Her arms began to tremble.

"Concentrate," Chase's calming voice intruded. "Hold the barrel steady."

She wanted so badly to do this, to make Chase proud of her. Callie curled her finger around the trigger. Her pulse hammered in her ears. *I can do this. I can—*

She yanked on the trigger.

BLAM!

Every muscle flinched at the deafening noise and the resulting kick of the fired weapon. Her nostrils burned with the acrid scent of gunpowder. She gasped and nearly dropped the rifle. Across the field, the sack remained untouched. She'd failed. Callie shook her head in disgust. "See...I can't..."

Chase moved behind her and pressed close. "Here...like this." He wrapped his arms around her and cupped his hands over hers.

Heat rushed though her and pooled in a tantalizing ball in her lower belly. She stuffed down a moan. Why was he putting her through this torture? First the gun and now the sweet agony of having him so close she could almost—

"See the metal piece at the end of the barrel?" His warm breath teased the skin at the back of her neck. She could barely manage a nod.

"Line it up with the center of the red circle on the sack and this notched rear sight." He tapped the rear piece with his thumb.

Callie suppressed another moan. How could she concentrate on what he said with his head just inches from hers, his body spooning hers so intimately?

"Now, gently squeeze the trigger," he said. "Don't yank on it." He clutched her finger with his and pressed lightly.

Before she could blink, the gun blasted out, its forceful recoil thrusting her backward into Chase's rock-hard chest. Her body burst into flames.

"There. That wasn't so bad, was it?" His voice was strangely hoarse.

Wasn't so bad? Sweet Mary, having him hold her like this was pure murder. The gunfire was nothing compared to the sweet ache filling her now.

Chase stepped away and began demonstrating how to eject the spent cartridge and feed another into the chamber. She could do little more than nod while he talked.

He handed the rifle back to her. "You try now."

Though she stood alone, her body burned as though he remained pressed against her. The sensation filled her with unwavering courage. She peered down the barrel and lined up the sights. Then, squeezing gently, she pulled the trigger.

The ear-splitting discharge and the rifle's painful recoil jabbed into her. She staggered back a step, but thankfully remained standing.

"You missed. Try again," he urged. "And keep the butt tucked tighter against your shoulder. It won't kick as badly."

Fine time to be telling me that.

Resisting the urge to rub her stinging flesh, she ejected the cartridge and loaded another round into the chamber. She cradled the rifle butt tight against her shoulder and focused all her attention on sighting the red circle. When the pieces lined up, she squeezed the trigger, this time, barely flinching at the ensuing blast.

Stuffing flew from the sack several inches above the bulls-eye.

"Nice shot, Missus Brooks," Private Brown exclaimed. "That would've taken out any Injun."

The other troopers joined in, praising her feat.

A swell of pride swept through her. She'd done it. She'd fired a rifle without falling into a hysterical heap.

Grinning broadly, Callie swung around to face the men. The troopers ducked and scattered before her. Her smile fell.

"Whoa," Chase admonished, pushing the rifle barrel towards the ground. "Don't ever point a firearm, loaded or unloaded, at anyone unless you intend to shoot them."

"I'm so sorry," she called out to the men. A rush of embarrassing heat flared in her face, yet the troopers' soft laughter and chiding comments eased her discomfort.

Her smile returned and she glanced up at her husband. She couldn't keep the adoration from shining in her eyes. Not any more. "Thank you, Captain. I'll never forget this. Ever."

"You're welcome," he replied. "You did very well. I hope you never need to fire a weapon, but at least you know you can if the need ever arises."

Darkness briefly clouded her sunny day. She hoped she *never* needed to either.

****

The Sutler handed her the paper-wrapped package. "Here you go, Mrs. Brooks. I'm sure Major Roy will enjoy your gift. That's his favorite pipe tobacco."

"Thank you, Mr. Bennett." Callie stuffed the parcel in her market basket. "I appreciate your suggestion. I had no idea what to get the post commander for his birthday."

"I'm glad I could help. Enjoy the party, ma'am."

She nodded and headed for the door. Callie doubted if she'd enjoy any part of the festivities tonight. She would be too busy worrying about the seductive ball gown Amanda insisted she wear. She'd considered feigning an illness, but didn't want to disappoint her friend. Amanda had worked much too hard getting the dress ready. She would have to cope with wearing the garment, despite her doubts.

Outside the Sutler's, she met Rose Franklin on the steps. "Good morning, Rose," Callie greeted. "Have you progressed any further into your primer?"

Rose cast a furtive glance around them and then answered in a soft voice. "Yes, Mrs. Brooks. I'm almost done."

Callie smiled. "That's wonderful news. You'll be ready for your second book when we meet on Tuesday."

149

"Yes, I imagine I will." Rose ducked her head. "If you'll excuse me, ma'am, I need to be getting inside."

"Certainly. I'll see you next week." Callie headed across the parade ground, wondering when Rose would warm up to her. She thought after two weeks of class, the woman would at least be able to look her in the eye.

A familiar figure loomed ahead, his lanky, six-foot frame casting a long shadow on the sun-baked earth. Her heart glowed with pleasure, and a smile found her lips.

"How do you know that *woman*?" Chase bit out.

Her smile dropped at his harsh tone. *Woman*? She looked over her shoulder, then back at her scowling husband. "You mean Rose Franklin?"

"Yes. Why were you talking with her?"

"She's one of my students."

"*One of your students*? How the hell did that happen?"

Callie frowned. "Rose asked if she could join my nightly classes. And I agreed."

Thunderbolts shot from his flinty eyes. "I don't want you to be involved with her."

"For heaven's sake, she only wants to learn how to read and write." She flung her hands into the air. "What's the harm in that?"

"The harm is that she's a whore. I won't allow my wife to consort with her kind."

Callie stared at him in disbelief. Rose? A prostitute? It was a difficult thing to imagine from such a quiet, unassuming woman. It might explain why Rose remained so reticent around her. But it didn't explain Chase's behavior.

"You won't allow me to consort with her kind," she threw back at him. "What nonsense."

"Nonsense?" His voice dripped with derision.

"Yes, nonsense. That's exactly the type of response I'd expect from Major Roy or his wife. As commander of Negro troopers and the recipient of many a bigoted remark yourself, you should understand how repulsive any form of prejudice is."

He narrowed his eyes and formed his lips into a pencil-thin line. "You don't know what you're talking about."

Her heart pounded. Where was the gentle man who had held her so tenderly the day before, the man who helped her overcome her fear and shoot a rifle? He'd apparently fled with his common sense. Frustration and anger bubbled inside her. She lifted her chin in defiance. "I know exactly what I'm talking about. I've heard about Major Roy's unwarranted slurs toward you and your troopers."

"It's not the same thing."

"It is, and you know it." She softened her tone. "It's not fair to judge Rose because of your mother."

He jerked his head back as though she'd slapped him. Raw pain glinted in his eyes. She ached to pull him into her arms, to comfort him as his mother should have done years ago. But she'd most likely only get a scathing rebuff for her efforts.

"Captain, I-"

He sliced the air with his hand. "Stop. I don't want to hear any more. You *will* obey me on this, Callie. Do I make myself clear?"

"Very," she choked out, unwilling to provoke him with further argument. If only he would trust her more. She was beginning to think there might not be a chance for their marriage.

"Were you on your way to the Forsythe's?" he asked.

At her nod, he snagged her elbow and nudged her forward. "I'll walk you there."

The tumbling gray clouds of the morning had scuttled away, leaving a broad expanse of blue sky in their wake. Uncloaked sunlight warmed the mid-April day to a pleasant temperature. Callie blinked away a rush of tears. She'd need more than balmy weather to dispel the chill that enveloped her.

Amanda greeted them at the door and sent Chase off with a wave. Her heavy heart aching, Callie followed her friend into the kitchen where a porcelain hipbath sat next to the cook-stove.

"Isn't this exciting?" Amanda gushed as she poured steaming water from a kettle into the tub. "I can't wait for the evening to arrive."

Callie forced a smile to her lips and worked to push aside her sadness. After all her friend had done for her,

Amanda deserved a more cheerful companion. She dipped a finger into the water. "It will be nice to bathe in a real tub, not a freezing creek or a rag-bath from a basin."

"I know how you feel. I had to beg Tom to purchase this for me." Amanda nodded at the tub. "You go first. I need to finish pressing my gown."

Callie undressed in the steamy kitchen and slid into the tub. Warm water wrapped her in a silky embrace. She gave a soft moan. It was almost pleasurable enough to banish her sadness. Almost.

After bathing, Callie toweled dry and then sat by the hearth in her shift. The fire's warmth lapped at her back. She closed her eyes and tried to relax. Chase's angry image floated before her, a ghostly reminder that she didn't yet have his heart. Maybe never would. Perhaps she should just get it out of her head that her dreams of being loved and cherished would never happen with Chase Brooks.

"You've been awful quiet," Amanda stated softly. "Did you and the captain quarrel?"

Callie frowned. So much for her attempt at feigning happiness. Was she to be a disappointment to everyone she loved? She heaved a frustrated sigh and opened her eyes. "Yes, I'm afraid tonight won't be such a pleasant affair for us."

"It will once he sees you in that gown."

Unease twisted at her insides. She still didn't think the revealing gown was such a good idea, especially after Chase's disturbing behavior earlier. Callie wished she felt more comfortable discussing her marriage with Amanda. Perhaps her friend could offer some comforting advice. Unfortunately, she didn't have the courage to reveal the details of her forced wedding, or discuss Chase's desire to keep their marriage in name only. It was much too intimate a subject to broach.

Amanda rose from the tub and tugged on a robe. As she tightened the sash, she glanced at Callie. "By the by, if you dance with Lieutenant Daniels tonight, watch out for your toes. He'll flatten them with those canoes he calls feet."

Callie shook her head and fingered a fold of her shift. "I doubt if I'll be asked to dance."

"Oh, you'll be asked all right." Amanda joined her by the hearth. "But I imagine your toes will be quite safe."

"Why is that?"

"Captain Brooks will most likely claim every dance with you."

Her belly somersaulted. She hadn't even considered the dancing aspect of the party. She'd be enfolded in Chase's arms, brushing against his lean body as they whirled around the dance floor...

Torment. It would be pure torment. Her scantily clad body would surely betray her. She squirmed, and the hearthstones dug into her backside. Maybe Chase would still be angry with her and wouldn't *want* to dance. Somehow that thought failed to cheer her.

"Let's see about your hair." Amanda began combing and winding paper strips around Callie's damp locks. After a few minutes, she stilled and gave a soft grunt. "Oh, another thing about the party. Beware of Betsy Alvis. She'll do her best to monopolize the captain."

Callie stiffened at the mention of Betsy Alvis.

Amanda patted her shoulder. "Don't worry. Chase barely gives that woman the time of day. What John Alvis sees in her is beyond me. Love must truly be blind."

Callie bit her lip. She knew one thing. Her love was *far* from blind. Just the thought of Chase dancing with beautiful, seductive Betsy turned her insides to stone.

****

Several hours later, Callie stood before the floor length mirror unable to keep her jaw from sagging. Entwined with rose-colored ribbons, thick, black ringlets fell to her shoulders from the elegant mass gathered atop her head. The satin and lace gown hugged her every curve. Sensual. Seductive. And nothing like she'd ever worn before.

"I can't believe it's me," she whispered.

"It certainly is you." Amanda entered the bedroom, looking exquisite in a cornflower blue gown gathered at the waist to reveal a white, ruffled underskirt. Matching blue ribbons adorned her upswept locks.

Callie glanced at her friend's equally exposed bosom and shoulders. At least she wouldn't be the only one indecently clothed.

Amanda drew next to her and peered into the reflection. "You look absolutely stunning."

Callie gave her a wan smile. "Not as lovely as you."

Amanda fluttered her lashes. "La, we'll be the belles of the ball."

She bowed her head and pretended to smooth out an imaginary wrinkle. Would Chase notice her transformation? She would find out soon enough. He and Tom were dressing in the captain's quarters and would arrive shortly to escort them to the gala.

Amanda clucked. "If I didn't know Chase was already in love with you, I'd bet my last dollar he'd fall for you tonight."

Callie jerked her head upward. Chase in love with her? Why would Amanda say such a thing?

The squeak of the front door stilled her question mid-breath. She snapped her mouth shut and glanced at the open bedroom door. The men had arrived. Pulse tripping, she trailed Amanda into the front room. Chase would finally see her in the decadent gown. How would he react? Delighted? Or disgusted? She didn't know which worried her the most.

Tom Forsythe stood just inside the front entry. He looked quite dashing in his dark, frock dress jacket lined with a double row of shiny, brass buttons and shoulder-enhancing, gold epaulets. The lieutenant swept off his feather-tipped hat and tucked it under his arm.

Callie arched her neck, trying to see beyond him.

Noting the direction of her gaze, Tom shook his head. "I'm sorry Mrs. Brooks, but the captain was detained. I'm to escort both of you to the party until he can join us."

"Oh, I see..." She donned a cheerful smile despite the pinch of disappointment.

Amanda gave her arm a reassuring squeeze. "Well then, let's go. Shall we?"

Callie nodded. Not much she could do about Chase's absence anyway. She slipped on her shawl and retrieved the major's gift from the side table.

In the waning light of day, they crossed the parade ground and headed for the mess hall. Callie walked in silence beside the lieutenant, struggling to fend off her festering gloom. Surely, Chase would come to the party.

He couldn't be that angry with her that he would miss the post commander's birthday gala.

The lieutenant's chuckle interrupted her musings. "Won't the other men be jealous of me? I have the distinct pleasure of escorting the two loveliest ladies to the ball."

"Oh, Tom," Amanda purred. "You say the sweetest things."

He groaned and shuffled his feet in an effort to maneuver between their hooped skirts. "Too bad you're also the ones with the widest gowns."

Amanda leaned forward and caught Callie's eye with a laughing gaze.

Callie hid a grin behind gloved fingers, her melancholy lifting with the Forsythe's playful antics. How fortunate she was to have such wonderful friends. Perhaps the gala wouldn't be so bad after all. She glanced at her exposed bosom and tugged her shawl tighter. If only she could wear her wrap the entire night. Then, she might be able to enjoy herself.

Ahead of them, three unfamiliar officers and an elegantly gowned blonde stood near the entrance to the mess-hall. The woman turned as they approached. Callie tensed. *Betsy Alvis.* She'd secretly hoped the woman wouldn't attend. So much for that wish.

"Lieutenant Forsythe," one of the men called out. "How'd you get so lucky as to have a beautiful lady hangin' on each arm?"

"Must be my charming personality," Tom replied as he assisted Amanda, and then her, up the stairs.

"Must be." The officer's freckled face split into a toothy grin, and he glanced at Amanda. "Don't forget to save a dance for me, Mrs. Forsythe."

Amanda groaned under her breath yet continued to smile at the grinning officer. "Certainly, Lieutenant Daniels. I'll be sure to put your name on my dance card."

As she trailed Amanda across the porch, Callie glanced at the lieutenant's feet. Like sled runners, his shiny, black brogans spanned at least three plank widths. She bit her lip to keep from grinning. She didn't envy her friend one bit. Amanda would surely have sore toes come morning.

A soft, feminine grunt drew her attention. Callie

lifted her gaze and stared into narrowed blue eyes. "Evening, Mrs. Alvis," she greeted, forcing the woman's name out of her mouth.

"Mrs. Brooks," Betsy responded with a slight nod before pursing her lips into a pout. "My, my, I surely do hope Chase can pull himself away from his duties this evening. He's such a *divine* dancer." The hussy's voice dripped with syrupy sweetness.

Bile burned in her throat. Where was John Alvis? The man needed to put a bridle on his wife. No, make that a gunny sack, pulled over her head and secured around her scrawny neck.

Before Callie could reply, Amanda snagged her arm and tugged her toward the open doorway. "Oh, never fear, Betsy," her friend shot back. "Captain Brooks will be here before long. However, I doubt if you'll be able to pry him away from his beautiful wife."

"The only reason you were invited, Amanda Forsythe, is because of your husband." Betsy's parting remark followed them into mess hall.

Fury bloomed in Amanda's cheeks. She slowed and released Callie's arm.

"Ignore her, Amanda," Tom warned softly. "She just wants to goad you into a fight. Don't give her the satisfaction."

"That mealy-mouth trol-"

"Amanda..."

"Oh, all right."

"Here's the coat table," Tom said. "Let me have your wraps, ladies."

Callie clutched her shawl like a lifeline. She already felt bared enough by the ugly encounter with Betsy. Maybe if she ignored him, the lieutenant wouldn't pressure her for her wrap. She pretended to admire the colorful banners hanging on the walls. Out of the corner of her eye, she spotted Amanda stalking toward her, a scowl creasing her brow.

Her heart nearly leapt into her throat. Amanda wouldn't.

Green eyes narrowed.

She drew in a sharp breath. Oh, yes she would. Callie released her death grip on the wrap, and it slid off her shoulders. Cool air swirled around her exposed skin. She tensed and flicked a frantic glance over the crowded hall. Small pockets of guests laughed and chatted amongst themselves. No one seemed concerned with her dishabille. She released her pent-up breath and handed Tom her wrap.

After setting their gifts on the nearby gift table, they moved farther into the gaily decorated chamber. Lanterns hung at intervals from the rafters and bathed the guests in golden light. The mess tables and benches had been pushed against the walls, leaving an open area for dancing. In the far corner of the room an impressive monument of rifles and flags stood in silent tribute to the regiment.

"You ladies are a treat for a travel-weary man's eyes," General Sheridan said as he joined them. He tipped his head in greeting. "Mrs. Brooks. Mrs. Forsythe."

"General," they replied in unison.

His lively gsze lit on Callie. "Captain Brooks should be arriving shortly, my dear. I left him at headquarters, wrapping up an urgent matter."

She inclined her head to him. "Thank you, General."

Her anxiety resurfaced, writhing like an eel in her belly. Chase would be here soon. She recalled his angry reaction to Rose and tossed a worried glance at the entrance.

God help her if he disapproved of her choice of gown.

TWELVE

"Evening, Chase," John Alvis greeted from the mess hall porch. Smoke curled from the cigar clutched between his fingers. "I expect Ben didn't have good news for us."

Chase removed his hat and climbed the short stairs. "I'm afraid not. Satanta has taken a hostile band and headed south toward Red River. The rest of the tribe remained with Black Eagle on the reservation."

"Damn. I knew it wouldn't be long before that rabid heathen started something. Are we sending a patrol after him?"

"Not right now. I dispatched a rider to Fort Richardson to alert the Sixth Cav."

"Well, let's enjoy tonight while we can."

Chase nodded and strode through the entry. He paused inside and scanned the lantern-lit chamber. Clusters of uniformed men and gaily-dressed ladies filled every corner of the room. The over-powering smell of perfume and warm bodies nearly made him gag.

God, he hated these things—having to endure clingy, prattling women and pompous, bigoted men. He'd rather have a tooth pulled by the doc. The only reason he'd shown up was Callie. He couldn't let her face this carnivorous crowd alone. They'd stay for a while and then head for the peace and quiet of their quarters.

He tossed his hat onto a nearby table and drifted further into the room. Out of the corner of his eye, he spotted Betsy Alvis making a bee-line in his direction. Chase groaned. *Godamighty.* Why couldn't the woman leave him be? He thought he'd made his disinterest quite plain.

"Captain Brooks," the blonde cooed as she drew next to him and placed a hand on his forearm. "I'm so glad you were able to get away from your duties."

Her flowery, stomach-turning perfume pricked his nose. "Evening, Mrs. Alvis," he replied in as bland a tone as he could manage without being rude. "Yes, I was able to get away." He yanked his head at the door behind him. "If you're looking for John, I saw him out on the front steps."

"I'm not looking for John."

You should be. "Well then, if you'll excuse me, *I* am looking for my wife."

"Now, Captain, surely you can spare a moment for a little chat."

"No. I can't. Good evening." He plucked her hand off his arm and moved away, ignoring her huff of indignation. God, didn't the woman ever give up? Her behavior was no better than that of a whore. He could never turn a blind eye to his wife's actions as John Alvis did, no matter how beautiful the woman.

Speaking of wives...

He searched the hall from corner to corner. The Forsythes stood at the far end of the packed chamber. Yet, there was no sign of his petite, dark-haired wife. Where the hell was she? He'd asked Tom to escort her to the party. Maybe she'd decided not to attend. Chase grunted under his breath. Suited him. He'd give the Major his regards and then—

The crowd shifted, exposing an exquisite figure staring at him from across the room. Tendrils of dark hair curled to her bared shoulders. Her gown hugged her trim figure, the low-slung neckline revealing a cleavage he'd only dreamed of setting eyes on.

"Jesus H. Christ," he swore softly, his loins tightening in response. With his eyes trained on the mesmerizing vision, he crossed the floor and reached her in seven healthy strides. "Sorry I was delayed," he said. "A scout reported in at the last minute."

"I understand," she murmured, her sweet voice and half-lidded eyes driving him further over the edge. "I'm just glad that you're here."

Before he could reply, a hand clapped onto his shoulder. "Captain Brooks, You didn't mention you had a wife." The hand tightened into bear-like squeeze. "Much less, one so beautiful."

He turned his head and gave the intruder a baleful glare. "For good reason, Sammy."

"Now, is that any way to treat an old friend? Introduce me to this enchanting creature."

He groaned inwardly. He knew coming to this party was a mistake. "Callie, this is Lieutenant Woodward. We served together during the War. He now has the distinct privilege of escorting General Sheridan around the countryside."

Callie dipped her lovely head. "It's a pleasure to meet you, Lieutenant."

"The pleasure is *all* mine."

A rosy blush stained her cheeks. She ducked her head, clearly embarrassed by Sammy's intense inspection.

Chase glowered harder at his friend. *Go find some other soul to pester.*

The lieutenant lifted an eyebrow. A knowing look crossed his face, and Chase stiffened. He knew that look. If Sammy thought Callie meant something to him, there'd be no end to the man's needling. Chase pressed fisted hands against his thighs and continued to glare at the irritating officer.

Sammy ignored his silent warning. "General Sheridan tells me you're President Grant's cousin, Mrs. Brooks. How is it that I missed seeing such a lovely lady at the Inauguration?"

A timid smile tipped her lips. "We didn't stay long."

The lieutenant chuckled. "Long enough to meet this lucky chap, it seems."

Chase's gut clenched. Christ, the last thing he wanted was the circumstances of his marriage aired to one and all. Before he could steer the conversation to a safer topic, soft music filled the chamber.

With a grin slicing his face, Sammy gave Chase's shoulder a final tweak and removed his hand. "You'll let me have one dance with her won't you, ole chum?"

"Probably not." Chase seized Callie's hand and led her toward the dance floor, away from Sammy, away from trouble.

She tried to wrench out of his grasp. "I-I don't care to dance—"

He stopped and pulled her close, cutting off her

protest. She stood before him, her luminous eyes widened in alarm. It appeared some of her shyness still lingered. He gave her hand a gentle squeeze. "It'll be all right, Callie. Just pretend it's only you and me dancing. Ignore the others."

She hesitated, tugging her bottom lip between her teeth as she considered his request. Creamy mounds rose and fell with each ragged breath she inhaled.

Fire surged through his groin. Chase sucked in a breath. Was he insane? He shouldn't dance with her. But, dammit, he just couldn't help himself. Not only was it socially required of him to dance the first dance with his wife, he was nigh onto exploding with the need to feel her in his arms.

Before he could withdraw, Callie gave him a cautious nod. He settled his hand at her tiny waist and swung her onto the dance floor. After a few minutes, the tension faded from her beautiful face. Her eyes turned soft and dreamy, and she followed his lead effortlessly. Damn, how he wanted to pull her closer and feel her lush body crushed against his. No. What he really wanted was to sling her over his shoulder and carry her back to his quarters where he could devour her sweet lips, taste more of the woman who had bewitched him.

Chase stiffened. Where was the control he so prized himself for? He snorted softly. It seemed to have flown out the window the moment he spotted his captivating wife standing across the dance floor.

The music soon trailed away, and the couples around them ceased dancing. Chase halted and stared down into Callie's entrancing eyes. He didn't want to move, didn't want to break the spell she'd cast upon him.

"May I, Captain?"

Chase groaned inwardly at the familiar, authoritative voice. *General Sheridan*. He couldn't very well refuse his commander's request, now could he?

With a quick nod, he relinquished her hand and moved off the dance floor. He shouldered against the far wall and watched as Callie and Sheridan began the intricate steps of a quadrille. His thoughts wandered to his earlier meeting with the general. Sheridan had warned him of President Grant's concern for Callie. Phil had orders to escort her back East should he find her being ill-treated. Chase fisted his hands. No one, not even President Grant, was going to take Callie away from him.

Not while he drew a breath.

As the quadrille ended, the fiddlers shifted into a lively reel, bringing a round of squeals and yips. Sheridan handed Callie over to a grinning Sammy. Chase frowned and glared at the lieutenant. *Tricky bastard. You'd best keep your hands where I can see them.*

"Turn your partner," the caller crooned to the dancers.

At the command, Sammy whirled Callie in a brisk circle. A laughing smile dimpled her cheeks.

Heated blood pounded through Chase's veins. He ground his teeth, tamping down hard on his rising jealousy. He wanted to look away, wanted to shield himself from the sight of his wife enjoying herself with another man. But he couldn't. Her pull was much too strong to resist.

Damn, he hated what she was doing to him, making him care, making him feel emotions he never wanted to feel again.

****

Chase found his patience thinning by the hour.

Every unattached officer danced attendance on Callie, bringing her punch, plates of cake, and even providing a handkerchief for her to mop the perspiration from her brow. He shouldn't begrudge the other men a chance to enjoy the company of a lovely female. Ladies were few and far-between in the Indian Territories. Besides, Callie deserved to have a good time. Life at the remote outpost must be awful dull compared to the social doings in Washington.

Yet, his good intentions disappeared when he spied her heaving breathlessly after a rollicking polka. Flushed breasts rose and fell with each breath she took, the lush mounds threatening to spill out of her gown.

His simmering blood finally boiled over. Chase marched across the dance floor and snatched her hand. "Looks like you need some fresh air." He tugged her toward the rear door, ignoring her faint protests.

Once outdoors, he spun her around. Light from the

162

shimmering moon illuminated her silky skin. She parted her pretty mouth and ran a pink tongue over her bottom lip.

Fire again flamed in his groin, threatening to consume him. His control in tatters, he seized her waist and hauled her against him. She molded him perfectly as if she were meant for him. He knew in that instant she was. No other woman completed him as Callie did. She was the light to his darkness.

Chase leaned over and captured her mouth with his own. Desire exploded in him, blasting all rationalization into a million pieces. He flicked his tongue across her velvety lips and then plunged inside to taste her sweetness.

Callie stiffened beneath his onslaught, pricking his shattered wits. *Slow down, Brooks. She's an innocent.* He eased his assault, content to tease her lips with his tongue and wait for her to relax.

His restraint was rewarded. She soon softened and melted against him, her faint moan drifting over his skin like warm butter. Satan's flames licked at his insides. Selling his soul, he slid his hand upward and cupped her breast, kneading the soft mound through the silky material of her gown.

A woman's laugh penetrated his lust-addled brain.

Chase lifted his head and stepped back with a quick glance at an approaching couple. *Damnation.* He sucked in a gut-deep draught of air and tilted his head back, staring at the stars until, inch by inch, his rebellious control returned. Enough to get him home, but not enough to stop him from having what his body craved.

He lowered his head and peered into Callie's upturned face. "Where's your wrap?" he growled. "We're going home."

She blinked and pursed lips reddened by his assault. "B-But we can't leave. The party is still—"

"We can, and we will. Where is your wrap?"

"O-On the table, near the front entrance."

He cupped her elbow. "Good. Let's go." He guided her back into the mess hall and through the throng to the front door.

As Callie rummaged through the collection of cloaks,

his gaze wandered over her trim figure. God, how he wanted to trail kisses down her slender neck, across her exposed shoulders, and delve deep between—

"Leaving so soon, Captain?"

Chase groaned and glanced at Woodward. "Yes, my wife isn't feeling well."

"Well, I'm sure you've got just the cure for her," the officer bantered under his breath.

Go to hell, Sammy. Chase snatched his hat from the table and aimed a hatchet-edged glower at the annoying lieutenant. Much more of this, and he'd have one less trooper to call friend.

Callie turned around, her shawl clutched in white-knuckled fingers. "I-I've found my wrap."

"Good." Chase pulled the garment from her grasp and tossed it around her shoulders.

"I hope you feel better, Mrs. Brooks," stated the undaunted lieutenant.

"Thank you, she will." Chase ushered Callie out the door before the obnoxious officer could goad him further.

As they crossed the darkened parade ground, only the seductive swish of silken skirts broke the silence. Chase inhaled in a frayed breath. He knew he shouldn't continue down the path he was taking, but he couldn't stop himself. He wanted Callie with a fierceness that surprised him. To hell with building a slow, natural relationship.

"W-Why did you tell the lieutenant I wasn't feeling well?"

He gave her elbow a gentle squeeze. "Did you want me to tell him the real reason for our leaving?"

Her soft intake of air sent a shaft of lightning slicing through his already smoldering loins. Chase ground his teeth. He didn't know how much more he could take without exploding like a Fourth of July firecracker.

Thankfully, they reached Officers' Row where the simple task of opening the door claimed his attention. Callie strode past him into the front room, almost knocking him flat with her sultry scent. He exhaled a hiss of air and fought his impatience to bed the woman who stirred him like no other. Christ, he was acting like an untried schoolboy, hot, excited, and ready to pounce. The last thing he wanted was to scare her with his eagerness.

Keeping his movements routine, he removed his hat and saber and hung them near the door. As he unbuttoned his jacket, a match flared to life in the darkened room, and then the soft glow of the oil lamp lit the shadows. Haloed by the golden light, Callie stood by the sideboard, wringing her hands together in a fretful ball.

His gut twisted. He hated seeing her so anxious. Perhaps she needed something to take the edge off. He knew he did. "Why don't you pour us a whiskey?"

She flinched at the sound of his voice, yet quickly regained her composure. Chin lifted, she tossed her shawl onto a chair and moved to the sideboard. The clink of glass rang out, then the soft gurgle of pouring liquor. A few drops spilled on the countertop. She frowned and swiped at the puddle with her fingers.

Chase eased toward her, taking slow, non-threatening steps. "Don't worry about that."

Her wary gaze lit on him. She swallowed and held out the drink. "Here."

He shook his head. "You have some first."

She hesitated a moment and then tipped the tumbler to her lips. Neck muscles convulsed beneath her silky skin as she took a healthy gulp. She lowered the glass and regarded him with gleaming eyes.

Chase pried the glass from her grip and set it on the tabletop. Still holding onto her wrist, he lifted her hand to his mouth and gently sucked the whiskey from her fingertips.

Nectar of the Gods.

Her eyes widened, mimicking the rounded "oh" of her mouth. With a faint moan, she tugged her hand away and rubbed her fingers as though he'd scorched them.

Chase reached out and caressed her cheek. So soft. So enticing. "I'm not going to hurt you, Callie."

"I know," she whispered. She closed her eyes and rested her cheek in his palm.

With a groan, he leaned forward and seized her lips once again. She tasted of brandy and of the tantalizing flavor of woman. His head reeled from the intoxicating rush. He wanted her, wanted her badly.

165

Damn, the consequences.

Chase moved his hand to her lower back and hauled her against him. Their bodies fused together. He deepened their kiss, delving his tongue between her parted lips. To his surprise, she met him, tentative at first, and then more daring as she entangled her tongue with his.

Heat seared his lower gut, flaming into a bonfire of desire. God she learned fast. Teaching her new things was going to be pure pleasure.

It took every ounce of willpower he had to keep from shoving her against the wall and tossing up her skirts. He didn't want her that way. He wanted to savor her, wanted to feel her writhing under him, calling his name and begging him to take her.

She shifted in his arms. Firm breasts pressed through the cotton fabric of his shirt and teased his senses. He could think of nothing more pleasing than caressing her naked flesh. That meant he had to get her out of a gown that seemed to be pasted on.

He slid his hands upward and fumbled with the knotted laces at the back. How the hell could she breathe, hog-tied as she was? After a few more tugs, the ornery laces gave way. The silk cocoon loosened and slipped away, revealing taut, rose-colored nipples.

Chase groaned. He had to see the rest of her.

He scooped her into his arms and carried her into the bedroom. She snuggled against him and pleasing heat pulsed through him. Prodded by the throb in his loins, he set her next to the bed and began to remove the rest of her clothes, wondering if he'd ever get her divested of all the things she'd worn under her gown.

Finally, she stood before him, her naked body glowing in the moonlight streaming through the window. "You're so beautiful," he murmured as he ran his hands along her smooth, silky sides and down to her rounded buttocks.

She trembled beneath his touch, but didn't flinch. "Is this truly what you want?" Her softly whispered words caressed his ears.

"Yes. God, yes." Eager to feel the press of flesh against flesh, he stepped back and began working on his own clothing.

Callie stood silently, watching while Chase stripped off his shirt, exposing taut muscles she'd only felt, never seen. Boots and trousers joined the cotton shirt on the floor. She inhaled a tattered breath and shuddered as cool air swirled around her bared body. Was she dreaming? Was her husband really about to make her his wife, his *true* wife?

The thought of what was to come frightened and excited her at the same time. She lowered her gaze, skimming the rippling muscles of his abdomen and halting at his engorged staff rising from a nest of golden curls.

She shouldn't stare. It wasn't proper. But, God in Heaven Above, he rivaled the sculptures of the Greek gods she'd once seen in a sketch book. And according to one of her other books...he would...she swallowed hard...they would...

Before she could think another thought, he moved closer. Her pulse leapt. *Oh, God, this is it.*

Callie took an anxious step back and collided with the bed. "I-I've read about...I don't..." She halted in an embarrassing tumble of words. Would her lack of experience displease him?

He placed a finger over her lips. "Shhh...I know you're innocent. Trust me."

Trust him. There was no one she trusted more.

He leaned forward and pressed her back onto the bed. The heat of his body countered the coolness of the quilt beneath her. Another shudder coursed through her, this one of pleasure and desire.

"You've haunted my dreams for too many nights to count," he whispered. "I can no longer deny how much I want you." His smoky eyes flared with passion. "Is this what you want as well?"

Is this what she wanted? Sweet Mary, it seemed as if she'd been waiting her whole life for this moment. "Yes. Make me your wife."

He lowered his mouth to hers and devoured her lips with fierce intensity. His hands roamed her body, caressing and kneading sensitive spots she never knew existed. With a groan, Chase abandoned his assault on her lips and moved downward along her neck, nipping and sucking her tender flesh. He halted at her breast and lathed her nipple with his tongue.

A flower bud unfurled inside her, opening up to the sunshine building between her legs. Instinct told her there was more, much more, and she wanted it with every ounce of her being.

His fingers slid downward along her belly, leaving a scalding trail in their path. He cupped her mound and began gently tugging and teasing her nest of womanly curls.

Unable to stop her response, Callie lifted her hips to meet his caress. She never knew she could feel such wonderful sensations. Nothing she'd read had prepared her for the thrill of a man's touch—the touch of the man she'd come to love with all her heart.

He draped a muscular thigh across hers and gently pried her legs apart. A second later, his fingers plunged into her heated flesh. Fire flamed deep inside her, building higher and higher until she thought she would explode. She gasped with the pleasure of it and writhed beneath his touch, her body crying out for fulfillment.

Amazed at Callie's abandoned response, Chase studied her face, wanting to forever etch her wanton expression in his memory. She was a precious jewel, and for the moment, she was his. He might not be able to love her emotionally, but he could definitely show her physical love.

He shifted atop her and braced his hands on either side of her shoulders. Sweat broke out on every inch of his skin as his body clamored for release. He hated the thought of hurting her, but he couldn't wait any longer. Chase drew in a ragged breath and worked to hold himself in check for a few seconds longer. "I'm sorry, sweetheart," he managed to get out. "But this is going to hurt. It won't last long, and I promise, you won't ever feel pain again."

She smiled up at him, her eyes filled with trust and something more. He didn't want to think about the *something more*. He had other more pressing things to occupy his mind, like controlling the urge to pound animal-like into her flaming flesh.

Chase covered her mouth with his and then using his knee, moved her thighs further apart. He hesitated, hovering just over her shimmering body. No easy way to do this but to...

In one quick motion, he thrust inside her, breaching the barrier that proclaimed her a virgin. Callie stiffened beneath him and gasped into his mouth.

Chase stilled his movements. "Relax," he whispered. "The pain will soon fade."

After several agonizing minutes, she finally began to soften. *That's it, sweetheart.* He moved to her breast and drew her nipple into his mouth, teasing the bud to a taut peak.

Sweet, ever so sweet. Like a summer-ripened berry.

She wriggled beneath him and shifted her hands to his waist. The tantalizing flutter of fingernails on his skin sent lava coursing through him. Unable to contain his desire any longer, he eased his staff out of her warmth and then returned, groaning as her heated flesh sheathed him like a well-fit glove.

Her soft, erotic cry washed over him. "Chase. Oh my, please..."

It was the first time he'd heard his name cross her lips. The sound pitched him into a wild fervor. He scooped a hand under her buttocks and lifted her to meet his thrusts.

When her pulsing climax began, she groaned into his mouth, a long, sensual moan that set his blood to boiling. Fire blasted through his insides. He gave one last plunge into her moistness and joined her at the peak of ecstasy, spilling his seed in pulsating spasms of pleasure.

THIRTEEN

Callie slowly drifted up from the grayness of sleep. Her body tingled with awareness of a warm body spooned against her back. She never knew she could feel so wonderful. Even while sleeping soundly, with his arm draped over her waist, Chase still aroused her senses.

She shifted onto her back and pulled the counterpane closer to ward off the morning chill. The tender flesh between her thighs throbbed with a faint, heated ache, albeit a pleasant one. Chase had definitely shown her the breathtaking pleasures a man could give a woman.

Had she pleased him as well? He seemed to enjoy their lovemaking as much as she did. She slid her hand under the quilt and absently stroked his firm, sinewy arm. She recalled his gentle strength as he'd held her tightly the night before. Heat rose in her at the memory of her wanton response. Was it acceptable for a wife to act so...so unrestrained?

"If you don't stop, you may get more than you bargained for." Chase's warm breath caressed her neck.

Callie jerked her hand away, not ready for such intimacy in the light of day. "I-I didn't mean to awaken you."

"I'd much rather be awakened by my beautiful wife than the trumpet of a bugle."

She gave a feeble laugh. "It's Sunday. No bugle will call you to duty this morning." Heart thumping, she inched toward the edge of bed. "Why don't I make us some coffee?" She winced at her overly bright tone.

Strong arms grasped her waist and tugged her back. "Not until I've had my good morning kiss." With a low growl, he gently claimed her lips.

She closed her eyes and enjoyed the wonderful sensations surging through her. All anxious thoughts fled as Chase tugged her against his rock hard body.

Sweet Mary, she loved this man. How could she not? He'd given her most everything she'd ever dreamed of having. The bulge of his rising manhood pressed into her belly. Though no words of love had passed his lips, she knew he wanted her. Love couldn't be that far behind. She would just have to be patient.

Hours later, after a second pleasurable frolic between the sheets, Callie stood outside the church with Chase and the Forsythes. On the far side of the parade ground, a group of troopers pitched horseshoes while others stood nearby watching.

Amanda grasped her elbow and pulled her off to the side. "You left the party early," she whispered.

Callie averted her eyes. "Yes, well..."

"I told you that gown would do the trick. Chase couldn't keep his eyes off you all evening."

Heat flamed up her neck. Did it *ever* do the trick.

"Lord, don't be embarrassed," Amanda chided. "I've been in your position plenty of times. A rousing romp will mend any marital rift." She gave Callie's belly a knowing look. "Perhaps you'll have an announcement to make in a few months."

Callie frowned in confusion. "An announcement?"

"Yes. The news that you're with child."

With child! Good heavens, she hadn't even considered the consequences of their joining. She pressed her palm against her lower belly, pleased at the thought of carrying Chase's baby.

"It'd be nice for my little one to have another child to play with," Amanda murmured.

Callie yanked her gaze to her friend's glowing face. A wide smile greeted her. "Oh, Amanda, how wonderful," she exclaimed. "Does Tom know?"

"I told him last night, although he already suspected."

"I'm so excited for you. When is the baby due?"

"Sometime in late fall. Tom wants a boy, but I'd love to have a sweet, beautiful daughter."

The lieutenant drew next to Amanda and placed a loving arm around his wife's waist. "Did you hear that, Captain? We're going to have a son in the fall."

Amanda thumped his chest with her palm. "A daughter."

"Congratulations," Chase said as he joined them.

Amanda gave him a wide smile. "Thank you, Captain. Perhaps you and Callie will soon have a similar announcement to make."

Oh, dear. Was that what he wanted? Callie risked a quick glance at his expressionless face. His flinty eyes widened a fraction before he schooled his features back into a stoic mask.

"Yes, well...perhaps," he muttered.

Her heart fell. Not quite the response she wanted to hear. Maybe he just needed time to become accustomed to the idea. He'd only come to accept her as his true wife last night.

Chase cleared his throat. "Callie, the Lieutenant is going to escort you back to our quarters. I have to report for duty as Officer of the Day."

She forced a smile to her lips in an effort to restrain her disappointment. "That's fine. I have some chores that will occupy my time." *Officer of the Day*. That task should be called Officer of the Day *and* Night. For the next twenty-four hours, Chase would patrol the garrison, ensuring that everyone followed the rules and regulations.

She would sleep alone, with no opportunity to indulge in the intimacies of the night before. Callie gave a soft sigh. Such was the life of a military wife. And she wouldn't have it any other way.

****

With a flick of her wrist, Callie swept the pile of dirt off the edge of the veranda. She paused and leaned against the broom handle, letting her thoughts wander to Chase and the unexpected yet welcome change in their relationship. Although they'd exchanged no words of love, she was certain, with a little more time, Chase would learn to trust her, would eventually be able to commit his heart to her. How could he not after the intimacy they'd shared.

A figure hurrying across the parade ground caught her attention. Bathed in the orange light of the setting sun, the unfamiliar woman kicked up puffs of dust as she

172

scurried toward Officers' Row. The slender brunette pulled to a panting halt at the bottom of the steps. "Missus Brooks?"

Callie nodded. "Yes."

"I'm Nellie S-Saunders, ma'am."

Was this another prospective student like Rose? She smiled down at the woman. "What can I do for you, Miss Saunders?"

The girl twisted a corner of her shawl in her fisted hand. "I'm sorry to bother you, ma'am, b-but you've got to come." Her wide brown eyes filled with tears. "You've just got to."

A band of fear tightened around her chest, cutting off her breath. Her smile fell. "Come where? What's happened? Is it my husband?"

"No, ma'am. It's not your husband. It's Rose. She's been locked in her room for days and refuses to come out."

Callie released her pent-up breath. Chase was all right. But apparently not Rose. She propped her broom against the wall and leaned inside the doorway to snatch her shawl off its peg. "Do you know why Rose refuses come out of her room?" she asked as she closed the door and stepped off the veranda.

Nellie shook her head. "I-I'm not sure. She won't talk about it. But I think it has somethin' to do with one of her customers, a Corporal Smythe."

Customer...as in someone who paid for a service. Callie fought the uneasiness welling inside her. Chase had forbidden her to associate with Rose. And here she was heading for Rose's lodgings—most likely a house of ill-repute. Her husband was going to be furious. Hornet-stinging mad.

But Rose needed her. And she couldn't possibly turn her back on a person in need, no matter what they did for a living. She'd deal with Chase later.

As they hurried across the parade ground, Callie's thoughts returned to Rose. What could possibly have happened to cause the woman to act so drastically? Shy, yet fiercely determined, Rose Franklin put forth a tremendous effort to learn whatever was taught her. She'd progressed well, surpassing many of the troopers with her reading and writing.

A nervous knot formed in Callie's belly. Whatever the reason for Rose's strange behavior, it had to be bad—really bad.

In the dying light of day, they raced past the Sutler's store and came upon a small, two-story cottage nestled at the edge of the garrison. Though in need of repairs, the building looked like any other wood-hewn cabin at the fort.

Callie followed Nellie up the porch steps and into the front entrance. She paused just inside the doorway to accustom herself to the diminished light. The overpowering smell of perfume, sweat, and some other musky, unpleasant odor filled the small foyer.

"You got us a new girl, Nellie?" came a deep, raspy voice. "Bring her here so's I can git a better look at her."

Female giggles followed the man's remark.

"No Ben Baker, it's not a new girl," Nellie scolded. "This is Captain Brook's wife."

Her eyesight finally adjusting, Callie peered into the adjoining parlor. Oil lamps flickered on the papered walls and cast a faint glow on several scantily-clad women—one reclined on a settee, the other perched intimately on the lap of a bearded man.

Callie's jaw sagged open. Sweet Mary. Chase was going to murder her for coming here.

Ben's whistle echoed into the foyer. "Captain Brooks' wife? Godamighty, Nellie, you done lost your mind, girl?"

"Hush, Ben," Nellie snapped. "I fetched her here to help Rose." She turned to Callie and nodded at the stairs. "Follow me, Missus Brooks. Rose's room is right up here."

Callie snapped her mouth shut and gathered her skirts. As she said, she'd deal with Chase later. Rose claimed her attention right now. She trailed Nellie up the narrow staircase to second floor.

The girl stopped midway down the corridor and rapped softly on a closed door. "Rose, it's Nellie." She grimaced and licked her lips. "I've brought Missus Brooks with me."

Only soft laughter drifting up from the first floor broke the stillness.

Callie stepped forward and knocked on the door. "Please open the door, Rose," she urged. "We're all worried about you."

More silence. Her insides knotted. This wasn't good. "Please, Rose. I only want to help." Callie held her hand against the wood panel, trying to reach the woman on the other side.

The shuffle of footsteps sounded from within. Then, a muted click rose from the lock. Callie watched as the knob turned and the door slowly opened. She suppressed a gasp of dismay at the sight that greeted her. Purple and yellow bruises littered Rose's face and neck. The battered woman peered through slits in her swollen eyelids.

"You shouldn't have brought her here, Nellie," Rose whispered.

Nellie wrung her hands. "I-I didn't know what else to do."

Callie reached out and gently rested a hand on Rose's arm. "I'm glad she did. Let's go into your room and talk, shall we?"

Rose bowed her head and turned to shuffle back into the bedroom. Callie followed, doing her best not to stare at the rumpled bed. As Rose sank onto a spindly-legged chair, she squatted beside her and reached for the battered woman's hand. Her stomach flipped at the sight of scabbed-over scratches marring the pale skin.

"Who did this to you?" Callie asked.

Rose ran her tongue over puffy, cracked lips. "It doesn't matter."

"Yes, it does matter."

Rose shook her head and then winced. "No, Mrs. Brooks. I appreciate your concern, but..." Her voice trailed away as she glanced around the room. "I should never have believed I could change what I've become."

"Oh, Rose. You can change, if you really want to."

A lone tear trickled down her mottled cheek. "I want to...Oh God, do I want to."

"You can. But you need to believe in yourself. Never give up on what you truly want. Trust me, I know." Callie gestured with a nod to the book resting on the side table. "Is that why you wanted to learn to read and write?"

"Yes. I've been saving my money. Soon as I had enough, I planned to go back East. Open a dress shop."

"There's no reason why you still can't. These bruises

will heal."

"You're wrong, Mrs. Brooks. That...that polecat stole all my money. Laughed at my dreams and said I owed him for all the lousy tumbles I'd given him. When I tried to get my money back, he...he did this." Rose heaved a dejected sigh and lowered her head.

The girl's forlorn expression knifed into Callie's heart. "Was it Corporal Smythe?"

Rose's slight nod was the only response Callie needed. She rose and faced Nellie. The girl squirmed in the doorway, hands twisted in the folds of her gown. "Nellie, go to the Headquarters building and get Captain Brooks. Tell him there's been an incident involving an Arbuckle trooper."

Eyes wide as saucers, Nellie nodded and fled from the room.

Callie remained by Rose's side, sickened by the defeated look on the young woman's face. Anger climbed in her like a spring-thawed creek cresting its banks. How could anyone do this to another human being? Corporal Smythe deserved the harshest punishment that could be meted out. She prayed Chase wouldn't allow his prejudice to interfere with his good judgment.

Twenty minutes later, boot heels thudded on the stairs. Then, a towering figure filled the doorway. Chase glared at her across the short distance, his jaws clenched tightly in suppressed anger. "Why are you here?" he demanded. "I thought I made myself perfectly clear the other day."

Callie pointed to Rose. "For God sake, Chase, look at her. I couldn't refuse to help her."

His fierce gaze moved to the woman sitting in the chair, head bent, hands folded quietly in her lap. He frowned and stepped further into the room. Rose lifted her head and looked up at him.

"Who did this to you?" he growled.

Callie answered for the battered girl. "Corporal Smythe. And he stole money from her as well."

He snorted. "An infantryman from the Sixth. I should've known. Do you need medical help? I can send for Doc Pearce."

Rose shook her head. "No, I'll be fine. Thank you,

Captain."

"The corporal won't get away with this, Miss Franklin. I promise you. I'll file charges against him tonight. You should receive a notice for a hearing of the garrison court in a day or so."

"You really don't need—"

"Yes, I do need to do this. What Corporal Smythe did to you is against the law. And I aim to see him punished." His voice was controlled and even, yet Callie sensed anger bubbling just below the surface.

"Very well," Rose murmured. "Thank you, Captain,"

Chase pivoted on his heels. "Let's go, Callie." He snagged her elbow in a vise-like grip and tugged her toward the door. "I'll walk you home."

She dug in her heels. "But, Rose..."

"You go on, Mrs. Brooks," Rose urged. "I appreciate your concern, but I'll be just fine." She formed a sad smile with her puffy lips. "Thank you for all you've done."

"Very well, but you send Nellie to find me if you need anything." She gave Chase a forceful glare, daring him to naysay her.

He remained silent, his anger palpable as they left the house. Upon reaching their quarters, he shoved open the door and motioned with a jerk of his hand for her to enter.

She swept past him and trudged to the hearth. With a heavy heart, she stared at the dwindling fire, hope fading in her chest like the dying embers. Chase didn't trust her. What did he think she was going to do, join Rose in her trade?

His imposing voice pierced her thoughts. "I'm going back to Headquarters. There'll be no more jaunts outdoors tonight. Understood?"

Hurt and confused, she faced him as he stood in the open doorway. She blinked back stinging tears and lifted her chin. "I'll not apologize for doing what I thought was best."

He reached for the door. "I didn't expect you would."

As the door clicked shut, she slumped in a chair and let her tears fall. What had happened to the gentle, caring man who left her bed that morning? Like a besieged knight, he'd retreated behind the walls of his fortress, shutting her out, shattering the beauty of what they'd shared.

It nearly destroyed her to think he'd only used her for his pleasure.

****

Major Roy's voice cut through the silence in the office. "I certainly hope things settle down for the rest of the night."

Chase stilled his pen and looked up from his paperwork. "My thoughts exactly, sir."

"Nasty business with Corporal Smythe. He's one of my best sharpshooters. Ah, well, finish writing up the charges. A hearing will be scheduled sometime tomorrow." The burly commander slapped his gloves in his palm and stalked through the open doorway and into the night.

Ass. Chase clenched his teeth together. The major's prejudice toward anyone he considered beneath him was infuriating. Callie would be heart-broken if Rose didn't get a fair trial. He'd do his best to see that Corporal Smythe got the punishment he deserved.

After scrawling his signature on the bottom of the report, Chase peered out the darkened window. He knew he'd overreacted to Callie's presence in the whorehouse, but, dammit, just the sight of her standing near that stained and rumpled bed pushed old torments to the surface. They'd risen inside him like a geyser. He'd unconsciously focused his rage on the only thing that had the power to hurt him, Callie.

He regretted his harsh words, but had been unable to stop them. His brooding had been one reason for his overreaction. For much of the day, he'd agonized over the fact that he'd consummated his marriage, had lost control and crossed a line he hadn't wanted to cross. He knew better than to touch her, to kiss her, but he just plain hadn't been able to stop himself.

Now, he would suffer the consequences. Callie would expect love and commitment from him, the two things he feared he could never completely give to any woman. And what woman could love a man who was frozen and empty inside? To further complicate matters, she could be with child, *his* child.

Jesus, what a mess he'd made of his life—and

Callie's.

With a frustrated growl, he rose and strode through the open doorway to the veranda. Stars twinkled in the ebony sky like gleeful fairies pleased their enchantment dust had worked so well.

"Too well," Chase muttered. Disgusted with himself, he shoved on his hat and set off across the parade ground. He'd make a quick check on Callie before making his rounds. It *was* his duty, after all, to look after her.

Upon reaching his quarters, he eased inside and walked quietly to the bedroom. Faint moonlight filtered through the window, illuminating the figure sprawled under the counterpane. Ebony hair spilled over his pillow. Pulse thudding, he crept closer to the bed. He reached out and rubbed a silky curl with his fingertips.

God, she was beautiful. Fire raced through his loins at the thought of their lovemaking last night. He tamped down hard on the desire to pull her into his arms and take her again.

His gut clenched. What had she done to him? He thought after one night with her, his hunger would be satiated. *Fool.* He should've known better. Now, he was obsessed with her, with wanting her. Like a drowning man, Chase fought the whirlpool pulling him under. He couldn't allow himself to desire her, to care for her. She'd only rip his heart clean out of his chest when she left him.

Chase hurried out of the room as if the hounds of hell were on his heels. He had to get her out of his thoughts, out of his blood. He would re-double his efforts to keep his military duties foremost. That would help keep her off his mind.

It had to.

Putting his avowal to work, he left Officers' Row and began making his rounds, inspecting the garrison for troopers who had not heeded the bugle call to be abed, lanterns snuffed, no talking. As he neared the laundress's quarters, female giggles and drunken, male voices issued from within. Frowning, he pushed open the door and stepped inside.

Sheridan's bearded, unkempt scout sat in a chair on the far side of the room, fondling a partially-clad woman sitting on his lap. Joe pulled a swig from a whiskey bottle and glared at him.

Chase frowned and shifted his gaze to the pair of Sixth Infantry soldiers scrambling to stand at attention near the potbelly stove. The two swayed on unsteady legs. Drunken fools. "Private Mitchell, Corporal Dunn," Chase said as he moved further into the room. "You are under arrest for being drunk and out of quarters after *taps*. You are hereby confined to your lodgings, pending a hearing of the garrison court."

Private Mitchell teetered to one side and bumped into Dunn, knocking the other solider off-balance. The corporal flailed his arms and struggled to regain his footing. He struck Mitchell in the face, triggering a howl of outrage from the red-faced private.

Dammit, he didn't have time for this. Chase leaned forward and trained a menacing scowl on the bumbling idiots. "Can you two make it back on your own, or do I need to call for a guard?"

"Cap'n Brooks, s-sir, we can...make it, sir," the corporal blurted.

"Be sure that you do. Dismissed." Chase watched as the two infantrymen saluted and stumbled past him through the doorway. He then turned his attention to the indolent scout who had remained silent during the encounter. The laundress woman had wisely disappeared.

Chase leaned back to his full height. "Joe, I expect you to return to your quarters as well. Drinking and carousing are not allowed after *taps*, even for scouts."

The bearded scout snorted. "You gonna be the one ta make me?"

"If I have to," he responded, keeping his voice low and forceful.

"I ain't takin' no orders from the bastard son of a whore."

Jackass. He glared at the malicious, buckskin-clad scout. He'd seen enough drunken men to know when one was in an ugly mood. And Joe was in one. Chase crossed his arms over his chest. "Get up, Joe. You don't want to start any trouble tonight."

The belligerent scout lifted his whisky bottle, took another swig, and then sucked air between his few remaining teeth. With slow deliberation, he set down the bottle and rose, standing with his feet planted wide apart.

Chase tensed. Christ, the fool wanted a fight. Not a very wise idea tonight.

Joe gave a scornful laugh. "You're the one with all the trouble, Cap'n. You'd best learn t' keep a tighter rein on that raven-haired filly of yourn."

Raven-haired. Why had Joe mentioned Callie? Chase unfolded his arms and lowered them to his sides. He pressed fisted hands against his thighs and forced himself to remain silent. He wouldn't be goaded into responding.

"Yessiree, that's one fine lookin' lady you got there," Joe foolishly persisted. "She took a shine to General Sheridan's journalist t'other day whilst we was toting yer new rugs back from the Sutler's."

Heated blood bubbled in his veins at the scout's words. Chase struggled to keep from ramming his fist into the man's filthy mouth. Joe didn't know what the hell he was talking about. The bastard was only trying to provoke him into a fight. And, after the day he'd had, a brawl should be the last thing the scout would want to start.

Joe's face split into a wide grin, exposing blackened gaps between his yellow teeth—teeth he wouldn't have for much longer, if he didn't shut up. "Yep, Cap'n, you'd best hope the major don't send you out on any patrols, lest you come back and find her gone off with that fancy writer from back East."

Unable to contain his fury any longer, Chase stepped forward with a snarl. "You filthy, loud-mouthed hillbilly, don't you ever speak ill of my wife again."

Joe's grin faded and he lifted fisted hands. Chase stiffened, preparing for an attack. It came a second later. Joe leaned in and tossed a right hook at him.

Chase ducked. Then, shifting his weight, he lunged forward and planted a fist into the scout's bony cheek. The sound of flesh striking flesh echoed in the small room. Joe's head jerked from the impact and he staggered back a step.

Chase's blood sang. *God that felt good*. All day long he'd wanted to hit something. And Joe had stupidly provided him an excuse by swinging first.

Joe spun faster than a drunk should. Chase grunted as pain exploded in his cheek. His mouth filled with warm, salty fluid. He spit a stream of bloody phlegm to the floor and then glowered at the weaving scout. Christ, he'd better concentrate or Joe would get the best of him.

Chase feinted to the right and Joe ducked. He rocked back and landed a punch to the scout's gut, doubling him over. He quickly followed with an uppercut to Joe's jaw. Bone and flesh gave way beneath his fist.

Joe sank to his knees, his breath coming in short wheezing gasps. The downed man coughed and spat a glob of blood onto the floor. A white tooth swam in the mixture. "Damn, Cap'n," he muttered. "That were a mean punch." He grimaced and worked his jaw back and forth.

Chase glowered at him. "There's more where that came from, if you want it."

Joe shook his head. "Nope. Had 'nuff."

"Smart man, for a drunk." Ignoring his throbbing knuckles, Chase grabbed Joe's arm and yanked him to his feet. After scooping his hat off the floor, he gave Joe a shove out the door and herded him across the parade ground. The scout cradled an arm over his gut and grumbled about having to leave behind a damn good bottle of whiskey.

When they reached the lantern-lit guardhouse, Chase called out for the sentry. The wide-eyed guard ducked through the doorway, rifle at the ready.

Chase shoved the swaying scout forward. "Corporal Williams, place Mr. Milner under arrest until further orders."

"Yes, sir, Captain Brooks." The trooper pointed his weapon at the scout. "You know where to go, Joe."

Joe glared at Chase before spitting another bloody mass onto the ground. He looked as though he wanted say more, but wisely remained silent.

As Chase headed back to headquarters, his mind twirled like a wind-tossed tumbleweed. Could there be any truth to Joe's remarks about Callie and Sheridan's journalist? He'd noticed the new rugs, but assumed she'd asked one of his troopers to help her. The fact that Joe knew about the rugs leant some credence to his taunting. Yet, he had a difficult time believing the ranting of a drunk. It just wasn't possible. Callie was too shy to strike up an acquaintance with a strange man. There had to be

182

some other explanation.

An idea surfaced. Maybe Joe had been at the Sutler's when Callie purchased the rugs. Yes, that had to be the answer. And, in order to provoke him into a fight, the scout had fabricated a story about Callie and Sheridan's journalist, a tale Joe knew would send him into a rage.

And dammit, it had. Why did he let the past haunt him? It had been well over three years since Miranda betrayed him, three years that he'd kept the memories at bay.

They rushed in now like floodwaters from a breached dam. Haunted by the horrible suffering and carnage of the War, he'd allowed the pampered daughter of a rich merchant to become a beautiful, alluring distraction. Despite the warnings in his head, he'd married her. Then came his assignment to Fort Gibson where it all started to unravel.

Accustomed to the luxurious, fast-paced life in Washington, his wife had turned into a waspish, discontented creature. He'd quickly realized he made a grave mistake in marrying Miranda. He didn't love her. Hell, he wasn't even sure he knew what love was. But his damn honor had kept him from ending his farce of a marriage. Perhaps if he'd been a better husband, she wouldn't have sought another man's arms. But, she had. And her treachery had led to her death. He'd buried his wife as well as his guilt, vowing never again to endure such pain.

Until his forced second marriage brought it all back to the surface. Would Callie turn out like his first wife? He was still incapable of offering his heart to her. Yet, he couldn't picture his reserved, unassuming new wife behaving like Miranda. No, Callie was nothing like Miranda. She genuinely cared for people and seemed to be settling into garrison life just fine. She'd even refused General Sheridan's offer to take her back East.

Despite his rationalization, a seed of doubt began to uncurl and wrap its roots around his thoughts.

FOURTEEN

Callie lingered at the table. The impatient tap-tap of her drumming foot filled the ominous silence. She pressed a finger into the spilled breakfast crumbs, scraped them back into her plate, then glanced at the front door for the hundredth time that morning. Chase's overnight duty would be over soon and he'd be coming home. Hopefully.

Her insides knotted. Had he calmed down enough to discuss Rose without exploding like a stick of dynamite? God, she hoped so. The tension that surfaced between them scared her. Sleep had been hard to come by. She'd tossed and turned, missing her husband's comforting presence in their bed.

Her cheeks flushed as she considered the other things she missed about his absence—his strong arms wrapped around her, his lips pressed heatedly against hers. She never imagined how deeply one night of lovemaking could change her entire perspective on marriage. No longer would she be content to just sit with him in the shifting, hearth light. She'd tasted what love could offer, and she wanted more of the deep, binding feeling.

Wanted it with her entire heart and soul.

A knock reverberated into the room. She frowned. Who could be calling? It was too early for visitors. Shrugging, she rose, crossed to the door, and tugged it open to reveal Sheridan's journalist standing on the veranda.

"Mr. O'Malley," she greeted. "What a surprise."

The Irishman removed his hat. Sunlight glistened in his short, auburn locks. "Sorry to be bothering you so early, Mrs. Brooks. But I wanted to give you a photograph I found stuck in my papers."

A photograph? How curious. She stepped back from

the doorway. "Please come in. Would you like a cup of coffee?"

"Oh, no. Thank you for asking. I'm meeting with the General shortly, so I canna stay but a moment." He removed his hat and stepped into the room, leaving the door ajar behind him.

Callie smiled. How thoughtful of him to think of propriety even at a remote outpost like this. She moved to the hearth and motioned to one of the chairs. "Have a seat, Mr. O'Malley."

"Please, call me Teague." He rummaged in his pocket as he crossed the floor and then sank onto the chair opposite her. "Here you are." He handed her a photograph. "'Tis a picture of your cousin taking the oath of office."

"How wonderful," she exclaimed.

His face dimpled into a wide smile. He leaned closer and tapped a well-manicured fingernail on one corner of the photograph. "If you'll look closely, I believe you can see your face among the family seated behind the President."

She tilted the picture to better catch the sunlight. "Why, so it is." She looked up and gave him a cheery smile. "Thank you, Teague, I shall treasure it."

He reached out and covered her hand with his. "And I shall treasure the delight shining in your eyes. 'Twill be a picture I shall carry with me on my long journey."

She glanced at their spooned hands. He was a nice enough gentleman. Someone she might have found intriguing back East in her Aunt's stuffy parlor. Yet, the Irishman's touch failed to produce the mind-numbing sensations that Chase's did.

A noise sounded in the doorway. She looked up and froze. Chase stood on the threshold, his condemning eyes boring into her.

The breath caught in her throat. Dear God. What this must look like to him. Without thinking, she yanked her hand from Mr. O'Malley's grasp like a child caught handling a forbidden object.

"Mister," Chase bit out, his voice edged with the promise of violence. "I suggest you take your leave while you still can."

The Irishman issued a startled squeak and catapulted from the chair. "G-Good day, Mrs. Brooks." He gave her a curt nod before tucking on his hat and hurrying for the door.

Chase moved aside only the merest fraction and glared at the journalist as the frightened man sidled past. Booted feet clomped on the veranda and then faded into silence.

Callie frowned and shifted uneasily in the chair. "I suppose you're angry I entertained a man alone. But I assure you, my chat with Mr. O'Malley was quite innocent."

Chase slammed the door shut and strode into the room. "Oh, it's Mr. O'Malley now. A moment ago, it was Teague."

"Chase, it's not what you think—"

"It's exactly what I think. You've done nothing but disobey my orders since the day you arrived, traipsing about unescorted, befriending whores, and entertaining strange men. I should've known you'd betray me."

Her heart thudded wildly. "Betray you? I'd never do such a thing."

"Do you deny allowing O'Malley and Joe Milner in our quarters while I was away?"

"No, I don't deny it. They offered to help with the rugs I purchased from the Sutler's. Amanda was present the entire time. It was a harmless gesture of goodwill."

Chase snorted. "And what do you call what I just witnessed."

"Mr. O'Malley merely gave me a photograph." She clutched the sepia to her chest.

"One you vowed to treasure," he snapped.

Pulse skipping, she rose and forced a sedate walk to her flinty-eyed husband. She ached to wrap her arms around him, to ease the pain she'd unintentionally caused him. But his thunderous expression held her back. He wouldn't accept such a gesture from her. Not now. Not after seeing her holding hands with Teague O'Malley, no matter how innocent the gesture had been.

She held the photograph out to him. "Look at this. You can see—"

He snaked a hand up and grasped her wrist in a

painful grip. His haunted eyes scoured her face. Then, with a strangled roar, he flung her hand away. The photograph slipped from her fingers and fell to the floor.

Her heart nearly leapt into her throat. "You're frightening me, Chase. Why are you acting this way? Of course I will treasure the photograph. It's a picture of my cousin Ulysses whom I'll probably never see again."

"Don't remind me. Your connection to President Grant is the only reason I find myself married to you. I should've stood by my convictions and left you in Washington."

Pain jabbed into her chest. Why would he say such a thing? What had she done that made him so angry, so contemptuous?

Before she could formulate a reply, he gave a harsh curse and stalked across the room. He yanked open the door and then stood on the threshold with his back to her. After a few agonizing seconds of silence, he looked over his shoulder.

"I've been assigned to form a detail to dismantle the old sawmill and haul it to Camp Wichita." His voice resonated with the venom of hurt and anger. "General Sheridan will be leaving in a few days, I'll ask him to escort you back to Washington when he goes."

She gasped and staggered backward. "Take me to Washington? Why, Chase? Please don't do this."

"You cannot change my mind, so don't even try. Be ready to leave with the General when he calls for you." He banged the door closed behind him, cutting her off, shutting her out of his life.

Ice coursed through her veins. Oh God, he was sending her away. Callie stuffed a fisted hand against her mouth to stifle the sob rising in her throat. She might as well try to stop a train crash. Grief erupted in gut-wrenching sobs that exploded inside her.

She fled into their bedchamber and flung herself onto the bed. *Why? Why? Why?* Why would he send her away? She'd done nothing wrong. It just didn't make any sense. Couldn't he see that she'd never betray him? She loved him.

Despair spread inside her, stretching and coiling its tentacles around her aching heart. She thrust a knuckle between her teeth and bit down. The physical pain did little to lessen the hurt. Chase's rejection meant only one thing—he didn't want her. He didn't love her.

And probably never would.

After what seemed like an eternity, her sobs subsided into soft hiccups. She rolled onto her back and stared at the ceiling. How was she to go on? She couldn't face a life without Chase. Not when she'd finally found the home, the husband, she'd dreamed of having.

The creak of the front door drifted into the bedroom. She bolted upright, her heart soaring with joy. *Chase.* He'd returned to beg for her forgiveness.

"Callie, are you in here?" a familiar voice called out. But not the one she wanted to hear.

Her battered heart plummeted to the ground like a wounded bird. She struggled to reply in a cheerful tone. "I'm in the bedroom."

Footsteps drew closer and her friend appeared in the doorway. "I knocked, but you didn't—" Amanda pulled her brow into a concerned frown. "What's wrong Callie? Why are you crying?"

"Oh, Amanda. My life is over," she sobbed. "Chase is sending me back to Washington. H-He doesn't want me here."

"What? Why would he do such a thing?"

"I don't know. H-He saw...Oh, God, I would never..."

Amanda crossed the floor and perched on the edge of the bed. She reached out and cupped Callie's hand. "Shhhh. Take a deep breath and tell me what happened."

Callie drew in a ragged breath and forced the words past the thickness in her throat. "Mr. O'Malley came by...to-to bring me a photograph of Cousin Ulysses. It was such a kind gesture. And th-that's all it was...an innocent gesture."

"I'm sure it was. Go on."

"Chase came home, and...and saw Mr. O'Malley holding my hand. Sweet Mary, he got madder than I've ever seen him. He threatened the Irishman...a-and...Dear God, I can hardly say it."

Amanda gave her hand a gentle squeeze. "Yes, you can. What did Chase do?"

"H-He accused me of betraying him." She closed her

eyes and felt the burn of tears behind her lids. "Oh, Amanda, I would never do such a thing. Why would Chase declare me unfaithful?"

Amanda wrapped comforting arms around her. "Oh, sweetie, you don't know about Miranda, do you?"

Miranda? She pried open her eyes. "Wh-Who is Miranda?"

"She was Chase's first wife."

Her heart skipped a beat. Chase had been married before? Was whatever had occurred with his first wife the cause of all his issues with her, his second, unwanted wife? She pulled out of Amanda's soothing embrace. "What happened to her?"

"Chase married Miranda right after the War ended and brought her with him to Fort Gibson." Amanda thinned her lips in displeasure. "Miranda never took to military life. After only one month at the garrison, she headed back East...with another man. Their stagecoach was attacked by hostiles. Miranda and her lover were killed."

Sweet Mary. Callie collapsed onto the pillow behind her. Breathing came only with difficulty. It was as if a boulder sat atop her chest, suffocating her. *Chase will never believe I'm innocent.*

"Yes, he will," Amanda replied.

Had she said that aloud? She peered at her friend through a watery cloud.

Amanda gave her a reassuring pat. "Give him time to calm down. Chase won't send you away. He loves you."

"Loves me?" She shook her head. "You don't understand. He was *forced* to marry me. He has never loved me...And he never will." Pain knifed through her.

"You're wrong, Callie. I don't care how your marriage came about, but I know one thing..." Amanda tilted her head to the side and lifted her lips into a gentle smile. "When Chase gazes at you, his eyes light up, and his face softens. That is the look of a man who is in love. He won't be sending you anywhere."

Callie looked away from Amanda's encouraging gaze. If only those words were true. Yet, how could a man in love behave as Chase had—treating her with such vile contempt? No, Amanda must be mistaken. He would follow through with his decision to send her back East.

She'd have to accept it, just as she'd accepted being unwanted for most of her life.

****

Chase leaned back in the desk chair and tipped the whiskey bottle to his lips. Rot-gut plowed down his throat and settled like a hot spring in his stomach. He grunted and lowered the bottle. Damn good stuff. It would make the night a whole lot easier to endure. Morning would be a different story. But he'd tackle that when he got there.

A soft scraping noise drew his bleary gaze to the doorway. Moses stood at attention on the threshold. "We're done for the evening, Cap'n. Another day and we'll be ready to haul the mill saw to Fort Wichita."

"Good. The sooner we leave, the better."

"Will there be anything else, suh?"

He shook his head. "No, thank you, Private. That'll be all."

The trooper tossed him a quick glance. Taut shoulders came down a fraction. His bland expression softened. Moses opened his mouth to speak and then apparently, thinking better of it, snapped his mouth shut without uttering a word.

Chase grunted. Wise man. "Dismissed," he commanded, a bit harsher than he intended. Company and the chatter that came with it was the last thing he needed right now.

Moses executed a brisk salute, pivoted, and pulled the door closed behind him with a soft click.

Chase grunted again and took another swig of whiskey. Through a haze, he stared at the framed map on the opposite wall. The Territorial lines blurred into indistinct shapes. He slid his gaze to the darkened window, not yet drunk enough to resist the pull of the distant, glowing lamp lights.

But he would be—as soon as he finished off this whiskey.

He knocked back another mouthful and then propped his legs on the desktop, crossing them at the ankles. Despite his efforts to keep them at bay, damnable images swam before his blurry eyes—the adoring smile Callie had given the Irishman, her soft voice telling him how she

190

would treasure his gift. And that Satan's spawn caressing her hand while murmuring sweetness to her, to Callie—to *his* wife.

Goddammit. He should've cracked that Irish bastard's skull when he had the chance. He didn't want to believe Callie had betrayed him, but he couldn't refute the evidence he'd seen with his own eyes.

His heart sank like granite in his chest. He didn't want to send her away either. How could he? She'd become everything to him. It scared the hell out of him to know how much he cared for her, how much he ached to pull her into his arms and make love to her again.

But he couldn't. She'd betrayed him, and he couldn't see any other resolution in the red fog of pain that engulfed him. He had to cut her out of his life. Now. End this marriage as he hadn't had the guts to do with Miranda, regardless of how bad it hurt.

****

Callie walked silently across the parade ground with Moses at her side. Although her heart ached, she couldn't allow her sadness to interfere with her teaching. At the moment, the troopers' eagerness to learn remained the only bright spot in her life.

She'd woken to an empty bed again that morning. Chase hadn't come home, not that she'd expected him to. Yet the pain of wondering where he'd slept—and with whom—nearly killed her. She'd wanted nothing more than to lie abed and let the world go on without her. But she hadn't. Somehow, she'd found the strength to endure.

And she would continue to do so.

Moses' soft humming drifted over her. She wanted to ask where Chase had spent the night, but pride prevented her from inquiring.

"Oh, I thought you'd likes to know, Missus Brooks," he said. "With the captain's testimony, the garrison court sentenced Corporal Smythe to three months in lockup. And Miss Rose done got her money back."

She'd forgotten all about Rose's trial. Well at least *something* good had happened on a perfectly foul day. Callie attempted a smile. "That's wonderful news. How is Rose?"

"She's doin' much better. I heared she was goin' back

191

East to open a dress shop."

"You heard correctly, Moses. That was Rose's dream, and now she's on her way. I'm so happy for her."

Chase had been kind to Rose, a woman who reminded him of his painful past. Did not she, his wife, deserve his understanding as well? She'd done everything in her power to make him happy. A heavy ache filled her chest. Obviously, it hadn't been enough.

Moses cleared his throat. "You know, ma'am. You might want to heed that advice you give to Miss Rose."

Advice she'd given to...how had Moses known..? No, she didn't want to know how he knew. Some things were best left unknown.

Her words to Rose rushed into her head like a raging river. *You can change your life if you believe in yourself and never give up.* Her stomach clenched. Had she stopped believing in herself? Given up?

A movement caught her eye. Dressed in a vivid yellow and black dress, Betsy Alvis looked like a hornet zipping across the parade ground toward them. No, more like a bat out for blood. The woman called out a greeting, and Callie suppressed a groan. Betsy was the last person she wanted to speak with right now.

"Mrs. Brooks, it's so good to see you out and about," the woman drawled as she drew next to them. She shifted her gaze to Moses and wrinkled her pert nose in disgust before looking at Callie. "We'd heard you'd taken ill."

Could the woman be any more obvious? Not wishing to expose Moses to any unpleasantness, Callie gave the trooper's arm a gentle squeeze. "You go on, Private. I'll be there shortly."

Moses hesitated and then with a frown furrowing his face, set off for the mess hall. At the top of the short steps, he turned and stood in the doorway, arms folded over his chest, chin elevated.

A smile crept to her lips. She should have known he wouldn't let her out of his sight. Callie returned her focus to Betsy. "Thank you for your concern, Mrs. Alvis. But as you can see, I'm fine."

Betsy sniffed, her icy eyes narrowing. "It seems Captain Brooks has been busy dismantling the old sawmill."

"Yes, he's been very busy." Where was the woman going with this conversation?

"Well, his absence during the day is quite understandable, but during the *night?*" Betsy flicked an indolent hand. "La, if I were his wife, I'd be quite put out by his behavior."

Heat rose inside her, not the familiar warmth of embarrassment, but the fire of anger, of bottled up emotions that suddenly exploded within her. Callie glared at the brazen woman and replied in the same cutting voice she'd heard many times in Eunice's parlor. "But, you aren't his wife, are you? So keep your pointy little nose out of my affairs."

Ignoring Betsy's indignant gasp, she sailed past the woman and headed for the mess hall. Yes, Chase *was* behaving badly. And thank you, Betsy Alvis, for pointing that out, for providing the spur she needed. Callie squared her shoulders. She would confront her husband and make him admit to his flawed judgment.

She'd done it before back in Washington. She could do it again.

****

Drat, drat, double-drat.

Every attempt she'd made to see Chase that morning had been thwarted. On such a small outpost, you'd think she'd be able to come across her husband at some point. Crouched near the edge of the creek, Callie clenched her teeth together and rubbed the sodden gown against her scrub board. Reddened knuckles protested the punishing chore. She ignored the pain and scrubbed all the harder. Though it didn't help her frustration, the muddied skirt hem was coming clean.

Amid the gurgle of the rushing water, feminine laughter rode the warm air. All around her, laundress women flanked the stream, washing uniforms of the men paying to have them cleaned.

One woman's raspy voice rose above the others. "What did Cap'n Brooks say to you?"

Captain Brooks? Callie froze mid-scrape and cocked an ear to catch the reply.

"Nothin'," came the other woman's response. "While he was shoutin' at the two soldiers, I ran and hid."

"And him and California Joe got into a fight?"

"Yep. Joe called the captain a bastard. Then, he started bad-mouthin' the captain's wife, saying she was foolin' around with some Irish journalist."

"Lordy, did the Cap'n kill him?"

"They traded punches until Captain Brooks finally knocked Joe to the ground and arrested him. That dumb scout lost another tooth. If'n Joe don't stop fightin' all the time, he's gonna be left with only gums."

Laughter echoed across the short distance. Callie fisted her hands around the wet garment. So, she had California Joe to thank for her current misery. She should have listened to her instincts and refused his offer of assistance at the Sutler's. Now she was paying the consequences of her foolishness.

She finished her wash in a fog of anger and frustration. Basket in hand, she followed the footpath back to Officers' Row. The thud of hooves and the rattle of wagon wheels filled the garrison. As she emerged from the path, Callie spotted the cause of the noise.

A small formation of riders headed for the exit followed by several mule-drawn wagons loaded with milling equipment and wood planks. A familiar figure cantered to the head of the detail.

Chase. The laundry basket slipped from her hands and thudded to the ground. She took a step forward and opened her mouth. Before she could call out, Zeus trotted through the gates and disappeared from sight.

A sharp stab knifed into her heart. He'd left without even saying goodbye. Hot tears burned in her eyes.

"Mrs. Brooks. Mrs. Brooks," a voice hailed her.

She dashed away her tears and turned to find Private White striding in her direction.

"Mail arrived this mornin', ma'am. You have a letter."

A letter? Who could have written to her? Certainly not the Boggses. She took the letter from him. "Thank you, Private."

The trooper regarded her with concern-filled eyes and then glanced toward the garrison entrance. "Don't you worry none, ma'am. The cap'n will be back soon."

But I won't be here when he returns. She gave him a

194

wan smile and simply nodded. She watched for a moment as the trooper headed toward the stables and then turned her focus to the letter.

Callie flipped the envelope over and immediately recognized Julia Grant's familiar handwriting. A smile crept to her lips. A small ray of sunshine had arrived to brighten her dreary day. She peeled open the envelope flap and extracted the scented letter.

Dearest Callie,

Ulysses and I were quite disturbed to learn of your forced marriage. Although Lyss assures me that he holds Captain Brooks in the highest regard, I am still concerned for your well-being. Having been around the military for most of my married life, I know how difficult such an existence can be.

Her smile faded. She hadn't wanted either of them to worry about her. It wasn't military life she was finding difficult. It was marriage itself. With a sigh, she tilted the letter to better catch the light and resumed reading.

This letter will probably find you ensconced on a remote outpost in the Indian territories. I persuaded Lyss to send a telegram to Phil Sheridan asking the general to check on your welfare. Knowing the irregularity of the mail, you may have already spoken with him. If not, just know that should you need anything, or wish to return to Washington, please do not hesitate to inform us. Lyss sends his warmest regards and prays for your happiness.

With all my love, Julia.

Callie bowed her head and let fall the tears she'd held at bay. Her cousin would have to pray several times each day in order to ensure her happiness. Unless she could convince her inflexible, distrustful husband otherwise, she would return to Washington, whether she wanted to or not.

FIFTEEN

Callie stood on the veranda and let her gaze travel over the sunlit buildings lining the parade ground. This would be her last day at Fort Arbuckle. General Sheridan had sent word they would be departing first thing the next morning. Her heart bled at the thought of leaving her new home. She loved every inch of the dusty, wood-hewn garrison. How could she possibly exist without the fort, without her friends—without Chase?

Through a watery haze, she saw Private Jackson approaching. He stopped at the edge of the veranda and removed his hat. "Missus Brooks, I'm ridin' with a small detail out to the Chickasaw reservation. We're going to barter for fresh meat and vegetables." He pointed at the mule-drawn wagon waiting near the flagstaff. "Would you like to join us?"

Visit the reservation? She frowned. "It's safe? The Chickasaws are a friendly tribe?"

"Yes'm, very safe. The settlement is only a few miles above the garrison on Wild Horse Creek. We been tradin' with them for years."

Perhaps an outing was just what she needed. "Well, I am feeling a little restless..." She managed a tiny smile. "Let me grab my shawl and bonnet."

A few minutes later, she met the detail at the wagon. Moses handed her in and then joined her on the seat. He released the brake and clucked to the mules. The wagon lurched forward, trailing behind the three outriders.

She glanced at the trooper's dusty boot propped on the footboard. "Is your foot feeling better, Moses?"

"A might bit. I still cain't put much weight on it, but Doc Pearce says it'll be fine in another few days."

"I'm sorry you were injured while dismantling the saw mill. But I have to admit...I was relieved it forced you to stay behind." She gave a soft sigh. "I've really appreciated your company these past few days."

"My granny used to tell me, 'things happen fo a reason, Moz.'" He bobbed his head. "I'm a firm believer in that saying."

"Well, I'm just going to enjoy the day." She tilted her face to catch the sun's warm rays. "It feels good to get away. You know, this is the first time I've been outside the garrison since my arrival."

"Yes'm. It's a mighty fine day, too. Hup mules." He slapped leather across the animals' rumps, urging them up the steep slope ahead.

Callie inhaled a deep, cleansing breath. Yes, it was definitely a mighty fine day. She wouldn't let thoughts of what tomorrow would bring spoil her outing. She would enjoy the day and savor this one last memory.

The wagon climbed higher and higher into the towering Arbuckle Mountains. Walls of rock rose out of the ground as if the earth had heaved them up from her bowels. Sprinkled throughout the hillside, budding redbuds added a dash of brilliant pink to the lush greens and browns.

They soon topped the steep rise and started down the other side. Below them, an enormous village stretched along a glittering creek. A large, rectangular building sat in the center of the settlement, surrounded by dozens of wood-hewn cabins. It looked more like a simple, civilized town rather than an uncultivated Indian camp.

As the wagon rolled to a stop, a large, eager crowd rushed to greet them. Women and children circled the wagon, chattering in a strange language. Callie stiffened. Though smiles lit their mahogany faces, a finger of fear scraped her spine. She leaned closer to Moses, thankful for his protecting presence.

Corporal Hayworth dismounted and headed toward a tall, buckskin-clad man. "Chief Solomon, it's good to see you again."

The Indian chief smiled and shook the trooper's hand. "Corporal Hayworth, it's good to see you as well." He waved to the lodge behind him. "Please, join me inside where we can conduct our business."

As the two men disappeared through the doorway,

Callie glanced at the strange mixture of people poking at the goods in the wagon bed. Trying not to let her apprehension show, she whispered softly to Moses. "There seems to be many different ethnic groups in this tribe."

Moses nodded. "The Chickasaw have taken in many people, from freed slaves to white Americans."

"And the women are wearing calicos and gingham dresses, not animal hides, as I expected."

"Yes'm. They's a very advanced tribe. Would you like to tour the village?"

She glanced at his foot. "What about your injury?"

"I kin manage. We won't go far." He gingerly dismounted and hobbled around to help her out of the wagon.

They wandered through the settlement, passing racks of drying fish and small clusters of women gathered around campfires. Some of the Indians plied needle and thread while others milled grain with mortar and pestle. Smiles and nods greeted them as they passed.

In the middle of the encampment, shouting children raced around a central lodge, toting lances and chasing a hide ball. Callie smiled. Children would be children no matter where they lived.

Moses waved at the youngsters. "The boys are playin' *chunkee*."

"*Chunkee*?" she asked.

"It's a native game where a ball is rolled 'cross the ground and the thrower must toss his lance where he thinks the ball will stop."

"It looks like a fun game."

Moses grunted. "It is *now*. Many years ago, the loser forfeited his life."

Her heart tripped. She glanced at the rifle propped on the trooper's shoulder and tried not to think the worst. She wouldn't let her wild imagination taint her impression of these seemingly friendly Indians.

Moses led her to the outskirts of the village. They topped a gentle rise and stopped. Below them, a large herd of cattle grazed contentedly in a grassy meadow.

"I didn't realize they had so many," she said.

"This tribe owns 'bout two hundred head of cattle. That's mainly what we come for, fresh beef."

Sunlight poured down from the cloudless sky, illuminating the glade in a dazzling glow and further warming the already balmy day. Perspiration beaded on her forehead. She adjusted her bonnet to better shield her face from the sun, then glanced at Moses. He had to be uncomfortable in his woolen uniform. Perhaps they should return to the shade of the village.

Before she could suggest going back, he stiffened. His eyes widened in alarm. With a jerk of his wrist, he swung his rifle into the air and discharged two simultaneous gunshots.

Callie flinched at the deafening noise. Sweet Jesus, why had he done that?

"Hurry, Mrs. Brooks." He grabbed her elbow. "Hostiles are raidin' the settlement!"

Hostiles! She peered over her shoulder and then wished she hadn't. Well over two dozen mounted Indians streamed across the meadow, scattering cattle before them as they galloped toward the village. Earsplitting howls and booming gunshots rent the air.

Moses tugged on her arm, pulling her out of her trance. She grabbed a handful of her skirt and broke into a trot beside him. Bullets zinged overhead. Panic clawed at her chest and climbed up her throat, strangling her when she needed air the most. She could feel her legs moving, could feel the grass swiping at her ankles, but it seemed as if she was stuck in an inescapable mire.

Callie fixed her gaze on the buildings looming in the distance. *Please, let us make it back in time. Please, please.*

Halfway to safety, Moses heaved a pained grunt. The grip on her elbow slackened. A second later, the trooper stumbled and toppled face first to the ground with a feather-tipped arrow protruding from his back. Blood spread from the shaft in an ever widening circle.

Horrified, Callie skidded to a halt. A scream bubbled in her throat. *No, no, no.* This wasn't happening.

The sound of pounding hooves penetrated her horror. She gave herself a mental shake and bent over her fallen friend. "Come on, Moses. You've got to get up."

"Run," he urged, his faint voice racked with pain. "Save yoself."

"I won't leave you. Please, Moses, get up." She tugged on his arm, straining to help him rise.

He managed to lift his head, but collapsed a second later with a pained moan. His eyes rolled back into his head and his body went limp.

Fear gripped her chest. She shook his arm. "*Moses*! Wake up."

A scalp-prickling howl pierced the air. Pulse thumping, she turned toward the sound. Fierce and menacing, the mounted Indians charged at her. The lead horseman lifted his rifle over his head and let go another ear-shattering yelp. Garish yellow and red paint slashed his dark face. Yet it was his eyes that held her immobile— black and brutal, as though they stared at her from the depths of hell.

The Indian leaned over the side of his galloping mount. Before she could blink, he scooped her into his outstretched arm and hauled her onto his lap, anchoring her in a muscular grip. The breath went out of her lungs with a whoosh. Day turned to night and then back to a sickening gray that whirled with darting stars. She sucked in a mouthful of air, wondering if she'd ever breathe normal again.

Her captor shifted his leg, and the pony veered away from the village. They galloped into the meadow, scattering cattle as they rode. Wind jerked at her bonnet laces, but she couldn't lift fear-frozen fingers to re-secure them. A few strides later, the straw bonnet sailed off her head.

The Indian pulled his pony to a halt at the far edge of the meadow. Eight bare-chested Indians emerged like silent shadows from the trees. Their cold, black gazes prickled the hairs at the back of her neck. She'd never seen such a raw, untamed hatred before.

Bile burned in her throat. Dear God, she was at the mercy of wild renegades—a mercy that probably wouldn't be forthcoming.

****

The pony's easy, rocking canter slowed and then shifted to a sedate walk. Callie yanked her bowed head upright and stared at the narrow path winding upward along a steep slope. On one side of the pathway, stone and earth formed a wall rising to the summit. On the other side, loomed a sheer, ominous drop-off. Her belly rebelled at the thought of navigating the treacherous route.

One misstep and...

Callie squeezed her eyes shut, refusing to imagine the rest of her terrifying thought. She had to remain positive. If she didn't, she feared she might shatter into a million pieces.

The pony climbed higher and higher, its hooves sending pebbles cascading to the rocks below. Her heart thumped wildly, threatening to leap right out of her chest. She tossed a prayer heavenward that their mount would be as nimble-footed as a mountain goat.

An eternity later, the pony slowed and stopped. Callie heaved a relieved sigh and opened her eyes. They'd halted on an outcrop littered with boulders and scrub brush. Her abductor slid off the horse and tugged her with him. Muscles, stiff from the long ride, screamed in protest and refused to hold her upright. Moaning, she slumped to the hard ground.

"Get up," the Indian barked.

She tried to stand, but only managed a low crouch before her legs gave way again. Her captor grasped her arm and pulled her to her feet. His grip strangely gentle, he propelled her over the rocky terrain toward a small stand of pines.

Her mouth went dry. What did these savages intend to do with her? Her mind whirled with the brutal accounts she'd read—of men relieved of their scalps with the flick of a knife, of beatings and torture, more vicious than even the Roman Emperor Caligula could imagine.

Callie sucked down the sob rising in her throat. No. She wouldn't succumb to fear. Instinct told her these ruthless Indians would respect courage more than cowardice. And if they respected her, perhaps they would let her live.

The Indian pushed her to the ground at the base of a tree. He pulled a length of rawhide from a pouch and lashed her hands together in front of her. The cord dug deep into her skin, bringing red whelps to the surface.

Callie bit the inside of her lip to keep from crying out. She refused show pain or fear. She was stronger than that.

With his face set in an impassive mask, the Indian wrapped another length of rawhide around her chest and secured her to the tree trunk. His task complete, he gave a satisfied grunt and then strode toward his comrades. Their guttural language drifted across the short distance. The deep, sing-song of their voices both intrigued and frightened. After a few moments, conversation halted, and the Indians settled among the rocks with rifles and bows at the ready. Like silent sentinels, they surveyed the ground below, clearly watching for any pursuers.

Her pulse tripped. There would be pursuers. There had to be. She closed her eyes and pictured a large formation of men in blue uniforms led by one formidable, gray-eyed officer.

The crunch of pebbles shattered the image.

She opened her eyes and was unable to contain a gasp at the sight of her captor returning. Dressed in a breechcloth draped over deer-skin leggings, the bare-chested Indian stopped in front of her and squatted. War paint slashed his high cheek bones, giving him a brutal, untamed appearance. He rocked back on his heels and scoured her from head to toe with dark, glittering eyes.

Callie drew in a sharp breath and mentally warned herself to be brave—a difficult undertaking, considering how badly her insides quaked.

"Pretty white woman," he finally said. He reached out and gently stroked her cheek with the back of his fingers. "Will bring Satanta good ransom."

A metallic tang flooded her mouth. She ground her teeth and forced herself not to jerk away from his touch. Despite her resolve to remain motionless, she was unable to control a tiny shiver.

The Indian frowned. "No need to worry. Satanta not hurt pretty lady." He unlaced a hide pouch from his side and lifted it to her mouth.

She clamped her lips shut and shook her head. It could be poison he offered.

"Water. You drink." He thrust the opening to her lips.

Callie leaned back a fraction and sniffed. No noxious fumes greeted her, only a dank, earthy smell. Her dry mouth puckered at the thought of a refreshing drink.

Well, maybe a tiny sip wouldn't hurt.

Placing her lips on the opening, she took a tentative swallow. It *was* water—warm and a bit stale—but satisfying nonetheless. She gulped down several more mouthfuls, enjoying the soothing sensation as the water eased her parched throat. Her thirst quenched, she pulled away and eyed Satanta warily. That drink could very well be the last pleasure she'd ever enjoy again.

The warrior lowered the pouch. "What is name?"

"M-Mrs. Brooks." *Stop stammering. You're braver than that. Remember Alice Grierson and Julia.*

"Why you at Chickasaw village?"

"I was with a Tenth Cavalry detail from Fort Arbuckle to barter for fresh beef."

Satanta grunted. "Buffalo soldiers. Worthy opponents to Kiowa."

Buffalo soldiers? She'd never heard the troopers referred to by that nickname. But Satanta clearly respected them. He should.

He glanced at her left hand. "You have husband at Fort Arbuckle?"

"Yes, Captain Brooks." And when he comes for me...Her empty belly seized. Dear God, would Chase come for her?

"Children?"

She blinked in confusion. "Pardon?"

"Mrs. Brooks have children?"

Callie rested a hand on her stomach. If she was with child, she would protect it with her life. She lifted her chin. "No. We have not been blessed with a child."

He grunted and lowered his gaze to her lap. "You will. Good hips for bearing children."

Heat flamed in her cheeks at his familiar comment. She shifted uneasily and glanced beyond him at the darkening shadows.

Satanta reached into a leather pouch hanging from his waist. He pulled out a piece of dried meat and held the morsel to her mouth. "*Wakapapi.* Pemmican. You eat."

Eat? How could she eat when her stomach churned like a raging river? She turned her head to the side. "I'm not hungry."

"You eat. Captain Brooks not pay good money for

skinny wife."

Her heart lurched. The captain might not pay good money for her period.

"Eat," the Indian growled again.

Annoyance climbed in her. Persistent man. Maybe if she ate the blasted thing he'd leave her alone. She teethed the pemmican into her mouth and began chewing. Not bad. A bit leathery, but flavored with some type of tart berry.

Satanta continued to stare at her as she ate. Callie averted her gaze, yet she could still feel his eyes on her, cold and assessing—and quite unnerving. *I'm eating. Now go away.*

As if he'd read her thoughts, the Indian grunted and rose to his feet. He eased away from her, effortlessly skimming the rocky terrain as he walked.

Relieved by his departure, she slumped against the tree trunk, ignoring the bite of the rough bark. Her thoughts fled to her husband. What would Chase do when he learned of her abduction? Would he feel she was worth the risk, to himself and his men, to attempt a rescue?

She closed her eyes and prayed with all her heart he would.

****

Chase lifted his hat and swiped at the sweat gathered on his brow. Christ, it was hotter than Hades. What happened to spring? It seemed the weather had jumped right from winter to summer in one day.

He settled his hat back in place and thinned his lips. Speaking of Hades, his own life had turned to hell—a hell of his own making. It'd been almost a week since he'd condemned Callie for being unfaithful, an accusation he knew, deep in his heart, wasn't true. He'd wrestled with his conscience, alternating between reality and the painful images his mind kept cooking up. He just couldn't shake the haunting picture of Callie and that damn Irish journalist.

And yet, he didn't want her to leave. He loved her—or at least what he thought was love. Why else would he ache to be near her, to touch her? To have her turn that sweet, adoring smile on him, and have her gasp his name as he plunged into her?

204

God, he hoped General Sheridan hadn't left Arbuckle yet. He needed to hold her, needed to see if he could exorcise his demons once and for all.

Sergeant Greaves's shout punched through his thoughts. "Rider headed in our direction, Cap'n."

Chase looked up and spotted a buckskin-clad horseman cantering swiftly toward them from the east. As the rider drew closer, he recognized Jim Eaglefeather, a half-white, half-Arapaho scout assigned to Fort Arbuckle. Though Jim looked more white than Indian with his green eyes and brown hair, he could track better than most full-blooded Indian scouts.

Chase lifted his hand and motioned the column to halt. Jim reined up in front of them, his mount sweat-soaked and blowing. Not a good sign. Not good at all. Chase frowned. "You heading for Fort Wichita, Jim?"

The scout nudged his pinto closer. "No, sir, Captain Brooks. I rode out to bring you the news."

His stomach fell. "What news?" he asked, though he wasn't sure he wanted to hear it.

"The Chickasaw reservation on Wild Horse Creek came under attack this morning. Several of your troopers happened to be at the village when the raid began."

Christ. "Were there any casualties?"

"Unfortunately, there were. Corporal Hayworth died from a bullet wound. Several Chickasaw natives perished as well. Doc Pearce is treating Private Jackson...he took an arrow in the back."

"Damn. Were they Comanche?"

"No, sir. Kiowa, about thirty braves led by Satanta."

"Satanta!" He grimaced and shook his head. "I knew we should've gone after that savage when he left the reservation."

Jim snorted. "I agree with you. We lost good men by holding back."

"Anyone going after them?"

"Roy sent Captain Alvis with a full patrol to trail them. Appears the raiders headed south toward Red River."

Forty men could handle the renegade and his bunch. Why, then, had Jim ridden hell-bent to meet up with *this* small detail? A sense of dread washed over him. "There's more, isn't there?"

"Yes, sir, there is." The scout paused, his jaw tightening with unease.

"Dammit Jim, spit it out."

"It's your wife, sir."

Ice filled his veins. "My wife?"

"She was with the detail at the reservation."

His heart slammed against his ribs. *Godamighty.* Callie had been right in the middle of an attack. If Moses had taken an arrow—that meant...

"Is she..?" Chase couldn't finish his question. By saying the words, he would be acknowledging that he would never see her again. And he wasn't ready to do that.

"We don't know, sir," Jim said. "Private Jackson stirred long enough to tell us she'd been abducted by Satanta. We found her hat in a nearby field."

His gut hardened into a rock-solid mass. She might as well be dead. Probably even wished she was dead. Callie was in the hands of the most brutal and untrustworthy Indian in the territory. Fear unlike any he'd ever felt coursed through him. "I'll take half my patrol—"

"You should know, Captain," Jim interrupted. "Major Roy refused to send anyone to notify you of the attack. Said he didn't want you going off half-cocked with your men."

"*Half-cocked!*" That arrogant bastard. Heat blasted through him. Chase fisted his hand around Zeus' reins. He *had* never and *would* never place his men in jeopardy with slip-shod leadership. Oh, he would go after Callie, all right. The major could be assured of that. And, if he was court marshaled for disobeying orders, then so be it. Callie meant more to him than any job in the Army.

"To hell with Major Roy," Chase ground out between clenched teeth. "I'm going after my wife. Thank you for riding out to inform me, Jim. I appreciate it."

The Arapaho nodded. "I felt you deserved to know."

"Damn right, I deserved to know," he snapped and then regretted his outburst. It wasn't Jim's fault the major was such an ass. "Sorry, Jim. Didn't mean to take it out on you."

Jim gave him a wry smile. "I understand, Captain. I saw the direction the renegades took. I'll be glad to act as your scout."

"You're already in enough trouble for warning me. Major Roy won't go easy on you, you know."

"I'll take my chances."

Chase grunted. Too bad there weren't more men like Jim, white, black, or red-skinned. "Well then, I'll take you up on your offer." He twisted in the saddle. "Sergeant Greaves, take half the men and the wagons back to Arbuckle. Inform Major Roy I'm riding with Jim and the rest of the patrol to intercept Captain Alvis."

"Yes, sir," the sergeant replied. A grim look sliced the trooper's face as he turned to make the assignments.

Chase glanced skyward. The sun had passed its zenith. Not much left of the day, but at least he was only hours behind the renegades, not days as he would've been if Jim hadn't ridden out to warn him.

His head swam with disturbing thoughts. Satanta was one mean, unmerciful Indian. The things he'd seen the bastard do...

Fury surged inside him. Dammit, if that savage harmed one hair on Callie's head, he'd rip him into little pieces with his bare hands.

SIXTEEN

A sharp noise punched through her fog of sleep. Callie wrenched her head upright and sucked in a startled breath at the sight of a man leaning over her and brandishing a sharp-bladed knife. The rosy glow of early dawn illuminated his high brow, obsidian eyes, and flaring nostrils. She fought the fear and despair rising in her. He was not the steely-eyed man who had filled her dreams—the man she'd wanted to wake up alongside.

She was still a captive.

Satanta sliced through her bindings. "Get up," he grunted. "We leave now."

With his unwanted hand on her elbow, she rose from the cold ground. Sharp pin-pricks stabbed her limbs, and she couldn't contain a gasp. Did she have any feet? If she did, she couldn't feel them. After sitting in one position all night, her boots seemed to be filled with ghostly appendages.

The Indian tugged her toward the waiting ponies. Callie winced as her feet came awake with painful shrieks. She stumbled and would have fallen without his support. A myriad of emotions bubbled inside her. Anger at his harsh treatment, frustration with her weakness. But mostly, anguish at the thought of never seeing Chase again.

She jerked out of the Indian's grasp and pulled to a stop. "Just wait a blasted minute."

He turned, his painted brow crimped into a menacing frown.

Icy dread doused her fury. She sucked in a breath. God, what had she done? The last thing she wanted to do was make him angry.

The Indian tilted his chin upward and crossed thick, muscular arms over his bare chest, much like another formidable man she knew. "Mrs. Brooks have moment for privacy," he said. "Then we leave."

Callie released her pent-up breath. Now that he mentioned it, she did need to relieve herself. She gave him a brief nod and hobbled toward a nearby boulder. Concealed behind the huge rock, she paused, waiting for her blood-starved limbs to recover. As she scanned the outcrop, a thought leapt into her head. She was out of her captor's sight. It would be the perfect opportunity to escape. Maybe the only one she'd have.

Yet, jagged rock walls surrounded her. The only way out seemed to be up. And she doubted she had the strength to climb such a tower. Callie sighed in resignation. Maybe another opportunity would present itself later. This clearly wasn't the one.

After taking care of her pressing need, she lumbered back to Satanta. "Thank you," she said. "I'm ready now."

He grunted an acknowledgement and lifted her onto his horse as though she weighed no more than a sack of potatoes. With surprising agility, he leapt behind her and gathered the reins. His bare chest brushed against her back. Warmth flamed in her face at the intimate touch. She straightened and tried not to lean against him. It was only a small gesture of resistance, but one that bolstered her waning resolve.

The fleet-footed ponies raced southward. They stopped briefly at midday to allow the horses to drink and to refill their water pouches. Near dusk, they reached the banks of a swiftly flowing river.

Images of the swollen, rotted body of Private Samuels swirled in her mind. Fear surged inside her. Surely they weren't going to...

Satanta urged the pony into the tumbling river. Pulse skipping, Callie squeezed her eyes shut. A gasp lodged in her throat as icy water churned around her legs and rose to her thighs. Halfway across, the pony stumbled, then righted itself. Callie dug her fingernails into the arm clamped around her waist. The animal lunged again, this time a stomach-wrenching hop that tossed her and Satanta into the fast-moving water.

She fought the tug of the current, kicking and flailing with all her might. Despite her efforts, her water-logged skirt pulled her under. Muddy water flooded into her mouth and nostrils. Her throat constricted. Oh God, she was going to drown.

Something brushed her arm. Callie clawed at the salvation, her panic almost as suffocating as the water. A firm hand wrapped around her wrist, but the river wasn't about to give her up so easily. She slipped out of her rescuer's grasp and sank back into the water.

Terrified, she kicked and paddled, trying to reach the surface. Her legs and arms burned with the effort. She ached to fill her blazing lungs, but knew it wouldn't be air she'd be inhaling.

The urge to fight ebbed. She slowed her movements, too exhausted to continue. Perhaps she should just give in. Let the river have her. Steely eyes swam before her. Callie tensed. She couldn't die. Not now. Chase needed her. And she needed him.

Please God, help me out of this river.

As if answering her prayers, powerful fingers dug into her hair and hauled her to the surface. Her scalp screeched from the mistreatment, but she didn't care. She was alive.

Callie spit out a mouthful of gritty water and drew in great gulps of fresh air. As she struggled to regain her breath, Satanta grabbed her by the waist and dragged her toward the shore. When her boots struck the comforting hardness of the river bed, she scrambled up the embankment and collapsed on the rocky bank.

Thank you, Jesus. She'd made it. There'd be no watery grave for her this day.

A pair of wet moccasins entered her line of sight. Fury welled inside her. Callie tilted her head and stared up at her captor. "You fool," she spat. "Why did you attempt a crossing here? I could have drowned." She glared at him, not caring if she angered him. The deadly dunking had frightened her way too much.

"Mrs. Brooks is all right?"

"No, Mrs. Brooks is not all right. I just swallowed half that blasted river."

He issued a bark of laugher and reached down to help her stand. Too exhausted to resist, she rose on trembling legs. Her cold, sodden gown clung to her. What she wouldn't give for a warm fire and a hot cup of coffee. Maybe after such an icy swim, Satanta would call for them to make camp.

The clatter of hooves lifted over the roar of the river. The remainder of the war party rode into view. One of the braves led their bumbling pony forward. Satanta took the reins and reached for her. Callie stiffened. They were resuming their ride? No camp, no fire...

"Can we not stop for the night?" she asked, unable to keep the weariness out of her voice.

"No, we ride further to village."

Before she could open her mouth to argue, he lifted her onto the pony and clambered behind her. For a while, she remained upright, refusing to lean against him. Eventually, an overwhelming exhaustion overcame her, and despite her efforts, she slumped against his rock-hard torso.

The contact reminded her of the one night of passion she'd shared with her husband. Chase had pulled her against his equally broad and muscular chest. Would they ever share such a night again?

Callie clamped down on the tears that threatened to fall. She wouldn't give in to her despair. She couldn't.

But she did give in to fatigue.

****

As the sun slid toward the horizon, Chase and his patrol intercepted D troop at the foot of a rocky incline. He cantered Zeus to the head of the column and reined in beside Captain Alvis.

John shook his head. "Why am I not surprised to see you here, Chase?"

He ignored the comment and nodded at the formation. "I see you only have half your patrol."

"The renegades split up after the attack. I sent Lieutenant Miller with half the men to trail one group."

"And this group?"

"Ben believes we are following Satanta and a smaller band of about eight braves."

Chase swallowed a gritty gulp. "Any signs of my wife?"

"I'm sorry, Chase. Nothing yet."

He grimaced and concentrated on guiding Zeus along

the narrow trail rising up an ungodly steep slope. Perspiration beaded under his armpits, further dampening his sweat-soaked shirt. He tried not to think about the horrifying possibilities of Callie's abduction.

She would survive. She had to.

After twelve hours in the saddle, Chase felt as though a hot poker jabbed into his spine. Every muscle in his body ached for a respite from the grueling pace. But he wouldn't rest. Not until Callie was safely tucked in his arms.

He uncapped his canteen and sucked down a mouthful of warm water, allowing himself this one tiny ration of relief. A shout echoed from the ledge above. His innards twisted. They'd found something. Callie's cold, lifeless face flitted before his eyes. Chase stiffened. No. He had to be positive. He wouldn't be able to keep going if he didn't.

The piercing screech of a hawk drew his gaze skyward. A lone raptor soared across the blue expanse, searching for prey. The absence of any circling harbingers of death gave him some measure of comfort.

No buzzards meant no bodies.

Chase fisted his hands around Zeus' reins and urged the animal forward. The sure-footed stallion navigated the narrow pass, his hooves sending pebbles raining down on the rocks below. The ominous ping rattled in Chase's head and clambered down his spine. He clenched his teeth around a bellow of frustration and fear. He had to stay strong. For both his and Callie's sake.

Five agonizing minutes later, Zeus crested the incline. Chase reined the stallion to a stop near a rocky outcrop, relieved to find no grisly remains littering the ground. He dismounted and joined the group gathered around a large boulder.

Ben Baker crouched and rubbed his hand across the dirt and pine needles. "Moccasins and unshod pony tracks." He nodded to the other side of the boulder. "And dried manure piles. Looks like they camped here during the night."

"Still the same number as before?" John asked.

The bearded scout nodded. "Yep. 'Bout eight of 'em." He focused on a nearby patch of ground and leaned closer.

212

A frown creased his leathery brow.

Chase's stomach lurched. "What is it, Ben?"

"Not sure..." He crept toward a knobby pine, eyes glued to the rocky terrain.

Chase trailed the scout. An uneasy combination of hope and fear surged through him. So far, there'd been no signs of Callie. Could this be the break they were looking for? Or something worse?

Ben stopped and hunkered over to study the ground.

"Find anything?" John asked.

The scout pushed aside a fallen pine bough and pointed to the rocky ground. "Small boot prints. Most likely made by a woman."

Chase sucked in a breath. The heathens did have her. But what had they done to her? "Any signs of..." He let his words trail off, unable to voice his thoughts aloud.

Ben shuffled around the base of the tree. "Nope. No blood. No signs of a scuffle." He tapped the trunk with a finger. "Appears they tied her to this tree."

Chase exhaled the breath he didn't realize he'd been holding. Callie lived. But for how long? Anger rose in him at the thought of taut rawhide cutting into her smooth, tender flesh. "How far ahead of us are they?" he ground out.

Ben frowned and glanced skyward. "I'd say 'bout six hours."

Chase fisted his hand around his saber hilt. That was six hours too many. "Let's ride, then. We have a lot of ground to cover."

He strode back to his horse and mounted quickly, not wanting to waste one precious moment. Callie's life depended on their swiftness.

If she died, he would die with her.

****

A sharply barked command jolted her awake. Callie snapped her eyes open and found darkness. Was it night already? How long had she slept? In the faint moonlight, she could just make out the conical outlines of several teepees. They had arrived at a village. Her heart sank. There'd likely be no more opportunities for escape. What would happen to her now?

Before she could dwell on that thought, Satanta

dismounted and plucked her off the pony. He carried her to a hide-covered lodge and set her down. "Mrs. Brooks stay here." He lifted a length of animal hide to reveal an opening. "Little Moon bring food."

Food. And a place to sleep. Both overrode any thoughts of being afraid. She ducked into the strange dwelling. Embers from a dying fire lit the interior in an orange glow. A variety of animal skins littered the floor around the campfire, forming an inviting, furry pallet. Callie lowered herself to the ground and ran a hand over the soft, wooly hides. It reminded her of the trip west and the tent she'd shared with Chase. The thought of his gentle strength comforted her.

Footsteps sounded outside the teepee.

Pulse skipping, she jerked her head toward the opening. The hide moved and a young Indian girl stepped into the lodge. Dressed in a calf-length, buckskin dress and knee-high moccasins, the raven-haired Kiowa crossed the dirt floor and handed Callie a wood bowl.

Unease turned to curiosity. Was Little Moon Satanta's wife? Sister? Betrothed? It was hard to tell with such a strange culture. "Thank you," Callie murmured.

Soft brown eyes flicked over her face before the maiden ducked through the flapped entrance and disappeared. Callie lowered the bowl to her lap. Was Little Moon curious about what Satanta intended for his captive? She knew she was—fearfully so.

The sweet aroma of venison and herbs drifted upward. Her stomach grumbled and she turned her attention to the stew. Thick chunks of meat swam in a thin, golden stock. Would it taste as good as it smelled?

Callie licked her lips and looked around for a spoon. Finding none, she gave a shrug and dug her fingers into the bowl. Hunger trumped manners in times like this. She selected a meaty chunk and popped it into her mouth. Tangy, flavorful juices bathed her tongue. She suppressed a groan of pleasure. The stew tasted much better than it smelled.

She finished off the meat, then lifted the bowl and drank the warm, flavorful liquid. Her hunger assuaged, she set the empty bowl aside and lay back on the furry pallet. Muted sounds filtered through the hide walls. A

214

dog barked and was quickly silenced. A woman's soft laugh rang out, followed by a man's deep-throated reply. All noises that she might've heard in any civilized town.

The rumbling beat of a drum thrummed the air. Callie bolted upright. *That* was not a sound she'd hear in any civilized town.

The hide covering shifted open. Callie clutched a hand to her thudding chest. She'd been fed. Was she now to be slaughtered?

Satanta stepped through the opening and padded silently across the teepee. He sank to the ground across from her and regarded her with dark, glittering eyes.

Disconcerted by his stare, Callie dug her fingers into the furry pallet. "What are the drums for?" she blurted out.

"Celebration."

"Celebration of what?"

"Successful raid."

Successful because they'd captured her? She wouldn't call that a victory.

He glanced at her empty soup bowl. "You eat stew," he said, more of a statement than a question.

She gave a slight nod. "Yes, it was very good. Tell Little Moon...your wife..?"

"Second wife."

Second wife. Dear God. Was the first still alive?

Satanta grunted. "Lone Wolf offered ten ponies for Mrs. Brooks."

His abrupt change of subject caught her off guard. She blinked in confusion and then found her voice. "Wh-Who is Lone Wolf, and what does his offer mean?"

"Does not matter. Satanta consider keeping Mrs. Brooks for third wife."

Her heart tripped. *Third wife*? Sweet Jesus, this couldn't be happening. She drew in a calming breath. "I thought you were going to hold me for ransom."

"Army captain not have much money."

"You're mistaken, Mr. Satanta." Was that how Indians were referred to? She didn't want to insult him with her ignorance.

"How mistaken?"

"Captain Brooks has lots of money. He received a

substantial amount when we were married."

He scoured her with admiring eyes. "Mrs. Brooks more valuable as wife. Fine, strong woman. Give Satanta many worthy sons."

She sucked in a sharp breath and gripped the hide pallet tighter. He wanted sons. That meant...A shudder of fear rippled through her. "I already have a husband," she finally squeaked out.

The Indian puffed out his muscular chest like a bantam rooster readying itself to crow. And he did. "Satanta make good husband. Many maidens wish to wed strong, handsome Kiowa Chieftain."

Strong? *Handsome*? He thought awful highly of himself. She stared at the flickering fire. How was she to get out of this log-jam without injuring the chief's pride? Without making him angry?

An idea took hold, and hope blossomed. She lifted her gaze and gave him an unwavering look. "I'm sure you would make a wonderful husband, Chief Satanta. However, wouldn't I better serve your people if you were able to purchase horses and food?"

He remained immobile, merely staring at her with those gleaming, feral eyes.

She spoke again, keeping her voice steady, though her insides churned around the stew, now soured and heavy in her belly. "Think about what keeping me would mean," she urged. "Do you want or need the aggravation of dealing with an unskilled, white woman while you flee from the Army?"

His jaw muscle twitched a mere fraction. Not much of a reaction, but just enough to let her know she'd struck a nerve. She pushed forward. "Because they will come after me. I can assure you of that. Imagine dozens of buffalo soldiers dogging your trail, day after day. Never resting..."

The Indian chief narrowed his eyes and studied her as though looking for some sign of deception. When he spoke, his tone was a stiff mixture of skepticism and expectation. "Captain Brooks have much money?"

Encouraged, she nodded. "Yes, enough to buy an entire herd of cattle. Two herds."

He grunted and furrowed his brow in thought.

Callie held her breath, waiting for his answer.

"Mrs. Brooks make good argument," he finally replied. "Satanta will think on it."

She exhaled a tiny breath of relief. Not quite the answer she wanted, but it would have to do.

The chieftain uncrossed his legs and rose. After giving her one last calculating look, he strode to the flapped entrance and ducked out of the teepee.

A cold clamminess invaded her body. Now, if only Chase would agree to pay her ransom.

****

Chase peered across the meadow at the lone Indian facing the formation of troopers. A white flag billowed from a bare branch clutched in the brave's hand. The Indian's mount, a brown and white paint, remained as motionless as its rider. Chase scanned the tree line for hidden threats. Seeing none, he motioned for his troopers to stay put and reined in beside Captain Alvis and Ben Baker.

John nodded at the waiting Kiowa. "Ready, Chase?"

"Been ready." He nudged Zeus forward. "Let's see what the heathen wants."

They rode across the meadow, casting long shadows in the ankle-high grass. Only a faint rustle broke the ominous silence. Early morning sunshine poured from the sky and heated the air to a stifling temperature. Hades hot. The perfect setting for this fiendish meeting.

Ten feet from the brave, Chase tugged Zeus to a halt and stared at the Indian from under the brim of his hat. The Kiowa returned his heated gaze. Chase's blood bubbled. *Heathen bastard.* He rarely allowed his emotions free reign during encounters with the Indians, but in this instance, pure, anger-driven hatred flowed through him.

The brave jabbed his flag-draped branch in the air and spoke in his deep, guttural tongue. Though he didn't understand the words, Chase understood the tone. Forceful and unrelenting. His gut knotted. Things didn't look too promising.

Ben interpreted the brave's words. "He says Satanta sent him to negotiate a ransom for Missus Brooks. If the deal ain't to his liking, the chieftain intends to keep her as his wife."

Chase fisted his hand around Zeus' reins. "Like hell

217

he will."

"Settle down, Captain," John warned. "Ben, ask the Indian what his chief demands for a ransom."

Marshalling his anger, Chase listened to the intense exchange between the warrior and Ben. After a few volleys, the Kiowa made a quick slash with his hand and fell silent.

Chase frowned. What the hell did that mean?

The bearded scout whistled softly and twisted around. "Your wife must've made a *re*-markable impression on Satanta, Cap'n."

"For God's sake, Ben," John barked. "Don't get Chase riled up any more than he is. What did the damn Indian say?"

"His chief wants thirty horses, fifty head of cattle, and a case of repeating rifles."

"No way in hell," Chase snapped. "I'll not give that heathen weapons he can use against me." He tilted forward and glared at the impassive Indian. "Ten horses and twenty head of cattle. *No* rifles."

At Ben's interpretation, the Kiowa's face reddened with fury. He shook his head and spoke in sharp, heated tones.

Chase ground his teeth. Too bad the Indian had come under a flag of truce. Right now, he wanted to strangle the heathen with his bare hands.

The brave fell silent once again.

Ben grunted. "He ain't backing down on the rifles, Cap'n." The scout leaned over the side of his horse and spit a stream of tobacco juice onto the ground. "Want me to seize him afore he rides off?"

"No," Chase ground out. "The bastard probably has a few well-hidden cohorts watching for that sort of thing."

"Chase is right," John said. "We can't put Mrs. Brook's life in jeopardy with a hasty act."

Chase shifted uneasily. Callie had best not be harmed. He glared at the Indian. "Ben, advise this brave to tell his chief no deal. And if Satanta harms my wife in any way, I'll personally track down his miserable, chieftain hide and kill him. Slowly." Without waiting for an answer, he wheeled Zeus around and cantered back toward the waiting troopers. He'd known what the outcome of the useless *pow-wow* would be before he'd even ridden out to meet the red-skinned envoy. And he hadn't been wrong.

There was only one way to free Callie.

On his orders, Jim Eaglefeather had ridden south, ready to trail the Indian and any of his Kiowa buddies back to Satanta's camp. Come hell or high water, Callie would soon be safe and back in his arms where she belonged. Nothing to do now, but wait—the hardest assignment he ever had to endure.

That night, unable to sleep, Chase stared at the shadows flickering among the trees. Images mingled with the dancing specters—Callie's luminous eyes filled with tears, her ashen face flashing with pain. It damned near killed him to know he was the one who had put it there.

He was a fool.

He'd allowed his fears to blind him to Callie's loyalty and devotion. His wife loved him. He'd seen it shining in her eyes and etched on her exquisite face. She would never betray him. God help him if anything should happen to her. He might never get another chance at a love so deep.

Chase shifted on his bedroll. Christ, he wished Jim would hurry back. He knew the scout needed to be extra careful to avoid being detected. And that would take time. More time than Chase wanted to spend sitting idle, but he didn't have a choice. Callie's life depended on Jim's success. That Satanta wanted Callie ate at him like a vulture pecking on carrion.

Bile rose in his throat. No other man had the right to touch her.

A whisper of a sound rode the wind. Chase jerked upright and scanned the tree line. A second later, a buckskin-clad figure emerged from the shadows. *Jim!* Pulse thrumming, he rolled out of his bedding and stood. "Did you find her?" he asked, unable to keep the worry out of his voice.

"Yes, Captain," the scout answered. "Three miles south of Lost Valley, a small encampment of about fifty braves and two dozen women and children."

Awakened by the noise, Captain Alvis sat up and blinked the sleep from his eyes. "What's going on?"

"Jim's back. He located Callie three miles south of Lost Valley."

"That's excellent news." John pushed to his feet. "The men and horses are well-rested from the wait. If we ride through the night, we should be able to reach the encampment by dawn."

Already on his way to saddle Zeus, Chase merely nodded.

Twenty minutes later, the eager detail rode out. They traveled south at a steady, yet cautious pace. With Jim's guidance and faint light from the half-moon, they were able to make good progress.

Near dawn, they navigated a narrow draw that opened up beneath a rocky ledge. Jim motioned for a halt and dismounted. He signaled for Chase to follow him.

Weary, yet anxious, Chase dismounted and tossed his hat and Zeus' reins to a nearby trooper. He flattened against the hillside and belly-crawled up the steep slope. He soon joined Jim at the top and extracted his telescope from his pocket. Chase carefully eased his head over the rocky lip and peered through the lens at the valley below.

Dozens of teepees dotted the ground along a wide, winding creek. A handful of figures moved about the quiet encampment, mostly squaws preparing the morning meal. At the far edge of the camp, tendrils of smoke snaked into the sky from the remnants of a bonfire. A celebration. His gut clenched. Celebrating what?

A tap on his shoulder pulled him back from his thoughts. He glanced at Jim.

The scout pointed at the prominent cliffs flanking the village. "Sentries are posted at each end of the valley," Jim whispered. "Four in all."

Chase grunted. "We'll take them out first. Quietly."

Jim nodded. "Your wife's in the teepee near the center of the village. The one where the paint is tethered."

Chase returned his focus to the spyglass and located the conical lodge. Icy dread shot through him. Not an easy target to get to in a hurry. Once the shooting started, Callie would be caught in the crossfire. If anything happened to her...

He drew up. *No.* He wouldn't allow himself to think along those lines. "Nice job, Jim." Chase collapsed the telescope and slid it back into his pocket. "Let's go work out the details of our attack with the others." He lingered a moment longer to study the layout of the village, then wormed his way back down the incline.

Chase joined Captain Alvis and Ben at the base. "They seem to be unaware of our presence and relying on the sentries for warning," he told them.

John nodded. "Good. What's the plan?"

Chase bent and drew a crude map in the dirt with the tip of his knife. "The village is laid out along a creek with access at either end of the valley." He looked up at the two scouts. "Ben, you and Jim split up and take out the sentries. John and I will position our men on opposite ends of the valley and wait for your signal. With the element of surprise and a coordinated sweep, we should be able to overtake them."

The two scouts nodded in unison and then set off to complete their assignments.

Chase straightened and peered at John. "Callie's being held in a teepee in the middle of the encampment. I'll go straight for her as soon as the attack begins."

John clapped him on the shoulder. "We'll get her out safe and sound, Chase."

His insides hardened. They *had* to get her out safely. There was no other option.

As John and his men rode out of sight, Chase glanced at the troopers gathered around him. They sat calmly, awaiting his orders.

Private White handed him his hat and Zeus' reins. "Don't you worry none, Cap'n. We'll get Missus Brooks back, whatever it takes."

The others nodded in agreement, their soft "yeahs" bolstering his confidence. A reassuring calm settled over him. His troopers were well trained. By him. And they would bravely follow him to rescue the woman he loved.

"I know you will," he replied in a warm, sincere tone. He tucked on his hat and quickly mounted Zeus. "Let's go get her, men."

SEVENTEEN

Callie awoke to the sound of the Indian camp stirring to life. Female chatter floated into her hide-bound prison, along with the faint odor of cooking meat. She draped an arm across her belly and fought the nausea that flooded her at the thought of what the morning would bring.

The day before, she'd been sitting in the afternoon sunshine, helping Little Moon sew colorful beads onto a pair of moccasins when a small band of warriors rode into the encampment. She and Little Moon had joined the parade trailing the riders.

After speaking with the newcomers, Satanta had marched in her direction. His horrible words still echoed in her head. *It is good you have started learning Kiowa woman's work. Captain Brooks refused to pay ransom. Tomorrow, you become wife to Satanta.*

Her heart ached from Chase's rejection—the second in less than a week. Tears burned in her eyes. Why had she ever come to this Godforsaken land? Her dream of becoming a poised, confident woman had brought her nothing but misery.

The swish of the hide flap punched into her dreary thoughts. Callie turned her head to the side. Little Moon entered the teepee and set a bowl near the fire. She glanced in Callie's direction. A fleeting expression of sympathy flitted across her bronze face before she ducked back through the entrance.

Callie ignored the stew. Food was the last thing on her mind. Besides, as unsettled as her stomach felt, she doubted the meal would stay down.

A hair-raising scream rent the air.

Heart pounding, she scrambled to her feet and started for the entrance. The resounding crack of gunfire blasted the stillness. She froze mid-stride. *Dear God, not another attack.*

Angry shouts and more gunshots rang out. The thunder of hooves drew near, then stopped outside the teepee. Footsteps pounded toward the entrance.

Callie held her breath and stared at the hide covering. *Go away*, she wanted to scream but could only manage a mouse-like squeak.

The hide moved and sunlight flooded into the lodge. A gun barrel appeared in the opening. Then came the brim of a blue hat and finally a familiar, tanned face. Worried gray eyes met hers across the short distance.

Her heart skipped a beat. It couldn't be. It had to be a mirage. She blinked once, and then again. No, it wasn't a mirage. It *was* Chase. She sobbed out his name and raced toward him.

He met her halfway and curled his arms around her, hugging her in a fierce embrace. "Thank God," he murmured into her hair, his voice strangely hoarse. "Are you all right?"

She cuddled against him, reassured by his strong heartbeat. "Yes, I'm fine. I can't believe you came."

"Of course I came. You're my wife."

Her heart plummeted. His wife. His duty. Of course he came. So he could send her back East as he'd promised. Callie stiffened. Not if she could help it. "Chase, I—"

Gunfire barked outside the teepee. He loosened his grip on her waist. "Later," he warned. "I've got to get you out here first." Chase pushed her behind him and moved toward the entrance.

An explosion of sound and movement burst through the opening. Chase grunted and stopped abruptly. His gun flew out of his hand and went sailing across the teepee.

Callie skidded to a halt behind him. Her belly seized as she spotted a tall, copper-skinned figure crouched near the entrance, brandishing a knife. *Satanta!*

Steel carved the air with a menacing swish. Before she could blink, the chief gave a hair-raising yelp and lunged forward. Like a panther attacking prey, he pounced on Chase. His momentum sent both men crashing to the ground.

Callie scurried backward until she collided with the

tent wall. She pressed a hand to her chest and watched, horrified, as Chase wrestled to gain an advantage. Satanta managed to end up on top and drove his knife toward Chase's heaving chest.

Nooooo. The scream welled inside her, but never made it past her fear-strangled throat.

Chase's neck muscles bulged as he held off the assault. Callie strained with him. *Come on, Chase. You can do this. Don't you dare die on me.*

As if hearing her plea, he arched his back and heaved Satanta to the side. The two men rolled over and over, tumbling toward the fire. Chase's boot scraped the embers. Sparks flew into the air.

The wink of firelight on metal caught her eye. Callie sucked in a breath. *Chase's pistol!* She should go get it. Her pulse skipped. But could she shoot the thing—at a man no less? She glanced at the battling men. Clearly tiring, Chase couldn't stop one of Satanta's swiping stabs. A grimace crossed his face as the knife bit into his arm. Red blossomed on his tattered sleeve.

Heated blood coursed through her. She had to do something. Now. Before Satanta killed the man she loved.

Callie raced around the campfire and grabbed the pistol. Though smaller, the gun had two sights and a trigger—just like a rifle. She held the weapon in her trembling hand. *Please God, let it work the same.*

As Chase taught her, she pulled back the cocking lever and lifted the pistol. More awkward than heavy, the gun wavered in her grasp. She clutched the grip with both hands in an effort to steady her aim.

Okay, she was ready. She hoped. Callie focused on the two combatants still locked in a violent struggle. Barely inches apart, they appeared to be one wildly flailing form. She hitched in a breath. They were too close. What if she shot Chase?

Her belly flipped as Satanta, once again, gained an advantage atop Chase. Straddling his opponent, the Indian landed a blow to Chase's temple, stunning him. Satanta reared back, knife upraised and poised to deliver a finishing thrust.

Daylight shimmered between the two entangled bodies.

Callie tensed. *This is it.* She lined up the two sights with the Indian's bronze chest and squeezed the trigger.

Blam! She flinched from both the deafening noise and the buck of the firing weapon. Satanta clutched his bloodied chest and lifted shock-filled eyes in her direction. Her knees wavered, and she locked them tight, fighting to say upright. Sweet Mary, she'd actually hit him.

Before she could think another thought, Chase lunged upward and slammed his fist into Satanta's jaw. The wounded chieftain collapsed to the ground and lay in a motionless heap.

Callie raced to her husband and sank beside him. His torn sleeve gaped open, revealing a jagged, bloodied gash. She sucked in a sharp breath and reached for his arm. "You're wounded."

"It's just a flesh wound."

A shiver wracked her. "Just a...Oh God, Chase, you could've been killed."

He gathered her in his arms. "Shhh...I'm fine."

"Cap'n Brooks?" a worried voice called from outside the teepee. "Everythin' all right in there?"

"Everything's fine, Ben," Chase answered.

The scout stuck his head in the opening and nodded. "Glad to see the Missus is all right."

"So am I." Chase relaxed his grip. "I don't hear any rifle fire. What's our status?"

"Under control, sir. We routed 'em pretty good. Cap'n Alvis is chasing down the stragglers."

"Excellent." Chase jerked a nod at Satanta. "Have someone retrieve that heathen and see to his wound."

Ben frowned. "He still alive?"

"Appears to be. Lucky for him, my wife only had one day of firearms training."

"Got what he deserved, I say." Ben gave a gruff snort and then disappeared from sight.

Callie glanced at the immobile, yet still breathing Indian. He *was* still alive. Thank Goodness. No matter how much she disliked the Indian, she didn't want him dead. She'd sleep easier at night, knowing she hadn't killed anyone. She swallowed around the lump in her throat and looked down at the pistol still clutched in her hand.

"You did the right thing," Chase said softly.

"I wasn't certain I could shoot the thing, but I had to try."

"I'm glad you did."

She looked up at him. "Chase—"

He pressed a finger to her lips. "We can talk later."

"But—"

Chase rose to his feet. "I have to see to the containment of the camp. Stay here. I'll be back shortly." He ducked through the opening and disappeared.

A few minutes later, two troopers entered the teepee and retrieved the wounded Indian chief. Unable to sit idle, Callie followed the men outside. Her insides twisted at the ugly sight that greeted her. Bloodied bodies and overturned teepees littered the ground. Scattered campfires smoldered and spit gray plumes into the air. The tendrils mingled with the smoky haze of burnt gunpowder drifting around the shattered village.

The acrid odor seared her throat. She covered a cough and glanced at the nearby creek. Half a dozen troopers stood guard over a subdued cluster of Indians. Little Moon. Callie anxiously scanned the captives, relieved to spot the young woman comforting a sobbing child. Though Little Moon had spoken few words, she had offered plenty of silent support. Callie could only hope to do the same.

Ben emerged from the side of the teepee. Callie turned and gestured at the captured Indians. "What will happen to them, Mr. Baker?"

"We'll escort them back to the reservation, ma'am. Satanta and his braves will face criminal charges."

"The women and children won't be punished?"

"Not if your husband has any say-so."

Callie nodded, reassured by the scout's comment. She was just as certain as Ben that her fair-minded husband wouldn't let Little Moon or the other innocents suffer any recriminations.

Captain Alvis and a small patrol materialized through the smoky haze, driving a small band of captured Kiowa before them. The moustached officer dismounted and walked toward her. "Mrs. Brooks, I'm glad to see you are alive and unharmed."

"Thank you, Captain. I'm relieved you were able to find me so quickly."

"Thank your husband. Satanta wanted rifles as part of your ransom. And Chase just couldn't agree to that. He wisely sent Jim Eaglefeather to trail the Kiowa envoy back to this village."

A fist clamped over her heart. Chase had refused to pay her ransom because he'd had to. No officer would willingly give hostile Indians weapons.

Why then had he come for her?

She excused herself and returned to the comforting confines of the teepee. With a heavy heart, she sank onto the furry pallet and absently added small twigs to the fire until the flames began to mount.

She loved Chase—loved him with all her heart and soul. Tears burned in her eyes. If only he could love her the same.

****

Chase paused outside the teepee and drew in a ragged breath. His wife waited within. *Wife.* Would he be able to continue calling her that? His accusations had cut deep, furrowing into her tender heart. He couldn't blame her if she refused to forgive him.

With a resigned sigh, he pushed aside the hide covering and stepped inside. Callie scrambled to her feet and regarded him across the short distance. Sad, luminous eyes gouged into him. His heart bucked. He'd put that pain on her face. It was up to him to take it away.

He tossed his hat to the fur-covered floor and in three brisk strides, stood before her. "It's time we talked." He motioned to the pallet. "Let's sit down."

Fire flamed in her eyes. She shoved back her shoulders and fisted her hands at her sides. "I don't care to sit."

What a little tigress she'd turned out to be. He would miss her indomitable spirit. His gaze strayed to her heaving breasts. And her passion. Chase drew in a steadying breath. "Callie—"

"No," she bit out. "I want to hear this standing up. And just so you know, I won't go back to Washington without a fight."

Won't go back...

His pulse rabbit-hopped. Did he dare hope? He lowered himself onto the pallet and reached for her hand. "Please. Sit with me."

She blinked as though surprised by his gentleness. A half heartbeat later, she placed a trembling hand in his and sat beside him.

Her flowery scent enveloped him—an aroma he would carry in his memory until the day he died. He squeezed her fingers, comforted by their warmth. "Callie, I'll never be able to make up for the pain I've caused you..."

His throat closed around the words. He briefly closed his eyes and fought for control. Muscles quivered from being held taut and rigid. He grimaced. A six day gun battle would've been less draining.

Inch by inch, his control returned. He opened his eyes.

Callie's concerned gaze met his. "Chase—"

"No. Let me finish." He swallowed hard and forced the words past the thickness in his throat. "I shouldn't have accused you of being unfaithful. I was wrong. My first wife cheated on me, and when I saw you with..." He inhaled a gut-deep breath. "I hope you'll forgive me."

Her expression softened. "There's nothing to forgive. Amanda told me about Miranda. I understand what you felt."

He shook his head. "I'm such a fool."

"Not a fool. Just human." She rested a gentle hand on his arm. "Chase, know this, I will never be unfaithful to you. Ever. I love you."

She loved him. His chest filled to near bursting. "I don't deserve you," he murmured.

Callie smiled. "Of course you do. You're the kindest, most unselfish man I ever had the pleasure to call husband."

He cupped her chin in his hands and stared down into her radiant face. "You don't know how special you are to me. You've shown me it's safe to trust again. Convinced me I'm worth loving. I never thought my empty heart could feel like this."

Chase covered her lips with his, gentle at first, and

then more demanding as she met his passion. After a few heavenly minutes of tasting her, he lifted his head. "I love you, Callie Brooks," he whispered. "You're my heart and soul. I still can't believe how lucky I am to have stumbled into the wrong hotel room."

She broadened her smile. "Sometimes, things happen for a reason." With a soft groan, she reached up and pulled his lips back to hers.

EPILOGUE

Callie stood on the veranda and stared across the frozen parade ground. The rising sun scattered glimmers of rose over the pristine snow. In the distance, white-capped trees sparkled like hand-blown crystal ornaments.

The faint creak of door hinges sounded behind her. A second later, Chase's strong arms enfolded her from behind. "Good morning, beautiful." Warm lips grazed her neck. "You're up early this morning."

She closed her eyes and enjoyed the comforting warmth pressed against her. "I couldn't sleep."

"Is your back still bothering you?"

She nodded and smiled as Chase slid his hands over her protruding belly and gently massaged the huge mound. "It won't be much longer," he told her.

"Dr. Giles says any day now." Callie opened her eyes, unable to stop a tiny shiver of apprehension. She wanted this baby with all her heart. But she had to admit, the birthing process frightened her. Having helped Amanda bring her daughter into the world, she'd seen the long, painful procedure firsthand. And she wasn't looking forward to her own ordeal.

Chase stilled his movements. "You're getting chilled," he said, mistaking her shiver for one of coldness. "Let's go inside."

She sighed and held her tongue. She didn't want to worry him with her fears. Chase was already anxious enough for the both of them.

He guided her back into the warm cabin. "Here, sit by the fire and warm yourself."

Callie lowered her ample body onto the settee in as lady-like a fashion as she could manage. A twinge of pain shot through her lower back. She grimaced and shifted around until she found a position that eased the ache.

Finally settled, she glanced up.

Chase stood before her holding out a paper-wrapped package. A smile dimpled his cheeks. "I have something for you."

Curious, she tilted her head to the side and eyed the present. "What is it?"

"I wanted to give you this at Christmas, but there was a delay in delivery to the Sutler's." He eased beside her on the settee and handed her the package. "It just arrived the other day."

She removed the brown wrapping to reveal a beautiful pewter picture frame. Her hand trembled as she ran a finger over the photograph of Ulysses accepting his oath of office. That Chase would give her such a present...

"Do you like it?" he asked.

"Oh, yes," she managed to say past the lump in her throat. "It's a wonderful, thoughtful gift."

"Turn it over."

She flipped the frame over and read the flowery inscription etched along the bottom edge—*To my loving wife, I commit my heart forever.* Her heart sang with joy. Callie lifted her gaze and peered through a haze of tears. "I love you, Chase."

"And I love you." He leaned toward her and covered her mouth with his in a tender, loving kiss.

Soft whistling and the clang of a pot intruded on their privacy. "Coffee's 'bout ready, Cap'n," Moses announced from the kitchen.

Chase stilled his assault on her lips and groaned.

Callie grinned and glanced at the open doorway. "Maybe I shouldn't have relinquished my household duties to him until *after* the baby was born."

"No maybe about it."

Callie chuckled and then rolled to her feet, using Chase's hand for leverage. She waddled across the floor to the sideboard and set the pewter frame on the tabletop. As she stepped back to admire the photograph, a fierce pain gripped her belly. A second later, a warm rush of water spilled between her legs. She stiffened and looked at Chase.

He jerked to his feet and rushed to her side. "What is it? Are you ill?"

"The baby," she whispered.

"The baby, what?"

"The baby's coming."

He widened his eyes. "Now?"

Another much stronger and more painful spasm clawed at her middle. She gasped and bent over.

"Moses," Chase shouted, his voice edged with panic. "Fetch Doctor Giles."

The private stuck his head through the doorway. "Sorry, Cap'n, but the Doc left early this mornin' for the reservation."

"Then fetch his nurse."

****

"You doin' all right, Capn?"

Chase glanced up from the stick he'd whittled to a nub. "I'm managing, Moses." Just barely. But enough to keep him from running through the garrison and howling like a madman.

His striker nodded and joined him on the veranda steps. "Birthin' can be a long process. Requires a lot of patience."

Chase peered beyond the trooper at the darkened horizon. A knot formed in his gut. "It's been nearly twelve hours...do you think..." he let his voice trail away, unable to say the words aloud. If he did, he'd admit that something had gone terribly wrong and he may never see the woman he loved again.

Moses snorted. "Twelve hours is nothing, suh. Why my Daisy took nearly a day and a half to deliver our son. Fine healthy boy, too."

A day and a half? He'd never survive a wait that long. And for Callie to endure such a delivery...

He shifted uneasily. "And your wife?"

"Up and working the garden in three days. Women are a lot stronger than we think they are. Missus Brooks will come through this just fine. You'll see."

Chase drew in a steadying breath. She had to come through this ordeal. He couldn't go on without her.

A baby's wail pierced the night. Chase jerked his head around and stared at the closed door. His heart galloped in his chest.

"Ain't that the sweetest sound?" Moses clamped a

hand on his shoulder. "Go on, Cap'n. Go see your wife and new baby."

Heart thudding, Chase pushed inside the cabin and strode to the closed bedroom door. He paused and tossed a glance heavenward. Please God, let her be okay. He couldn't bear to loose Callie, not when he'd finally found the love he never believed he could have.

Before he could move, the door opened and Rose Franklin smiled at him from the threshold. "You may come in, Captain. Callie is doing just fine."

He heaved a sigh of relief. "Thank you, Miss Franklin. I appreciate you bringing her through this."

She smiled up at him. "I wouldn't have it any other way. You go on in now. Callie's waiting for you."

He nodded and moved into the bedroom. His gaze locked on the lovely vision resting against a stack of pillows. Ebony hair tumbled around her like a silky halo. Though ringed with weariness, her eyes glowed with love and contentment. His heart soared. She was alive.

Callie looked up at him and smiled. "I have a late Christmas gift for you too, Chase." She lifted the tiny bundle cradled in her arms. "Come meet your son."

His son. He eased next to the bed and gingerly accepted the tightly swaddled bundle. The tiny, ebony-haired infant opened his rosebud mouth and yawned. A strange, tender ache filled his chest.

Chase raised the bundle to his lips and kissed the soft, fuzzy forehead. "Welcome to the world, Alexander Ulysses Brooks. You've got a lot to learn, but if you're half as smart and plucky as your mother, you'll make a superb, little cavalry officer." He moved his gaze to Callie and returned her loving smile. "He will carry on the family tradition and become a trooper," he added proudly.

"No doubt," she said with a shake of her head. "And he'll be a brilliant, compassionate commander, just like his father."

A word about the author...

Born, raised and still living in Richmond, Virginia, Donna discovered a love of reading at an early age. Combing through her grandma's massive bookcase, she eagerly devoured such works as THE HARDY BOYS and NANCY DREW. Once she reached an age deemed appropriate, she was allowed to read the hallowed romance collection.

Donna soon turned her hand to writing. In high school, many of her works were published in the school's literary magazine. Prose, poetry, no genre was off limits to her fertile imagination. After seeing her two sons graduate, she focused on her writing career and joined the Virginia Romance Writers and Hearts Through History RWA ® chapters. She hopes her readers will enjoy her curl-in-the-chair, let-the-house-fall-in-around-you romance novels and will come back for more.

Visit Donna at www.donnadalton.net